DYING FOR LOVE

Also in Rita Herron's Slaughter Creek series

Dying to Tell
Her Dying Breath
Worth Dying For

DYING FOR LOVE

A SLAUGHTER CREEK NOVEL

RITA HERRON

Text copyright © 2014 Rita Herron
All rights reserved.

Published by Montlake Romance, Seattle

www.apub.com

Amazon, the Amazon logo, and Montlake are trademarks of Amazon.com, Inc., or its affiliates.

ISBN-13: 9781477825112
ISBN-10: 1477825118

Cover design by Marc J. Cohen

Library of Congress Control Number: 2014907477

Printed in the United States of America

To my twin—and my very best friend!

Prologue

I wish I could leave my body behind. I'd take my mind to another place, somewhere nice and soft and warm. Someplace with bright, pretty colors, where I had friends and a mom who'd sing to me at night.

Then the monsters could do whatever they wanted to me, and I wouldn't feel any pain.

I try so hard to make it happen. To levitate and leave the room. To float to another place far away so I can tell . . .

Help me. Please help me, I cry.

But I'm only a kid and nobody listens. Nobody hears me cry at night. No one comes to help me.

No one says it'll be okay.

Because they don't tell lies where I am. And they don't care if you're afraid.

Death whispers in my ear a thousand times a day. "You can run, and you can hide, Zack. But I'll get you anyway."

No . . . I will escape one day.

The room is dark. Cold. Cement floors. Concrete walls. Musty smelling.

Outside my prison it's quiet.

Except for the footsteps of the leader. Left, right, left, right. Coming closer.

My stomach pitches. He's coming for me again.

I pick up the nail I found under my metal bed and scratch a picture on the concrete wall. A drawing of the monster who keeps me locked up. It has hideous features, distorted and bulging. Coppery eyes that shoot daggers dripping with blood at my feet.

And sharp fangs that snap at my skin and tear it off into pieces like rags.

The woman's voice drifts through the cold halls. The lullaby she is singing. Only it isn't a lullaby but a call for the dead. A warning of what is to come.

The room is black. The door bolted. The keys turning in locks down the hall screeching like banshees.

I shiver at the idea of banshees.

I know what they are. They're creatures of the night.

People who are about to be murdered see them.

I hear her mourning call from the woods outside.

She's washing the bloody clothes of someone who just died.

Is she coming for me next?

Chapter One

———— o ————

The nightmares refused to leave Amelia Nettleton alone. She glanced at the bottle of pills on the table. The medication would quiet the voices, numb the pain. Make her forget . . . at least for a little while.

They also numbed her to everything else.

With a shaky hand, she pushed the bottle away. She'd come too far in her therapy to go back to that place where she floated in and out of reality. Where life was nothing but a blur, and she wasn't really living at all.

Determined to purge the haunting images of the past from her mind, she mixed the paints, dark grays and black and reds, and began to fill the blank canvas with the images. Fast, furious, terrifying—she put it all on there.

Body parts filled the jars on the shelf on the wall—fingers, toes, a hand, a tongue . . . then eyes . . . bloody and ripped from humans as if a wild animal had scavenged them for food.

The eyes were the worst. They stared at her in shock and terror, accusing and full of hate. Why had she let this happen?

How could she love a man who was a monster?

Ting. Ting. Ting.

She painted the wind chimes on her porch outside. They tinkled, then clanged together, banging in the wind.

Then the monster turned on her, reaching inside her chest, tearing out her heart with his long, icy fingers, ripping through muscle and tissue, cracking bones and puncturing blood vessels until they gushed red like a river running down her chest. Pain tore through her, her body convulsing.

Her eyes were torn out, blinding her, making empty sockets in her face, the black holes endless and evil looking. Then her tongue was slashed, leaving her gagging, swallowing blood and rasping out a silent scream, her breath coming in shallow spurts as death called her name.

Amelia dropped the paintbrush, red paint splattering on the floor like blood.

Chilled from the inside out, she walked to the window to look out, wishing for daylight to chase away the darkness hovering over her. But the pull of death and despair threatened to consume her as night dragged on.

The chill of February raged through the mountains, lapsing into a sea of endless gloomy skies, winter holding on with a vengeance. Twigs snapped and broke off, flailing to the ground while the wind whistled through the mountains, shrill and eerie sounding.

Bare tree branches swayed and shook icy sleet onto the snow-crusted ground, the leaves dead and buried beneath the layers of frozen, muddy slush from the deluge of storms that had descended on Slaughter Creek.

I'm coming for you, a gruff voice whispered. *Wait for me, Amelia.*

She shivered at the sinister tone. Six's voice was filled with the shock of betrayal.

Six—her former lover and the man the town called "the Dissector" because he'd mutilated his victims and stored their body parts in the same type of mason jars her granny had used to can beans and peas from the garden.

Body parts he kept as treasures. Trophies.

For a brief second, his image appeared in the shadows of the woods as if he were watching her. She blinked, her heart hammering.

No . . . it wasn't real. He was locked away. She was safe.

Wasn't she?

———————— , ————————

There were too many damn missing kids in the U.S.

But six-year-old Darby Wesley was one TBI, Tennessee Bureau of Investigation, Special Agent John Strong hoped to find.

Wind bit at his neck and fluttered leaves around his feet. His boots crunched the frozen snow as he crept toward the clapboard house deep in the mountains. Night sounds echoed from the woods, the dark keeping him hidden as he clutched his handgun at the ready.

The countryside was desolate with its dead trees and icy sludge crusting the ridges.

Had the kidnapper brought the little boy here?

Various scenarios raced through his head. A large percentage of the missing children cases involved parental disputes turned kidnappings. There were hundreds of runaway teens. Kidnappings for ransom. Abductions by mentally disturbed individuals desperate for a child of their own.

The reasons went on and on.

Some of the lost children were already dead. Some they'd never find or know what happened to them. Others were being abused or tormented.

Worse were the child traffickers. Bunch of sick fucks.

And then there were the pedophiles . . .

Even sicker fucks.

What were they dealing with this time?

Not a parental dispute, he knew that already. Parents were dead. Darby was in foster care.

John's partner, Special Agent Cal Coulter, gave a quick nod from the opposite side of the house where he had a view of the front window, indicating he had visual confirmation the suspect was inside. John prayed the kid was, too. Darby had been missing less than twenty-four hours.

Every hour that passed decreased the chances of finding the boy alive.

But they'd caught a break when a gas station clerk had heard a noise coming from the back of a white utility van.

A noise that sounded like a little boy's scream for help.

The clerk had played it cool, but scribbled down the van's tag number, then called 911 as soon as the driver peeled out of the parking lot and headed into the foothills of the mountains.

A helicopter search had narrowed down the location.

John inched around to the left, checking the side windows. Years of grime and dirt coated the windowpanes, making it difficult to see inside. Birds had nested on the windowsill while termites had eaten at the wood.

He crept to the back door. Rotting wood, no glass. But a small, narrow window offered a view inside. More dirt and grime on the panes, but they were clear enough for him to see the hallway. "No visual on the child," he said into his mic.

"Suspect is passed out on the couch," Coulter replied. "Should we call for a warrant?"

Technically they should. But John didn't always play by the rules. "No way. If we catch hell, I'll deal with the fallout later."

After all, a kid's life was in danger. That was all the probable cause he needed.

John jiggled the doorknob. Unlocked.

Either they had the wrong man, or the bastard was so cocky, he thought he'd already gotten away with his crime. That he was so far off the grid no one would find him.

That he could rest up before doing whatever heinous thing he'd planned with the child.

That wasn't going to happen on his watch.

Unless he had already hurt the boy . . .

Two hours had passed since the 911 call. Two hours was a long damn time.

The suspect could have killed the child and ditched him someplace in the woods or thrown him off a ridge and no one would know. It might take days for them to recover his body. In that time, there was no telling what the animals might do to him.

Nausea tied John's stomach into a knot.

Days that would be torture for Darby's foster mother, who was already crazed out of her mind with worry and guilt.

Hand clenched around his Sig Sauer, John crept inside the kitchen. Musty odors. Cigarette smoke. French fries.

His gaze swept the room. A pizza box on the counter. A fast-food bag with a kid's toy.

The man definitely had a child with him.

Fear squeezed John's chest. The room was too quiet.

———————— . ————————

Exhausted but still unable to sleep, Amelia turned on the TV to distract herself from her thoughts while she put the last touches on her painting.

"This just in, a late-breaking story," the reporter said. "A bomb exploded earlier at a women's clinic in Knoxville. Three were killed, including two doctors and a nurse on duty. At this time, police are unsure of the motive but are investigating."

Amelia stored her paints and immersed her brushes in cleaning solution, then crawled into bed, her nerves frayed as the reporter continued.

"Witnesses report a young man about fifteen years old walked into the clinic with a bomb strapped to his chest and set off the explosion."

A shudder of horror ripped through her as the cameras panned to show the carnage. God . . . what was the world coming to?

Unable to stand watching any more, she punched the TV set off.

The wind whipped a branch against the window, its jagged edges scraping the glass as if they were gnarled fingers trying to claw their way in.

Six's voice taunted her in the silence.

Why did you betray me, Amelia?

She battled the panic, desperate to banish his words—and her guilt.

She'd *had* to turn him in. Had to stop him from killing again.

She took a deep breath and pulled the quilt her gran had made for her over her, tracing her finger over the fine stitching and odd shapes. Gran had called this a crazy quilt because its pattern consisted of random shapes and fabrics mingled together.

Just like she was.

She glanced at the chest where the other quilt had been folded and stored. The wedding-ring quilt Gran had made for her marriage bed.

Her sister Sadie had hers on her bed now.

A sadness enveloped Amelia. She'd never get to use hers. Never get married or have a family. Not with her dark past and troubled soul. What man could possibly love her?

Thoughts of Gran gave her comfort, though, and she finally slipped into a deep sleep.

A voice seeped in.

Not Six's this time. A child's.

Help me, Mommy. Help.

The earth spun and she felt as if she were free-falling. When the world cleared again, she was in a hospital. Machines beeped. Voices sounded. The scent of antiseptic filled the air. A cart moved, trays rattled.

The sanitarium—she was back there, in a room. White coats all around her.

"Push, Amelia, push. The baby's coming!"

Pain ricocheted through Amelia's abdomen, fear choking her. What if something went wrong?

"Come on, you can do it."

Hands lifted her shoulders. A voice ordered her to grip her knees and push again. She heaved a breath, fighting through the pain of the contraction, imagining the moment she would hold her newborn in her arms.

Her newborn . . . she was finally having the baby . . .

Tears blurred her eyes. She wished Sadie were there. Wished for Papaw and her grandmother and all the people she'd lost when they'd locked her up.

The bright lights blinded her, and the room blurred, spinning in circles. White coats with nameless faces floated past, the sound of voices echoing as if they came from a faraway place. As if they were in a tunnel.

"She'll never know."

"Don't tell her."

"She's too crazy to have a baby."

"No one can ever find out what we did."

She struggled to discern who was talking, but another contraction gripped her, then another. They were right on top of each other.

"One more push, come on, Amelia."

She gritted her teeth, clutched the bed, and pushed.

Two more times and a baby's cry echoed through the room.

Her baby's cry.

"It's a boy," someone said through the chaotic haze.

Tears blinded Amelia, but she blinked them back, then reached out her arms. "Let me hold him . . . "

But another pair of hands pushed her down on the bed. Restraints snapped around her wrists.

Amelia fought against them, kicking wildly. "Please, give him to me! Let me hold him!"

The lights dimmed. Something sharp stung her arm. Hushed voices drifted. The baby's cry grew more distant.

A man's face appeared in the corner, just a flicker from the shadows . . . who was he?

Then there was another voice, another face . . . one she recognized.

The man she hated and feared most. The Commander.

And she fell into the darkness.

Amelia startled and jerked to a sitting position. The same dream . . . delivering a baby . . .

God . . . why had she dreamed that again?

The clawing sound drew her gaze to the window once more. The tree branch? Or was someone outside?

Trembling, she pressed her hands over her ears, forcing the voices and images away as she climbed from the bed and hurried to the window. She looked outside again, hoping for the sun, but it was still the middle of the night, and a gray fog loomed over the woods.

Was someone out there watching her?

She searched the shadows and trees and saw movement. Her stomach tightened. She'd had the feeling of being watched all her life and for good reason—the Commander and his people had been watching.

What about now, though?

Seconds later, she spotted antlers and realized it had been a deer.

Sucking in a sharp breath, she grabbed her robe and pulled it on, clutching the lapels as she went to the kitchen to make some hot tea.

The disturbing painting of the mason jars mocked her from the corner. But her gaze was drawn to another canvas.

The painting of a man's face. One that had been slipping into her dreams for weeks now.

He was tall, muscular, broad shouldered. A soldier's body. Square jaw. Stubble.

Dark, stormy, mesmerizing eyes.

She had sketches of him all over her studio. For some reason, he kept reappearing as if he was someone important to her.

But he wasn't real . . .

Just like the baby in her dream wasn't real. She'd never given birth.

Maybe she was experiencing some kind of twin jealousy because Sadie was pregnant and due any day.

That had to be the reason. She'd always had a connection with Sadie.

Her phone trilled.

Something had to be wrong.

She raced to answer it. When Sadie's name appeared on the caller ID, her hand began to shake.

"Hello."

"Amelia, it's Jake. Sadie and I are at the hospital. The baby's coming now."

——————— , ———————

John eased through the kitchen, glancing sideways into the bedroom to his left. He'd considered waiting for more backup, but decided to strike during the night, hoping to catch the kidnapper off guard.

It was dark inside, but he spotted a rusted metal bed with a quilt thrown over it. A pair of men's work boots. Overalls on the floor.

No Darby.

Dammit.

Coulter was waiting on him so he moved swiftly into the hall and checked the second room. A twin bed, blue comforter on top.

Shit. A bed for a little boy.

But he didn't see Darby inside.

Heart racing, he crept to the edge of the living room and spotted a big guy on the couch, sprawled out, arms dangling to the side. He looked scruffy, a patchy beard growing in, a gut overflowing his pants.

A rancid odor hit him. Sweat. Beer. Body odor like the man hadn't bathed in days.

His snores punctuated the air, almost deafening.

But a shotgun sat propped by the couch within a finger's reach of the man's right hand.

Coulter acknowledged that he saw John in the doorway, raised his fingers in a one-two-three count, then kicked the door open with a bang.

"TBI!" Coulter shouted, his gun aimed at the man.

The meathead on the couch jolted upright and reached for his gun.

"I wouldn't do that," John said in a lethal tone.

The suspect jerked his head around, and John pointed the barrel of his Sig Sauer in his face. "Where's Darby?"

"Get the hell out of my house," the man snarled.

Coulter took a step closer, closing in. "Tell us where he is, and I won't put a bullet in your brain."

The bastard was just stupid enough to ignore the warning and lunge for his shotgun.

John and Coulter fired at the same time. Coulter's bullet hit the man between the eyes while John's pierced his heart.

The bastard collapsed, blood and brain matter splattering.

Dammit, they'd done what they had to do. Still, rage ripped through John. If little Darby wasn't in the house, they might never find him.

———————— , ————————

Amelia hated hospitals. The machines beeping, the strong odor of alcohol and antiseptic, the nauseating whites of the uniforms, footsteps shuffling, coming closer with the medicine carts, the blinding lights from the ceiling . . .

All a terrifying part of her imprisonment at the sanitarium. But worry for Sadie forced her to fight her fears.

She inhaled sharply, stepped inside, and walked to the waiting-room area of the maternity wing. Even though it wasn't morning yet, the waiting room was half-packed.

Ayla, Jake's daughter, lay sleeping against her nanny, Gigi, who was like a grandmother to Ayla.

A soul-deep ache seized Amelia. She'd give anything to have the kind of love Sadie and Jake shared. To have a family and a future to look forward to.

Jake suddenly stepped into the hallway, his face glowing. "It's a boy."

Amelia breathed out. Her dream had to have been just twin stuff, nothing more.

Ayla stirred from her sleep and jumped up, looking tired but excited. "Can I see him, Daddy? Please, please, please . . . "

Jake swung Ayla around, and Gigi gave him a hug. "Of course you can. But remember, Sadie's tummy might be a little sore so we have to be gentle when we hug her."

"Is Sadie okay?" Amelia asked.

Jake grinned, eyes glittering with pride. "She's great. Come on and meet our son."

He waved for them to follow him, and Amelia's nerves settled slightly. A baby was a happy occasion.

This hospital visit was nothing like her others.

As they entered Sadie's room, she saw her twin propped against several pillows, a tiny bundle wrapped in a blue blanket cradled in her arms.

Amelia's heart stuttered at the sight. Déjà vu hit her again, immobilizing her—and she saw herself holding her own infant.

Then a scream reverberated in her ears as someone took her son away.

Ayla and Gigi raced over to dote on the child, and Jake lifted Ayla onto the bed. Sadie wrapped her arm around Ayla and whispered low to her, smiling as Ayla examined her little brother's fingers.

"Congratulations, Sis," Amelia said, striving to banish the nagging voice of worry.

Sadie stroked the newborn's head, a smile on her face. "We're going to name him Ben."

Amelia swallowed hard. Ben, after their father. They'd lost him along with their mother when they were only two. "He's beautiful, Sis."

Amelia backed toward the door. "Jake, can I talk to you for a minute?"

Jake gave her a curious look, but nodded. "We'll be right back, Sadie."

As soon as they stepped into the hallway and the door was closed, Amelia clutched Jake's arm.

"Jake, I'm scared."

"What's going on?" Jake asked.

"I've been having these bad dreams, nightmares about having a baby, then someone takes him away. I think the Commander is there, that he's behind it."

Jake heaved a weary breath. "Amelia, the Commander is dead. We found his signet ring and finger. The DNA proves it was his. Maybe you should talk to your therapist—"

Amelia twisted her hands together. "You're right. Maybe I'm making something out of nothing, but Sadie and I have always had a connection. I'm afraid the dream is about Sadie." Her heart hammered. "That it's some kind of sign that Ben is in danger."

Chapter Two

——— o ———

"A melia, please don't go worrying Sadie with statements about something bad happening to the baby."

Amelia's dream flashed back. It was so real. Was it a premonition? "I love Sadie," Amelia said, "and I just want Ben to be safe."

Regret deepened Jake's voice. "Listen, Amelia, I know you've had a terrible time, and that my father was responsible for it. You have no idea how sorry I am. But I . . . I want to move past what he did to us all and be happy."

So did she, more than anything.

But all her life she'd been tormented by residents of Slaughter Creek staring at her as if she were insane.

Because she'd suffered from dissociative identity disorder.

God knows she'd tried so hard this last year in therapy to get well. She'd managed to merge her different alters and felt stronger than she'd ever felt.

But would it ever be enough? Would people always see her as the psychotic twin?

Would Sadie always have to be embarrassed by her? "I'm sorry, Jake, you're right. Go back inside and enjoy your family."

His gaze met hers. "Amelia—"

"Go." She gave him a gentle shove toward the door. "Tell Sadie I'll see her and the baby later."

Hating that she'd tainted the day for Jake, she turned and fled down the hallway, tears clogging her throat.

John swept the house while Cal called in the shooting and requested the medical examiner and CSI team.

He checked the man's bedroom first, glancing at the tangled sheets in disgust. The stench of his body odor permeated the room. A ratty duffel bag sat in the corner, empty.

But thankfully there was no blood or signs that the child had been there. He searched beneath the bed, then in the closet, but found nothing but work boots, worn clothing, and a few empty liquor bottles.

A shoebox on the top shelf of the closet held photos of Darby in the park with his foster mother, in the schoolyard with a friend, and one shot of him sleeping in bed.

Sick creep. He'd obviously been stalking the child before the abduction.

Satisfied Darby wasn't in the room, he hurried to the second bedroom. Dust motes floated in the air by the window.

A twin mattress lay on the floor. Sheets rumpled. Pieces of rope on the mattress. His mind traveled to a dark place as he imagined what kind of demented games the pervert had intended for the child.

Dammit, where was he? He shouted his name. "Darby, you're safe now. I'm with the police. Tell me where you are."

He paused, listening, straining, and hoping to hear the child's voice.

Instead the sound of mice skittering greeted him. Then the kind of quiet that made his gut knot. Had the bastard killed him?

Or maybe he'd handed him off to another party.

"Darby! If you can hear me, make some noise!" He strode through the room again, checking the closet for a secret door. Nothing.

The hall was dark, but he spotted a bare lightbulb dangling from the ceiling and pulled the string. The light was just enough for him to see the cord to the attic.

Outside, a siren wailed, and he assumed Coulter rushed to greet the CSI team and the ME.

John yanked on the cord to pull down the stairs, shaking off the dust and cobwebs that rained down on him as he settled the bottom of the ladder onto the floor. Slowly he inched up the steps, listening again. More mice skittering. A furnace groaning.

Breath tight, he lowered his voice so as not to frighten Darby if he was hiding.

"Darby, I'm here to help you," he said softly. "I want to take you home."

He peered through the dark interior with his flashlight, and spotted several boxes filled with junk and old clothes. A trunk and an old wardrobe were pushed against the far wall. Dust motes swirled in the moonlight. A dank, musty odor hit him. He used his flashlight to light a path and crossed the room, the wood floor squeaking beneath his boots.

"Darby, are you up here? The bad man is gone. I'm here to take you home."

He paused to listen again, and heard a soft tapping sound. It was so light it was barely discernible. But it was coming from the corner where the trunk and wardrobe sat.

"Darby, make some noise," he said. "Let me know where you are."

Another tapping sound, a little stronger this time.

Adrenaline surged through him, and he raced to the wardrobe. The lock required an old-fashioned key to open it, but he removed a lock-picking tool from his pocket and jammed the tip inside.

"Hang on. I'll get you out of there in a minute." He jiggled the tool until the lock clicked open.

He yanked open the door, his heart pounding when he spotted the dark-haired child hovering inside, his knees drawn to his chest, eyes bulging with fear.

But he was alive.

"You're safe now," he whispered as he knelt and held out his hand. "Come on, let's go."

Tears trickled down the boy's cheeks, a sob escaping him as he launched himself into John's arms.

———————— , ————————

Dawn cracked the sky as Amelia drove back to the condo where she'd lived while undergoing therapy. Sadie had helped her make a painting studio out of the front room, her safe haven from the world.

She shivered as the bitter wind swirled around her, hazy white clouding the air as more snow flurries seeped from the dark clouds. Icicles clung to the awning and windows of her studio like jagged knives. Occasionally one cracked, the brittle ice tapping against the glass as it snapped off in the wind.

She flexed her fingers, which were numb from the cold. As she entered, the scent of her paints gave her comfort, although the dark images of the body parts on the canvas disturbed her.

She shoved that one in her closet.

The paintings of the handsome, strange man from her dreams were less creepy, although perplexing, and made her wonder about her sanity.

Why did she keep dreaming about the same man? Had she seen him somewhere or known him at one time?

Or was he simply a fantasy her mind had fabricated because she was alone and always would be?

And why had she dreamed she'd given birth to a child?

She'd had a male alter before—Skid, a teenage boy who'd protected her when things had gone wrong.

Was this man in her dreams another alter trying to emerge?

Terrified at that thought, she brewed a pot of coffee, poured herself a cup to warm her hands, then flipped on the television to listen to while she started another painting.

This time she'd capture something happy—Sadie and her newborn son.

Another recap of the Slaughter Creek Sanitarium scandal was airing. Brenda Banks, a local reporter and Amelia's friend, had covered the CHIMES, Children in Mind Experiments, story since it broke, revealing the frightening details of the project orchestrated by Commander Arthur Blackwood. An experiment that had used her and several other children. They had been assigned numbers to replace their names. She was Three.

Brenda continued, "Police now know there were ten subjects instead of seven. Subject Six was recently arrested as the Dissector, the serial killer who murdered several women in Slaughter Creek."

Amelia shivered. Six had reappeared in her life a few months before, and they'd shared a torrid affair. She touched her belly, the dream disturbing her.

Was the image of her delivering a baby an omen of the future? That she might be pregnant with Six's child?

No, impossible. If she was pregnant, she'd know it by now.

It had been months since his arrest.

"Commander Arthur Blackwood and former Secretary of Defense Carl Mallard spearheaded the project years ago. But police and TBI agents tracked them to a hospital, where they tried to flee the country." A photo showed a picture of a helicopter exploding in midair, then another image appeared of the carnage scattered across the trees and mountains—charred, smoldering metal along with rescue workers and a body bag. "Both men died in the explosion."

Amelia shuddered as the Commander's photo flashed next. He had the coldest eyes, eyes that seared you as if you'd been burned.

But Jake was right. There was no way anyone inside that chopper had survived.

Sadie and her baby were safe.

She was safe.

"This late-breaking story," the newscaster broke in. "On the heels of the bombing at the women's clinic in Knoxville, we have a success story to report. Yesterday an Amber Alert was issued for six-year-old Darby Wesley, who was abducted from his foster family."

Amelia paused with her paintbrush in midair and angled her head to see the photograph of the boy. He had brown hair and big brown eyes, and was wearing a red T-shirt and jeans.

"Today TBI agents John Strong and Cal Coulter rescued Darby Wesley from his abductor." The reporter turned toward the two agents and pushed the microphone toward them.

"Special Agent Strong, how did you find Darby Wesley?"

The camera zoomed in on his face and Amelia gasped.

Agent Strong was the man she'd been painting from her dreams.

———— , ————

John despised the camera. Despised the media attention.

Hell, he did not want to do that interview at all.

He was nobody's hero, just a man who hated child predators and would die trying to get justice for kids who were too little to take up for themselves.

But the story was too public for him not to give a statement, so he'd agreed to meet the press on the front steps of the court-house. "We received reports that the van the perpetrator was driving when he kidnapped Darby Wesley was seen at a gas station, and we used our helicopters to track down the vehicle from there. Special Agent Coulter and I approached the house and found the suspect inside, passed out on the couch.

"We identified ourselves as agents, but the perpetrator reached for his gun, and we were forced to fire. He died at the scene. While Agent Coulter called an ambulance and crime team, I searched the house and discovered the boy locked in a wardrobe in the attic."

"Do you have any idea why the man abducted the child?"

John gritted his teeth. He could speculate but refused to go there. Only the psychiatrist who was evaluating Darby at that very moment could tell them if the child had been hurt.

Agent Coulter stepped up. "At this point, all we know is that the kidnapper was a man named Curtis Billingsly. He had no priors, so it's possible this may have been a crime of opportunity."

"Did the family receive a ransom note?" the reporter pressed.

Coulter shook his head. "No, they did not."

Which meant the perpetrator's intentions had not been good. All the ugly possibilities ran through John's mind, from abuse to child trafficking . . .

And the one detail they had decided to keep quiet—the crime team had found a large duffel bag of cash hidden in Billingsly's van.

Enough money to draw suspicion that he'd been paid to kidnap the little boy.

———————— , ————————

He listened to the news report about the Wesley kid's rescue in disgust as he drove by the next house on his list.

Fresh snow nearly blinded him, making him slow to a crawl. The damn weather would make it harder to snag the kid when he was outside.

And he'd have to cover his tracks. Leave no footprints behind.

Fucking foster families didn't want other people's leftovers, didn't love them, treated them like they were nothing.

He rubbed the scar on his arm beneath his shirt, then the one on his chest. He had dozens of them. Scars that had made him cry when he was a kid.

Scars that made him tough as a man.

Just like the one from the pin in his leg. That asshole had beat him with a baseball bat, thrown him out on a freezing night. Bloody and nearly unconscious, he'd crawled under a bridge and tried to find shelter. But his fingers and hands and feet had nearly frozen.

And his leg had been permanently damaged.

He massaged the ache. But those scars made him who he was. Had taught him to be strong.

Just like he had to teach the boys.

Poor little Darby Wesley would get lost now. They'd put him back in that system where they shuffled kids around like a stack of cards.

That stupid Billingsly had fucked up big time. Not only had he been spotted at a gas station, but he'd taken the kid to his own damn house instead of to a motel where he couldn't be found.

Loser. Good thing the cops had shot him. He would have killed Billingsly himself if he'd had the chance.

What had the idiot done with the cash?

If he'd left it lying around for the feds to find, they'd be digging around for answers, wanting to know who'd paid him.

If not for the money, they'd probably have chalked the case up to a pedophile and celebrate that the sicko was dead.

But the money indicated they'd know Billingsly hadn't been working alone.

But they would never find out the truth about who was behind it.

No, hell, no.

Not until he wanted their asses to know.

The wind beat at his car so hard that the windows rattled. More snow and ice on the way. More nights when the poor kids who slept in shelters and on the streets would go hungry and cold.

He parked at the old wooden house, took out his camera, and used his telephoto lens to look through the window. This damned woman was like the old woman in the shoe.

She had so many fosters she didn't know what to do.

The familiar childhood rhyme echoed in his head, except he'd invented his own verses:

Eenie, meany, miney, mo
Catch a child by his toe
Turn him loose and watch him go
Eenie, meany, miney, mo

Laughter bubbled in his chest. Except when he caught them, he didn't plan to let them go.

He'd turn them into soldiers.

He'd learned well from his mentor and would continue to honor his legacy.

Because he had his own cause now.

One that would change the world and help these unwanted boys go down in history.

Chapter Three

———— o ————

Amelia sank onto her couch in a stupor.

She had seen the agent before.

That was the only explanation for the portraits she'd painted of him.

But where had they met?

Outside, a storm brewed, the winds rolling off the mountains and beating at the house. The furnace groaned, struggling to keep up with the drop in temperature.

The news faded to the weather, another sleet storm on its way. Roads were being shut down, cars were stranded, the mountain roads were treacherous with black ice.

The wind chimes tinkled in the background, drowning out the story and carrying Amelia back to the lost years of her life. She was in the basement of that sanitarium. Screams echoed around her. The scent of a strong antiseptic turned her stomach.

She tried to shout for help, but her voice wouldn't work. Her hands and feet were strapped, holding her down on the cold steel table. The drugs infused her system and her mind blurred as voices tapped at her thoughts.

The Commander's sinister laugh . . .

You're weak, Amelia. But you're pretty. We're *pretty*, Viola said with a throaty laugh. *Let me find a man to take care of us.*

Shut up, Viola, you're a whore, Skid said harshly. *I'm the strong one. I'll take over.*

Shut them out, Bessie whispered. *It's dark in here and I'm scared.*

A shudder coursed up Amelia's spine as she remembered the subtle ways the alters had guided her, confused her.

But no more. Now she was in control.

Her hands felt clammy as she twisted them together. Was she in control?

If she was in control, why did she still have nightmares? Still feel like someone was watching her . . .

God . . . she had so many holes in her memories. Dozens of nowhere nights when she'd slipped into a fugue state as one of her alters. Days and nights she'd do things, talk to people, go places—only to forget it all when she transformed into Amelia again.

Amelia the lonely, crazy girl with too many people in her head.

She looked back at her painting of the man. What was it about him that haunted her?

She took each of the canvases of John Strong and lined them against the wall.

She had captured his square jaw. His olive skin tone. Thick dark brows. Blue-black hair.

Intense, dark-brown eyes.

Eyes that had looked troubled even as he'd been heralded for saving the child.

But the pain in the depths told a different story. Those eyes were dark. Simmering. Self-loathing.

He didn't see himself as a hero.

And he didn't want to be in the limelight.

Lord knew she understood that feeling. Except she had her own reasons for avoiding reporters and cameras. Her involvement in the Slaughter Creek experiments had become worldwide news.

Suddenly she was famous and everyone wanted to probe her mind as if she were a bug under a microscope.

People not only thought she was crazy, but they looked at her with pity. She was a *victim*. They said it like it was a four-letter word.

But she was also unpredictable, and she recognized the wariness in people's eyes, as if they thought she might burst from her own body and turn into a raging lunatic.

Or a killer.

Six, Seven, and Eight *had* become killers. And another subject had been a cold-blooded hit man.

No . . . she was a survivor.

Desperate to know more about Agent Strong, she rushed to her laptop and googled his name. Seconds later, links appeared, most of them articles about the TBI agent's heroic work.

Six years ago, John Strong had joined the TBI. She skimmed the headlines.

SPECIAL AGENT STRONG RESCUES ANOTHER MISSING CHILD

AGENT JOHN STRONG FINDS LOST LITTLE BOY CHAINED IN BASEMENT BY HIS STEPFATHER

THREE CHILDREN ABANDONED BY THEIR MOTHER FOUND NEARLY STARVING IN CABIN ON LOOKOUT MOUNTAIN

Another case had drawn national attention—

Woman in western Tennessee sold her son for ten thousand dollars to a couple who intended to use him as a child laborer.

The mother, who claims she needed the money for drugs, has been arrested along with the couple, who refused to talk to the police.

Adrenaline pumping, Amelia searched for more information on Agent Strong's background, looking for any clue as to where they might have crossed paths. But there was nothing about him prior to the date he'd joined the TBI.

Nothing about him ever being in Slaughter Creek or being connected to the sanitarium.

———————— . ————————

John cleared his throat, speaking into the mic again. "If you have any information about this man Billingsly, please contact the authorities. Police believe he was not working alone, and we are looking for his accomplice."

The reporter repeated the number to call and John turned to leave. He was anxious to speak to the doctors evaluating Darby Wesley.

And to Darby. Maybe he'd heard something, like the name of the accomplice.

Who had paid Billingsly to abduct Darby, and why?

People didn't kidnap kids for no reason. John wanted to know what that reason was, and if it was an isolated incident.

Or if whoever paid Billingsly was looking for another victim.

He tugged his coat collar up around his neck to ward off the bitter chill. Winter was almost over, but Tennessee had been racked with snow and ice that year and record low temperatures.

He went inside the courthouse to meet with the child psychologist.

Darby's foster mother, Shayla Simms, was already seated in the viewing room in front of the two-way mirror that allowed them to watch the interview. She kept wringing her hands together as if she feared what Darby might disclose.

Because she'd been in on the kidnapping?

Of course, she'd been questioned unmercifully by the police when the boy had first gone missing. Every parent or guardian of an abducted child experienced guilt, but the officer she'd first turned to for help had practically accused her of child neglect and implied that if she'd been watching Darby, he wouldn't have been kidnapped.

He didn't blame the officer. He didn't expect Darby to go home with the woman either.

The psychologist, Dr. Catherine Rowen, was known for handling difficult cases with children.

"I'm so glad to meet you, Darby. You're a very brave little boy."

Darby shrugged, his teeth worrying his lip.

"I understand the past couple of days have been hard for you, but I'd like to ask you some questions. Would that be all right?"

He shrugged again, then released a wary sigh.

"Do you like to draw?"

"I guess so," he said in a low voice.

She smiled, then slid some paper and crayons in front of him. "Can you draw me a picture of yourself?"

He stared at the blank paper for a moment, then chose a brown crayon and drew the outline of his face and body. He drew two long oval shapes for his eyes, then colored them in with the brown.

"That's good," Dr. Rowen said. "Like I told you, you're a very brave boy."

She paused, and he drew his mouth, although he wasn't smiling or showing his teeth. His mouth was a straight, harsh line.

"Darby, I know you had a scary time," she said softly. "Can you tell me about the man who took you?"

Darby looked up at her, fear flashing across his face. "He was mean."

"Did he hurt you?" Dr. Rowen asked.

Darby shrugged.

The psychologist stroked his back gently. "Tell me what happened."

Darby chin's quivered, then he dropped his head forward and began to draw again, this time a sketch of his foster mother's house. "I was playing in the yard making snowballs, and he grabbed me."

"Did he have a weapon? A gun or a knife?"

He shook his head. "No, he just grabbed me real tight. He said he was taking me to a better place."

Dr. Rowen's mouth turned downward. "Did he tell you where this better place was?"

"No . . . he said my foster mother didn't want me anymore. That she said I was too much trouble, and that I had to go with him."

John's chest clenched, and he angled himself toward the foster mother.

"Did you tell Darby that?"

"No," Shayla shrieked. "That's not true."

"How about neighbors or friends? Did you tell anyone that you wished you hadn't taken Darby in?"

"Of course not. I told you all this before."

"You also said the state didn't pay you enough for all the kids. Did this man offer you money for Darby?"

Shayla crossed her arms, her voice brittle. "You think I sold him?"

"It happens," John said, deadpan.

The woman sagged against the chair. "I may not have been the best mother, but I tried. I . . . Darby was just rambunctious sometimes."

"And you had to scold him?"

"All kids need to be reprimanded."

He made a note to check the doctor's reports for physical abuse. If there were signs, he'd personally get Darby removed from the home.

But if she hadn't cooperated in the kidnapping, the abductor had used a mental ploy to draw Darby away from the house.

"Then what happened?" Dr. Rowen asked.

"He tied a cloth around my eyes and put me in his van." Darby dropped the brown crayon, picked up a black one, and drew the rag over his eyes with angry lines. John didn't have to be a shrink to realize he was depicting the terror he'd felt when he was blindfolded.

"Did the bad man say where he was taking you?"

"No." Darby's voice cracked. "Just that one day everyone would know who I was."

John grimaced. Darby had been compliant. Maybe that had saved his life.

"Did he talk to anyone on the phone or meet up with someone while you were with him?" Dr. Rowen asked.

A long second passed, fraught with tension.

"Darby?"

"He talked on the phone."

"What did he say?"

Tears swam in Darby's eyes. "He said I was a good one."

"A good one?" Dr. Rowen asked. "What did he mean by that?"

Darby clenched the crayon so hard it broke. "That I did what he told me to do."

"What else did he say?"

"That he'd deliver me the next day."

John fisted his hands by his sides.

When he found this guy, the bastard would never see the light again.

———————— , ————————

Nerves tingled along Amelia's spine as she checked over her shoulder before entering the doctor's office. She couldn't shake the feeling that someone was following her.

A car zoomed past her. Three strangers were walking across the street, then a shadow caught her eye.

She froze, digging her hands into the pockets of her thick winter coat. The gray fog of winter made visibility difficult, but the shadow disappeared into an alley.

She took a deep breath, telling herself she was imagining things. She stepped inside the doctor's office and greeted the receptionist.

"She's waiting on you," the petite blonde said, then turned back to her computer.

Amelia rapped on her door, then pushed it open. Her therapist, Dr. June Clover, waved her in, and Amelia sank onto the sofa. Dr. Clover had been using hypnosis to help her recover memories and sort the truth from delusions.

"Tell me what's going on today, Amelia," Dr. Clover said with a smile.

Amelia hesitated. All morning she'd debated whether or not to tell her therapist about the dream. She didn't want to sound crazy.

But the doctor had promised to help her.

"Amelia?" Dr. Clover said. "What is it? Did something happen to upset you?"

She released a wary breath. "I've been having a recurring dream," Amelia explained. "I'm in the hospital delivering a baby."

"Your twin sister just gave birth, didn't she?" Dr. Clover asked.

"Yes," Amelia said. "A baby boy. They named him Ben." She held up a hand when Dr. Clover started to speak. "I've already considered the possibility that this dream is some kind of jealousy over Sadie and her marriage and family."

"A very astute observation."

Amelia smiled wryly. "I've been in therapy for months."

Dr. Clover laughed softly. "Does that mean you don't need me anymore?"

Amelia wished that were true. "No. If this is some kind of envy dream, I can accept that. But in the dream, someone takes my baby from me."

"Who takes him?"

Amelia fidgeted. "I can't see his face, but I think it's Commander Arthur Blackwood."

Dr. Clover sighed. "That's understandable. Blackwood robbed you of a normal life for years, isolating you from your family. Maybe your subconscious is working out your emotions and anger because you feel you would have had love and a family like your sister if he hadn't made you a subject in the experiments."

"Maybe." On a rational level, Dr. Clover's comments made perfect sense. "But it feels so real."

Dr. Clover raised a brow. "It's hard for you to believe he's dead, isn't it, Amelia? That it's finally over?"

Amelia nodded. "Of course it is. But Jake assured me that it was his finger and his DNA in the carnage from the crash."

Dr. Clover leaned forward, her gray eyes penetrating Amelia's. "He hurt you so much over the years that it's understandable you have residual fear. Even rationally knowing he's gone, the mind plays tricks on us."

Amelia nodded. That had to be what was happening, just like outside when she'd imagined being followed. But the feeling seemed to have grown stronger lately.

Amelia fidgeted. She wanted to talk about the man in her dreams as well, the one she'd painted.

Dr. Clover grew quiet. "Would you like to try hypnosis again?"

Amelia agreed. She'd do anything to find the answers and be rid of the constant fear consuming her.

———————— . ————————

The winter storm continued to rage across the mountains as John let himself into the cabin he'd rented on the river, a migraine pulsing behind his eyes.

After the interview with Darby Wesley, he'd checked into Shayla Simms. He hadn't liked what he'd found out.

The doctor's report indicated bruises that had been months in the making.

Darby wasn't going back there.

But his other options weren't good either. The poor kid needed a loving mother to comfort him after the trauma, but he had none.

Life fucking sucked sometimes.

He staggered toward the kitchen counter and leaned on it, closing the blinds to shut out the light. Wind crashed against the windows, and the woods behind his log house were covered in a blanket of snow and ice. The cold made his head hurt worse.

With the holes in his past had come the headaches. Sometimes so severe he had to take a pill to knock himself out.

He popped a couple of aspirin, and chugged a glass of water hoping to ward it off before it immobilized him.

There were too many unanswered questions in his past. Too many blanks that hadn't been filled in and might never be.

Not since he'd woken up in the hospital with no memory of who he was, where he lived, or what he'd done with his life.

And not a damn clue as to why he'd been driving a hundred miles an hour on mountain roads, ultimately plunging over a ridge.

Doctors said the head injury had caused amnesia and that he might never regain his memories. Without ID, the police had dubbed him a John Doe.

When he'd been released, one of the nurses had assured him he was strong and would survive, so he'd changed the Doe part to Strong.

Of course he'd searched for information about himself, but he came up with nothing.

A fact that perplexed him even more.

Maybe it was the mystery of his own life that had driven him to join law enforcement. Working cases was where he belonged.

The only place he belonged. Instinctively he knew he'd been a loner before, that he always would be. That he'd done something bad in the past.

Something he didn't want to remember.

It had taken a multitude of psych reports to clear him to become an agent, but he'd made it. And last year, a missing child case had cemented his decision to focus on other similar cases.

The little girl had been three and missing a week before the mother even reported it. She'd been high and too afraid to call the police.

By the time he'd found the child, she'd died from the elements. Buried in a pile of tree branches that had fallen during a storm.

The breaking news of the Slaughter Creek experiments had played into his decision as well.

Too many innocent kids being hurt and taken advantage of. Someone had to do something.

Maybe helping others would somehow bring salvation for his own lost soul.

He slung his jacket onto the coat stand, removed his weapon, and placed it in the desk in his home office. Articles and photos of the investigation on Slaughter Creek covered his wall.

Why that case intrigued him, he didn't know. But like the rest of the country, he'd gotten caught up in following the story.

When local reporter Brenda Banks had begun her profiles on each of the subjects, his interest had intensified. The experiments had altered the subjects' lives drastically. Some of them suffered psychological and emotional problems as well as exhibited violent behavior. Some had become killers themselves.

Others . . . had survived.

Like Amelia Nettleton.

Her story had been plastered everywhere.

When he'd read about her mentally blocking out events from her life, he almost felt a kinship with her.

Why did some victims crumble after trauma, while others thrived and became stronger?

He was determined to be a survivor himself.

One day he would find out who he was and why he'd been in the mountains that fatal night.

The night whoever he was had died and John Strong had been born.

He just wasn't sure he was ready to face the truth yet.

———————— · ————————

The man's ice-cold eyes bore holes in Zack. "Get inside."

"Please don't lock me up," Zack cried.

"You spit on me, you little shit." The man grabbed his arm with hard fingers and dragged Zack down a long dark hall.

"Stop it, let me go!" Zack beat at the man with his fists. He hated him. Hated everything they wanted him to do.

A sharp hand slapped him across the face. Zack tasted blood, but he refused to cry.

Crying only made the big man madder.

He dragged him through a door that he used a key card to get through. A heavy metal door that slammed shut.

Like a prison.

Zack tried to pull away and run the other way, but the man caught him around the waist and lifted him like he was a sack.

A key jangled as the man unlocked another metal door and tossed Zack inside. He hit the concrete floor with a thud. His shoulder snapped in pain.

"Next time will be worse. You have to learn to obey."

Zack spit blood at the man. For a second, his eyes spewed fire at Zack. He took a step forward, and Zack thought he was going to hit him again.

But the phone on his belt buzzed. "Lucky for you," the man snarled.

He clicked his boots together, then marched toward the door. A second later, the heavy metal screeched and slammed shut.

Zack looked up to see where he was. Concrete walls. Cement floor.

It was freezing inside.

No bed or blanket. Nothing inside to fight with or make a weapon.

He rubbed at the blood on his mouth, then crawled to the corner. A small window.

Pushing himself up, he looked outside. He had to find a way to escape.

But the woods were dark. Thick with snow. Tree branches scratched at the window like a witch's fingernails.

A noise sounded. Faint. Far away. A plane.

He lifted higher, trying to see it above the trees.

If he could get out there, maybe the plane would see him. It would take him far, far away where no one could find him.

He pressed a hand to the glass. It felt like ice. Frost covered it. Would it break if he shoved his hand through it?

He stretched on tiptoes and tried to see where the woods ended. Was there a town nearby? A road where he could hitch a ride?

All he could see were the barbed-wire fences. The sharp razor wires at the top would stab his hands. And then there were the men with guns.

Guns that could shoot and kill people.

Were there more boys here? Sometimes he heard voices. Sometimes he thought he was all alone.

That the only other boy was the one who lived in his head.

Sometimes he knew others were there. But they always kept him separate. Why?

Suddenly lights flickered outside. He saw another boy. Older than him.

He was running.

If he got away, maybe he'd send someone back to help him.

"Go!" Zack whispered. "Run faster!"

A gunshot blasted.

The boy went down. A big man stood over him.

Zack's throat hurt. "Get up," he moaned. "Get up and run!"

But the guard picked him up and threw him over his shoulder.

The boy wasn't moving.

A sob caught in his throat. The boy couldn't help him now.

Chapter Four

———— o ————

The ticking of the clock echoed in Amelia's head as she emerged from the hypnotic state. The sweet scent of strawberries filled the air, relaxing and comforting, reminding her of the jam Gran used to make.

But she wasn't at home or with her grandmother.

It was the candle burning on the table. Part of Dr. Clover's relaxation techniques, along with soothing music.

"What happened?" she asked Dr. Clover.

Dr. Clover frowned slightly. "You described giving birth. Then you became agitated when someone took the baby from you before you could hold him."

"That's my recurring dream," Amelia said.

"You described it as if it were actually happening," Dr. Clover said. "It's possible you either experienced this or were with someone who did, and you're projecting those memories into your own psyche as if it happened to you, as if you gave birth to a child."

"So you think I am delusional?" Amelia asked, a knot forming in the pit of her stomach.

"That's not what I said," Dr. Clover replied.

Amelia jumped up from the sofa and began to pace. "Did you meet another alter?"

Dr. Clover shook her head. "No, in fact your voice inflection never changed. Neither did your mannerisms, as they did when you slipped into a fugue state."

Amelia paused, contemplating the doctor's comment. "So it was just me?"

A soft smile curved the doctor's mouth. "Yes, I believe so."

"Then you think I'm just jealous of Sadie?"

"*Are* you jealous of her?"

"No," Amelia said. "At least not in a bad way. I mean I'm happy for her. Sadie sacrificed a lot for me."

"But she's not the one who suffered in the experiment."

"She did suffer though," Amelia said. "And I'm happy she found Jake again and that they're married." Although it was hard not to be bitter. Not at Sadie but at what life had done to her.

"But you want that for yourself?"

"Doesn't everyone want that?" Amelia said, her voice brittle. "Isn't that normal?"

Another smile from the doctor. "Yes, Amelia, wanting love and a family is very normal."

Her words registered, offering some comfort. But part of her knew she would never find love. That she didn't deserve it. Not after the things Skid and Viola had done. "So I'm dreaming about a family, but the baby is taken away because I'm afraid if I find love, it won't last? That someone will take it away from me again?"

"That's one explanation," Dr. Clover said. "Have you discussed this with your medical doctor?"

"No."

Amelia placed a hand over her abdomen. If she had given birth, workers at the sanitarium would have known. Ms. Lettie could have drugged her to make her forget. And Dr. Tynsdale . . . he'd believed she was delusional and would have protected her from the traumatic memory. He might have even decided that putting the baby up for adoption was better for the child.

Better than being raised by a mother suffering serious psychiatric problems. "Thanks, Dr. Clover. I'm going to make an appointment today with my ob-gyn."

———— . ————

Darby Wesley's face haunted John.

Although the man who'd kidnapped Darby was dead, someone had paid for the boy, and John was damn well going to find out who.

Anxiety needled him with every passing minute they had no answers. Whoever had wanted the boy would be looking for a replacement.

Which meant another child might be abducted any minute.

He accessed the files of children who'd disappeared in the state over the past year and attached them to the whiteboard, noting the dates of the disappearances, places the children had been abducted, and their family circumstances.

Finding commonalities, if they existed, would help them track down any unidentified subjects, or unsubs, as the team called them.

Child predators typically stuck to a pattern—they chose victims of a certain age and gender. But child traffickers sought all types, especially if they had orders to fill.

Slaughter Creek wasn't far from Atlanta, Georgia, a hub for human trafficking. The unsub could easily hide out in the mountains, then drive to Atlanta to meet with a broker or buyer.

It could have been what Billingsly was planning to do with Darby.

———— . ————

Amelia stared at the ob-gyn in shock. It had taken all her nerve to go to the appointment. But she had to have answers. "You're saying I've given birth?"

"Yes." The doctor looked at her over his bifocals. "I can confirm that."

The sterile white walls swirled around her. The scent of a cleaning chemical was so strong, she had to exhale to keep from being nauseated.

"I understand you were given a variety of drugs while you were in the sanitarium. Do you remember anything about being pregnant?"

Frustration made fresh tears well in Amelia's eyes. "No. Just the dream of the delivery. What about the narcotics they gave me?"

A sick feeling clawed at her. Maybe that was the reason the baby had been taken away. Because it had been deformed or stillborn.

No, she'd heard the infant's cry . . .

Hadn't she?

Or was the dream her subconscious forcing her to face another brutal truth?

"It's difficult for me to say at this point," the ob-gyn said. "Is it possible the doctor who held you captive stopped the drug regime during the pregnancy?"

"I don't know," Amelia said. But someone would know.

Dr. Tynsdale was dead. But there was Ms. Lettie. The woman she'd trusted. The woman who'd deceived her by working for Arthur Blackwood.

John's head throbbed, but he refused to give in to the pain. He had to find this unsub.

The list of missing children mocked him from the whiteboard. What was the connection?

Devon Ruggins—seven, Caucasian, abducted from the neighborhood park after a youth softball game. The mother had turned her back for a moment to talk to her boyfriend. Other parents had said she'd yelled at Devon for missing the ball, and twice she'd forgotten to pick him up, leaving him to wait for an hour or more. No one had seen or heard anything the night he went missing, though. Not a scream or a panicked cry. Zilch.

Next Regan Ludson—six, Caucasian, abducted from the sidewalk as he walked home from school. Another kid living with a single mother, who worked the graveyard shift at a local factory. An elderly grandmother kept the child at night, although Social Services had been called because a neighbor was concerned the grandmother suffered from dementia and often wandered off, leaving the boy alone. Neighbors claimed they saw a white van in the neighborhood during the days before the kidnapping, although no one witnessed the boy's abduction or saw the driver of the van.

And last, Corey Olson, nine. Slightly older than the other victims, but he was small for his age. If the perp had been looking for a younger boy, Corey could have looked the part.

He lived with his father and was a latchkey kid.

The crime team had the photographs from the box found at Billingsly's place and were comparing them to the database for NCMEC, National Center for Missing and Exploited Children. CSI had also scoured Billingsly's property in search of graves or bodies, but had come up empty.

A relief. But that didn't mean he hadn't kidnapped others and handed them off to his contact.

It was still anyone's guess where they had gone from there.

Amelia gulped in a big breath as the prison guard escorted her to the visitor's room. It was cold. Empty. The table where she sat was scarred with crude words.

She knotted her hands on top of it, studying her wrists where, at one time, she'd slashed them in an attempt to end her own misery.

So much of her life had been wasted because of Arthur Blackwood and this woman.

She hadn't seen or spoken to Ms. Lettie since the woman's arrest. She was the one person Amelia had trusted, the one she thought was protecting her from the Commander.

Instead, Ms. Lettie had protected the Commander and the secrecy of the project by keeping Amelia drugged. As long as her mind was too foggy to remember the truth, her behavior was too disturbed and erratic for anyone to believe her.

Amelia had been shocked to learn the truth about her caretaker.

Sadie had suggested that it might be cathartic for her to confront Ms. Lettie, but the thought of facing the woman who'd betrayed her had hurt too much.

Now she had no choice.

The door squeaked open, and Ms. Lettie shuffled in, shackles around her bony ankles, her wrinkled hands cuffed. She'd aged drastically since Amelia had last seen her.

The orange prison uniform hung on her thin shoulders. Her hair had grayed and was pulled back in a bun at the nape of her neck, accentuating the sagging skin of her neck and chin.

Her skin looked pale, liver spotted, and held a yellowish cast, and dark circles made her eyes look sunken and weak, like she was hollowed out.

When she looked up at Amelia, a spark of anger flared. "I figured you'd eventually come."

In spite of her anger, Ms. Lettie's voice sounded worn and defeated, old as if she might be ill.

Amelia summoned her courage. "You owe me some answers."

Ms. Lettie studied her for a moment, then dropped into the metal chair opposite her, cuffs jangling. The guard looked at Amelia, and she gestured that she was okay. The guard nodded, then assumed his position beside the door.

"Funny, you know," Ms. Lettie said with a harrumph. "He thinks an old lady like me could fight him."

Despite the fact that the woman had betrayed her, Amelia's heart ached with grief. For years, she'd considered Ms. Lettie a friend.

That anguish surfaced now. "How could you have done that to me, Ms. Lettie? I loved you. I trusted you."

Ms. Lettie looked down at her arthritic hands, her fingers gnarled as she curled them into her palms. "I had my orders."

"So I was just an assignment to you? I thought we were family."

Ms. Lettie sighed, her false teeth clacking. "I thought it was best you not remember, Amelia. The drugs kept you calm, kept the bad stuff at bay."

"The drugs made me crazy," Amelia said, disgusted. "They made me dissociate so I could never have any kind of normal relationship. Or life."

"I'm sorry," Ms. Lettie said. "I . . . there was nothing I could do."

"That's your excuse?"

Ms. Lettie looked up at her with sad eyes. "What do you want from me, Amelia?"

She wanted to know that she was sorry. But everything about the woman had been a lie. Maybe the Commander had brainwashed or threatened Ms. Lettie as he had the subjects.

Amelia would never understand her logic or motives.

"I've been undergoing hypnosis and remembering details from the past. I know I had a child."

"Amelia—"

"Don't lie to me again," Amelia said. "I saw an ob-gyn, who confirmed I gave birth."

A long minute passed, the handcuffs jangling as Ms. Lettie shifted. "Have you ever considered that it might be a blessing you forgot things? That you didn't know everything that was happening to you?"

Amelia shook her head. "No, because those moments were stolen from me. And how can I move forward if I don't know all that happened in the past?"

"Let it go, Amelia. You're just opening up old wounds."

Amelia stood and slammed her hand on the table. "Tell me, dammit. I have to know. What happened to my baby?"

"Lord help me, child, I don't want to talk about this."

"I don't care what you want," Amelia said. "I need to know."

Ms. Lettie heaved a breath. "I hoped you would never remember." She waited another minute under Amelia's scrutiny, her breathing heavy in the silence. "It was six years ago. You tried to escape when you went into labor."

Relief mingled with anger and a deeper sense of betrayal as she sank back against the chair. "What day was my son born?"

A hesitant pause. "July fourth. The Commander wanted to terminate the pregnancy, but I convinced him not to. Looking back, that was a mistake."

Her child had not been a mistake. "Did you drug me while I was pregnant?" Please, dear God, no . . .

"No, we eliminated the drugs for months. But once they were out of your system, you started having memories, figuring out what had happened to you and the others. That's when the Commander realized the experiment was unsuccessful, that the effects weren't permanent."

"Because without the drugs, there was a chance I'd be normal."

Ms. Lettie murmured yes.

"You held me hostage anyway?"

"It was too dangerous for the Commander. If you'd gotten free and revealed details of the project, it would have ruined all of us."

Rage at the injustice balled in Amelia's stomach. "I didn't remember the pregnancy until now because you started drugging me again after the birth?"

"Yes, the Commander ordered a combination of drugs and brainwashing techniques to erase your memory."

Amelia leaned forward, pinning Ms. Lettie with a glare. "You believe it was okay to ruin my life and my baby's?"

"We didn't think you'd ever learn the truth."

"That doesn't make it right. He stole my life."

Ms. Lettie rubbed at a spot on the back of her neck, then stood. "I don't know what you want from me."

"The truth," Amelia cried.

Ms. Lettie turned to leave, but Amelia shouted, "What happened to my baby? Was he okay?"

Ms. Lettie hesitated a little too long.

"Tell me, dammit. You owe me that."

"After the birth, I left the room. Then Blackwood came out and said the infant didn't make it, that he'd bury him beside his own daughter's grave."

Zack looked out the window again, straining to see in the dark. Shouts. Angry voices and grunts.

Then a shovel hitting stone.

His hand shook as he lifted it to the freezing glass. Ice crystals were woven in a pattern like a spiderweb.

He hadn't seen the boy after the guard had picked him up.

But he knew his name.

Devon.

A noise sounded. A shovel. They were digging again. Making a big hole out in the woods. Flashlights shined across the dirt. Rocks and dirt crunched. An animal howled.

Terror clogged his throat. They were digging Devon's grave.

That's what happened when you tried to run.

Chapter Five

------- o -------

A melia stumbled from the prison, anguish eating at her. Learning she'd had a child and that the baby had died was almost too much to bear.

Snow flurries dotted the air, her shoes crunching the icy particles as she pulled her coat around her and rushed to her car.

Freezing, she flipped on the defroster and heater, giving them a minute to warm up as she tried to absorb the shock. A prison bus left, hauling a group away just as she pulled from the parking lot.

The desolate wilderness of the mountains passed by in a blur. By the time she reached the outskirts of Slaughter Creek, she'd hoped to be calmer, but her emotions were on a roller coaster. She spotted the pond where children and families gathered to skate.

Still reeling from her encounter with Ms. Lettie, she parked in front of the pond and sat hunched inside her coat. Two mothers helped their little girls tie their skates, then led them out onto the pond and stopped to show them how to balance.

A little boy of about five raced across the ice like a pro, his bigger brother chasing him. Their mother waved, laughing at their antics.

Her son would have been about that boy's age.

If he'd lived.

But he hadn't survived.

She choked on a sob. Finding out she'd had a son and that she'd lost him was almost more than she could bear.

If he'd survived and she'd gotten to keep him, what kind of mother would she have been? Would she have had the patience to teach him simple tasks? To reprimand him without being harsh? To soothe his worries at night?

Or would her own neurosis have kept her from giving him the love he should have had?

Another thought made her insides chill. Who was the baby's father?

She had no idea . . . She'd been drugged, locked away. Was he someone who worked at the hospital? One of the Commander's men?

Sickened at the thought, she swallowed back bile. How would she ever know?

Maybe she could try hypnosis again . . .

Or . . . the answers might be in her journals. But the alters had destroyed those . . .

Hands shaking, she started the engine and drove to the graveyard where Ms. Lettie said her son was buried. It was the same cemetery where her parents, Papaw, and Gran had been laid to rest.

Sadie had told her about Jake and Nick exhuming their sister's grave there, that she'd supposedly been buried by their mother. But when they'd opened the casket, their sister hadn't been inside.

The Commander had made everyone think she was dead so he could put her in his experiment.

Discovering that empty coffin, Jake and Nick decided to exhume their mother's grave to verify that she had died, that the Commander hadn't locked her away somewhere. Her body was in the grave, but they discovered she hadn't died in childbirth like the Commander had claimed. The Commander had killed her and lied about that, too.

Dead flowers littered the snowy ground, plastic ones swaying and fading in the weather, as she searched the tombstones for Mrs. Blackwood's name. Fallen, dried leaves looked like ashes on the graves.

She paused at the monument. It was obvious the grave had been disturbed.

Arthur Blackwood had lied about his daughter Seven being buried just as he'd lied about so many other things.

What if he'd lied about her son? Was he in that grave?

———————— , ————————

John looked up from his desk at the TBI office, his eyes narrowing as Amelia Nettleton walked inside.

The receptionist had alerted him that Amelia had requested to see him. Meanwhile, he'd done his research on her.

Not that he didn't recognize the name. Her face and story had been all over the news. Hell, he even had those pictures and files at home.

But what was she doing at the office?

He stood, his pulse kicking up as his gaze rested on her face. He'd seen her picture from Brenda Banks's profile, and before that, when she'd been arrested for allegedly killing her grandfather.

But he wasn't prepared for the bolt of awareness that shot through him when he looked into her eyes. Mesmerizing, haunted eyes that reflected the strain of the horrific torture she'd endured.

Eyes filled with pain and sadness as if she'd lost herself along the way.

An artist's eyes.

He knew that from her profile as well. Had seen a few of the canvases she'd painted depicting the trauma. A dark bleak painting of Alcatraz. A portrait of herself chained inside a cell. A canvas of psychedelic colors reminiscent of the hallucinogens she'd been given.

For a brief second he felt connected to her. Both had lost parts of their past, had empty voids of time and memories.

But he didn't share anything about himself with anyone. Sharing meant opening yourself up to caring.

Caring meant being vulnerable.

Besides, this woman was trouble.

"Miss Nettleton." He extended his hand, and she stared at it for a moment as if afraid to touch him.

Then her gaze flew to his, and something akin to attraction sparked in his gut.

Good God, no. This woman had emotional problems. She was strictly off-limits.

"Agent Strong."

Her voice sounded soft and lyrical, seductive, another distraction he didn't need.

"Sit down and tell me what I can do for you."

Her hands clenched the folds of her peasant skirt as she sank into the chair. "I saw you on the news, when you rescued that little boy Darby Wesley."

John claimed his own seat, dragging his gaze away from her so he could focus. "Yes, we caught a break on that one."

"The little boy is okay?"

"Other than being emotionally traumatized, he wasn't harmed." He leaned forward, sensing she hadn't come to congratulate him on an arrest. "But you didn't come to me about that case, did you?"

"No." Those mesmerizing eyes met his. "You know who I am?"

He nodded. Hell, who didn't? She was famous in Tennessee. "I followed the Slaughter Creek story. I've worked with Agents Hood and Blackwood as well. In fact, isn't Nick Blackwood's brother married to your sister?"

Uncertainty flared in her eyes. "Yes. But . . . I wanted to talk to you."

He arched a brow. "Why me?"

She fidgeted. "Because I don't want to bother my family right now. My sister just had a baby, and Nick is working that suicide bomber case."

"Go on."

Amelia ran her fingers through her long auburn hair, hair that curled around her face and made her look delicate and sweet. But he'd heard she had different sides. Alters, they called them.

One of them, a teenage boy, was supposed to be violent. Police had suspected Amelia of her grandfather's murder, but later learned the Commander had committed the crime.

She was supposedly in therapy to deal with her disorder, but he had no idea if she was making progress.

"Just tell me what's on your mind," he said, ignoring the pull of attraction tugging at him. Pretty women in trouble had a way of turning him into an alpha dog, stirring his protective instincts.

And getting him entangled in their lives.

He had his own mess to deal with.

She drew a deep breath. "I just learned that I gave birth to a baby boy six years ago. It was during the time I was hospitalized at the sanitarium."

Not what he was expecting to hear. "You know this how?"

"I've had recurring dreams about the birth. At first I thought it was just that—a dream. But I underwent hypnosis, and apparently I've been reliving a memory from my past instead."

So she was still in therapy. "And?"

"I spoke to Ms. Lettie, the nurse who cared for me years ago, and she confirmed that I had delivered a child. But she told me Arthur Blackwood buried him beside his daughter. We know he lied about burying his daughter, so he might have lied about my baby."

John shifted, his interest piqued.

"Will you help me?"

God, he had his hands full with this kidnapping case. "Why not go to Sheriff Blackwood?"

She wet her lips with her tongue and started to say something, then bit her lip. "I told you that I don't want to bother him now. Besides, I did some research. Finding missing children is your specialty."

John grimaced. What else had she learned about him? That he'd lost years of his life? "We don't know that your child is missing, though."

Amelia stood, anger radiating from her. "Is that a no?"

He leaned his hands on the desk. Dammit, after all she'd been through, how could he tell her no? Because she was right.

Arthur Blackwood had lied and used innocents for his own purposes for years. He could have taken her baby and started another damn project in another city. Or another state.

———————— · ————————

Amelia wanted to tell John the rest, that she'd seen him in her dreams. But he obviously knew of her mental problems, and she didn't want him to run like most men did from her.

She needed his help.

"I have to ask you something," he said. "What if you gave the baby up yourself, Amelia? You were young, troubled. Confused. Maybe you thought it would be best for the child to go to a loving two-parent home."

His words mimicked the deep fear in her heart. But she didn't believe it. That child would have given her a reason to fight.

"Because I remember begging the doctor to let me hold him," she said. "But they took him away, then drugged me again."

John folded his arms. "So what will you do if you find this

little boy alive? What if he's happy in a loving home? Will you uproot him from the only life he's known?"

Uncertainty engulfed her. "I don't know," she said. "You obviously think he's better off without me."

"That's not what I said," John replied. "I'm just cautioning you to think about the little boy."

"Just exhume that grave so I'll know the truth," Amelia said. "You have the power to do that, don't you?"

"Yes," John said with a frown. "After all, if this matter is related to Arthur Blackwood in any way, a judge will readily agree."

True. The man had faked deaths before. And he'd kept secrets regarding highly classified government projects.

Secrets he'd taken with him to his grave.

"You said he's allegedly buried beside where Blackwood's daughter was supposed to be?"

"Yes."

"I'll make the phone call now," John said.

Amelia extended her hand, and when he clasped it, a warm tingle spread through her. An awareness that sparked familiarity inside her.

And the feeling they'd been lovers.

But that was ridiculous. Unless . . . Viola had met him somewhere.

But John didn't seem to know her.

It didn't matter. He was the best at what he did, at tracking down missing children.

And that was all she needed from him.

It took John twenty-four hours to set up the exhumation. Against his advice, Amelia insisted on being present, so they met in the cemetery at noon. The snowstorm had temporarily eased, but the ground was still four inches deep in snow and ice.

And the temperature was dropping. Hell, he could see his breath puffing out in front of him.

Ice crackled below his boots as he made his way to the gravesite. If they found the remains of an infant in the grave, it would be difficult for her. But hopefully she could accept the loss and move on.

If not . . .

He'd investigated enough cases to know that kidnappings and illegal adoptions occurred. If the child had survived and Arthur Blackwood had given him to someone else, the child could be anywhere.

That family would be attached and vice versa.

Ripping apart a family was always painful.

The crew had already arrived and set up privacy tarps. A heavy fog fell over the graveyard, adding a dismal feel as John approached. Amelia had beat him there and stood by the small grave, her face pale in the gray light, her body shivering inside her long black coat.

She looked so fragile that for a moment he was tempted to pull her up against him and comfort her.

But he had a strict policy against getting personally involved with anyone. Getting involved meant opening yourself up. And how could he do that when he had no idea who he'd been before? When he sensed he'd blocked out his past because there were things he didn't want to remember? Things he was ashamed of.

Besides, something from his past might come back to haunt him any day.

There were times he had flashes of incidents . . . incidents that made him question if he'd been a criminal himself.

Other times he had the horrible sense he'd hurt someone, that he'd done something wrong that he couldn't take back.

That no one could love him if they knew the truth about him.

Maybe that was the reason he'd joined the Bureau. He was making an effort to atone for his transgressions.

"Thank you for doing this, John," Amelia said as he approached her.

He gave a clipped nod. "You don't want a friend or family member with you?"

"I don't exactly have a lot of friends," she admitted. "The only family I have left is Sadie, and I don't intend to upset her with my problems."

Her love for her sister stirred his admiration. Not that he understood family dynamics.

He didn't even remember if he had a family. Where were his parents? Were they alive? How had he grown up? In a happy home?

No . . . somehow he knew he hadn't . . .

Neither had Amelia. Although, even with her dissociative identity disorder, she still had a sister who cared for her.

Somehow he knew he didn't. That he was alone in the world. That he deserved to be alone.

Shovels sounded as they hit dirt. The wind tossed dried flowers from another grave across his feet. Twigs snapped and broke, raining down across the tombstones. The wind whistled a ghostly sound as if to say the dead below did not like to be disturbed.

The hearse was waiting to transfer the remains to the morgue for an autopsy. They would have to confirm the identity of the infant inside, whether or not it was Amelia's child, and the cause of death.

If there was foul play, a full-fledged investigation would be ordered. Amelia would want answers.

Hell, she deserved answers.

Only she might not like what she learned.

———————— · ————————

He studied the foster home from his vantage point where he'd parked on the street, searching for the best way to get inside. His phone buzzed, a startling sound in the quiet of the storm. His second-in-command.

He hoped to hell the man was following orders.

"What happened to that Devon kid?"

A Honda rolled by, and he ducked low so the driver wouldn't see him.

"He tried to escape. We moved him to the rehabilitation facility for further training."

That was the last step. The kid's last chance.

"Buried a guard, though. Asshole tried to help the kid get away. We had to make an example of him."

His breath rushed out in the harsh night. "I understand."

"If Zack doesn't conform soon, we'll move him as well."

"Fine. But remember, he's hands off."

"Of course." A hesitation. "Did you find a replacement for the Wesley boy?"

Excitement of the hunt sparked inside him, and he rubbed his injured leg where it throbbed. "I'm working on it now. Will be in touch."

Still, caution made him hold off. It was dangerous to snatch another kid so soon. But he had his calling. And so did the Brotherhood.

Chapter Six

---○---

The graveyard stood amid the woods, eerie and dark. Ghostly shadows floated between the bare trees, the images shimmering against the white snow.

Cemeteries always reminded Amelia of the loved ones she'd lost.

She could practically hear the cries of the dead in the shrill wind. See the gruesome skeletal bones reaching up through the dirt begging to be saved.

See her tiny baby's remains lying on the satin . . .

John placed his hand at the small of her back. "Perhaps you should step away while we open it, Amelia. You might not want to see this."

A cold sweat raged over her body, but she steeled her back and shook her head. "No, do it." She would face whatever they found. She'd have to.

John gave them the signal. Snow and ice fell away from the coffin as they opened it.

Amelia's breath caught, a chill skating up her spine.

Only a teddy bear lay inside, macabre-looking against the blue satin pillow where it had been locked away beneath the ground, forgotten and unmourned, as was the little boy who was supposedly inside.

The teddy bear was clean though, well preserved, almost as if it had been purchased new before being placed inside.

As if someone had wanted to honor the baby it was meant for.

She swayed slightly at the thought. That bear . . . it was just like the one her alter Bessie used to have.

Arthur Blackwood had put it inside as some kind of cruel message.

John cleared his throat. "Burying the teddy bear probably indicates that whoever did this . . . cared."

It took a moment for her voice to work. "No, it was a taunt to me. My child alter Bessie always slept with a teddy bear just like that one." Amelia swallowed back her revulsion. "He must have thought that one day I might remember and come looking for my baby."

John's expression darkened. "I'll have forensics look for evidence linking the teddy bear to the Commander or an accomplice."

Another scenario made Amelia's throat thick with fear. What if the Commander or one of his cohorts took her baby because he was disfigured, or mentally or physically challenged?

Blackwood's techniques twisted normal men into soldiers who would have no remorse over killing innocents as a casualty of their cause.

Her heart ached as she watched the workers load the casket to transport to the lab. "I thought when the Commander died and Six was arrested, it was finally over." She turned to John. "But it's not. I can't rest now until I find out what happened to my son."

* * *

The scent of damp earth beneath the snow suffused John, the biting cold stinging his hands. He kicked off the dead flowers that had landed at his feet, his eyes glued to the hearse as the men drove the casket away.

Was Amelia right? Had the Commander put that bear in the coffin as a message to her?

The missing children cases he'd worked blurred together, the common denominator being the fear that nearly incapacitated the parents.

Fear of the unknown and the endless, heinous possibilities of how their child might have suffered.

Guilt compounded the emotions.

Now Amelia was feeling all those things. The Commander's sick way of continuing to torture her even though he was gone.

A parent's job was to protect their offspring at all costs. To fail brought unspeakable pain, grief, and a sense of failure that was impossible to overcome.

And if that child was found dead . . .

Hell, it went against the natural order of life for a parent to bury a child.

"I'll get to the bottom of this," John said, knowing he could no more walk away from Amelia or this case than he could quit searching for the truth about his own past. Because if Commander Blackwood had hurt Amelia's baby or used him as an experimental subject as he had Amelia, the child might still be in danger.

And if he hadn't, if he'd given the child to a couple to adopt, Amelia deserved to know that, too.

If the child was alive at all.

He braced himself for Amelia to fall apart. If she was as unstable as reports had indicated, he might have to call her shrink.

"Thank you," Amelia said.

He hardened himself. "Don't thank me yet. I have conditions. You have to be honest with me. If you remember something, if one of your alters takes over, or if one of them knows the truth, you have to tell me."

Her jaw twitched slightly as if she was trying to deflect the blow he'd given her, making him feel like a heel.

Dammit, he had to set some rules though.

He'd investigated too many cases where parents or friends of the family had lied to him, leading him in a thousand different directions chasing false leads.

He wasn't in this for the parents but for the children. He didn't sugarcoat anything or worry about hurt feelings.

"Where do we start?" Amelia asked.

"*We* don't start anywhere," he said, determined to make it clear that he worked alone.

"But I have to help," Amelia said. "We're talking about my child."

"Then work with your therapist and see what other memories you can recover."

"I will do that," Amelia said, as if that was a given. "But I need to know what's going on."

The temptation to comfort her needled him, but touching her would be a mistake. A dangerous attraction to her loomed in his gut and spiked his blood.

They were both too troubled, both had too much baggage. Both were lost souls.

His head pounded just trying to remember his past, a reminder he was running from dark secrets.

Amelia had suffered so much that she deserved someone whole. Someone who could give her the life and family she wanted.

"Trust me to do my job, Amelia."

A bleakness clouded her eyes, as desolate as the gray skies above. "I don't trust anyone, John. That's one lesson I learned a long time ago."

He didn't blame her, but he could not let himself get suckered into caring about her.

She was a case, nothing more.

Despite the fact that her sweet feminine scent was intoxicating, he tried for logic. "You came to me for help, remember, so let me do my job. But I'm warning you—not every case turns out well."

Amelia squared her shoulders. "I don't expect a happy ending," she said, her voice sad. "At least not for me."

Dammit, that made him want to help her find closure so badly his chest throbbed. Made him want to give her that happy ending.

But he gritted his teeth, biting back false promises. The last thing he wanted to do was tell her he'd bring her child back when the truth was, they had no idea if the child was even alive.

Amelia wrestled with her emotions as she parked at Sadie's house and walked up to the front door. The shock of finding that empty grave had given her a chill that wouldn't ease.

What else had Ms. Lettie and the Commander kept from her? How much more would she have to endure from that horrible man?

Footsteps sounded inside, dragging her from her shock.

The snowman Ayla had built seemed to wave to her from the front yard. Sadie and Jake had probably helped, adding a carrot nose and one of Sadie's scarves. Amelia imagined the family out throwing snowballs and rolling them to make the snowman, and her heart ached.

She wanted a family like that. But if her little boy was alive, he might not even know she existed. What had Blackwood told him about her?

That she didn't care or want him?

That she would have been a terrible mother?

Was her little boy in danger, being drugged and tortured like she'd been?

She shuddered, nausea rising to her throat.

But she swallowed the bile and punched the doorbell. Guilt pricked at her when she looked through the window and spotted Sadie coming to the door.

What kind of sister had she been that she'd neglected to visit her new nephew?

Admittedly at times, she'd felt like Sadie had deserted her, but Amelia understood why her sister had left town years ago, and no longer felt that way. Guilt dogged Amelia like a demon, though. Because her sister had suffered the stigma of being the twin of a lunatic.

Yet their bond was strong, the very reason she'd first believed her dream was about Sadie and her newborn.

Sadie's face glowed with radiance from newfound mother-hood as she opened the door.

"I've missed you," Sadie said as she reached for a hug. "I thought you'd come by when we first got home."

The heavenly scent of cinnamon and apples filled the air inside. A homey scent that reminded her of Gran.

Amelia's throat thickened. Jake had been right to tell her not to worry Sadie. "I figured you needed some time with your family first and didn't want to intrude."

Sadie's smile wilted slightly, and she pulled Amelia inside the foyer. "You're my family, too, Sis." Sadie squeezed her hand. "And you're never intruding. I moved back here to be with Jake *and* you."

Amelia was touched. "Thanks, Sis. By the way, motherhood agrees with you. You look beautiful."

Sadie gave a self-deprecating laugh. "Yeah, right. I'm still in maternity clothes, I'm sleep deprived, and I haven't even show-ered today." She ran a hand through her tousled hair. She was wearing sweats and no makeup, but she still looked happier than Amelia had ever seen her.

Amelia warmed at the sight of the fire roaring in the fire-place. "But that little guy you brought home is worth it, isn't he?"

"Absolutely." Sadie tugged at Amelia's hand. "Come and see Ben. He's sleeping, but it's almost time for him to eat again."

Amelia followed Sadie to the den, a cozy room with lots of throw pillows, a comfortable couch, and a toy corner for Ayla, complete with a kitchen set and doll cradle.

Unlike her own home, there were no dark paintings of Alcatraz or prisons or death in Sadie's house. Only paintings filled with the deep, rich colors of the mountains in fall, a landscape of the creek in winter, a light watercolor depicting spring with Ayla running through a sea of wildflowers, and a bright, sunny painting of Jake and Ayla digging in the sand on a beach with the ocean glimmering in the sunset.

Ben was sleeping on his back in a bassinet in front of the window, a pale-blue blanket wrapped tightly around him, a tiny white teddy bear tucked beside his arm. Amelia couldn't take her eyes off the bear.

"Isn't he beautiful?" Sadie whispered.

Amelia blinked back tears. The fresh scent of baby powder and newborn suffused her. "Yes, he is." Slowly she laid a gentle hand on his chest.

Ben wiggled beneath the blanket, his tiny hands curled by his face, a squeaking sound coming from him as he stirred.

Sadie stroked the baby's cheek. "I can't believe he's finally here. I . . . don't know what I'd do if anything ever happened to him."

Amelia tensed. "I can understand that, Sis. But Ben is safe, and you and Jake are wonderful parents."

Sadie brushed at her eyes, where tears had formed. "I don't know what's wrong with me. One minute I'm giddy with happiness, the next I'm terrified I'll do something wrong. Sometimes I sit and watch his chest rise and fall just to make sure he's breathing."

Amelia didn't blame her. "Hormones," Amelia said, trying to comfort Sadie.

Sadie laughed. "You're probably right."

The baby whimpered, and Sadie gently scooped him up. "Do you want to hold him before I nurse him?"

A deep breath caught in Amelia's throat as the memory of begging to hold her own son surfaced.

"He won't break," Sadie said, oblivious to the turmoil eating at Amelia.

Sadie eased the infant into Amelia's arms, and she cradled him close to her, rocking him gently back and forth. He whimpered, then opened his eyes, squinting at the light as he kicked at the blanket.

"He's so precious." Amelia smiled at the way he curled his little hand next to his cheek. He felt so sweet in her arms, so tiny and innocent, that love for him overwhelmed her.

Sadie wrapped an arm around Amelia and hugged her. "He's going to love his aunt."

Amelia brushed at a tear. Would he?

If her son was alive, would he want to see her? If he knew about her mental illness, would he be embarrassed that she was his birth mother?

"What's wrong?" Sadie asked.

God, she wanted to confide in her sister.

But that would be selfish.

The baby squirmed again, saving her from answering when he began to fuss.

Amelia traced a finger over the newborn's soft dark hair, noting his features. Jake's square chin and blunt nose. Sadie's eyes.

"Ah, it's okay, buddy, Mommy's going to feed you," Sadie said softly.

A hollow emptiness filled Amelia as Sadie took the baby from her, and she turned away so Sadie wouldn't see more tears in her eyes.

Several pictures of Ayla, from birth to kindergarten, hung on the wall. The photos chronicled the little girl on holidays, and as she learned to crawl and walk. Ayla's mother had abandoned her when she was small, leaving Jake to raise her alone.

In the last photo, Ayla, Jake, and Sadie posed together, beaming at Sadie and Jake's wedding.

Sorrow wrenched her heart.

Her son would have been about the same age as Ayla.

Maybe the doctor who'd delivered her baby had taken him because he knew she was crazy. Incompetent. That she couldn't take care of herself, much less a child.

Maybe her son was better off where he was, never knowing about her.

———————— , ————————

John shook off his concerns over Amelia as he stepped inside his office and punched Agent Liz Lucas's number. He'd heard Liz was considering taking a leave from the TBI, that she and Rafe Hood were marrying and adopting a little boy. But she had connections that might help him.

Besides, it wasn't his problem to worry over how Amelia would take the bad news if his investigation didn't turn out as she wanted.

And in spite of the fact that she'd claimed she didn't expect a happy ending, he knew that deep down she hoped for it.

That was human nature.

Still, she'd learned the horrors of people and life, and he couldn't blame her for wanting the truth. If he were in her place and his child had been taken, he'd do everything humanly possible to find the kid.

The phone trilled a fourth time, then Liz picked up. "Agent Lucas."

"Liz, it's John."

"What can I do for you?"

"Didn't you work with a social worker regarding files related to the CHIMES project?"

"Yes, why?"

"This is strictly confidential, but I have reason to believe that Amelia Nettleton may have given birth while she was locked in that sanitarium."

"Good heavens."

"The nurse who drugged her admitted that Amelia delivered a little boy." He explained about the exhumation and finding the coffin with the teddy bear. "Forensics is processing the casket and bear. I need you to ask your contact if she can track down the names of any baby boys born on July fourth of that year. There might be a record of an adoption."

"I'll call her office, but actually she took a leave of absence. I'm working with a new social worker named Helen Gray," Liz said. "I'll have her phone you."

John's other line buzzed. "Thanks. I've got another call coming in."

John punched connect to answer the call. "Agent Strong."

"John, it's Coulter. There's been another kidnapping."

Hell. "Another child?"

"Yeah, a boy just like the others."

Chapter Seven

—————— o ——————

The bad weather forced John to slow his speed, making the drive to the foster family's house longer than it should have been. Worse, a tree had fallen in the middle of the road, making it impassable, and he'd had to turn around and find an alternate route.

He parked in front of the house and cut the engine. Snow had piled on the roof and frost coated the windows, icicles dangling from the awnings.

The house had once been white but now looked dingy yellow. Toys, a sandbox, and a rickety swing set were scattered across the fenced-in yard.

His mind raced. They'd known Billingsly hadn't been working alone.

Fuck. Billingsly's partner had probably taken this kid.

In spite of the cold and snow, two little girls with stringy brown hair and big doe-like eyes climbed a metal jungle gym, the tire swing next to them creaking as a redheaded little boy of about six pushed it back and forth.

At least the kids wore coats and gloves.

The kid pushing the swing looked the same age as Ronnie Tillman, the boy who was taken. Why take one boy and not both? Why had he left the redheaded kid behind?

So far the unsub hadn't discriminated by hair color. And the boy was the right age and gender.

Coulter was already on the scene, standing with a woman in a brown coat and faded jeans at the edge of the playground. She appeared to be visibly shaken, one hand clutching a wad of tissues as she held a baby on her hip.

John analyzed the scene with a critical eye. Since the house sat on the corner of two streets, the playground was visible from the street, easy access for a predator.

One of the little girls dangled her legs from the top of the jungle gym. "You a cop?"

He nodded and flashed his badge. She shrugged, and he decided she'd probably dealt with police before.

"One of the boys who stays here is missing?" he asked.

She twirled the fringe on the end of her snow hat. "That's what Ms. Terri said. The kids were playing hide-and-seek. But we looked everywhere and can't find him."

John ground his teeth at the wariness in the little girl's face. Foster kids usually came with baggage. They were distrustful, had attachment issues, had experienced domestic abuse, were angry from being moved from one home to the next. "Has he ever run away?"

She shook her head. "Ronnie ain't been here long. Just a couple of days."

"What do you know about his family?"

The little girl rocked back and forth, sending snow falling from the metal bars. "His mama's a meth addict. Got locked up for it."

Yeah, this kid was already world-weary. "And his father?"

"Shot and killed himself."

Good Lord. Poor kid.

"If he ran away, where would he go?"

The little girl shrugged. "I don't know. He didn't like the cold or to play outside so we looked in all the closets. But he ain't in there."

The foster mother approached, tugging her hood over her ears. She looked a little rough about the edges, her skin milky pale and dry, her eyes tired. "I'm Terri Eckerton. Ronnie didn't run away."

"You're sure about that?" John asked.

She nodded, jiggling the baby. "He's not that kind of kid. Not adventurous or the kind to wander off."

Coulter walked over to question the girls. Maybe he'd glean some information John hadn't. Sometimes witnesses or family members offered different stories, or added details they might have forgotten.

John directed his comment toward Terri. "So Ronnie was happy about being here?"

"None of the kids are happy about being here," Terri said with a note of sad acceptance in her tone. "They all miss their mamas and daddies. But I do the best I can to make it a decent place for them."

That wasn't John's experience, and he'd grown cynical.

"Besides, Ronnie has asthma and knows he can't be without his inhaler." She gestured toward an army-green backpack on the ground by the fence. "It's in there, along with the picture of his mother he keeps. He wouldn't leave that behind."

John couldn't argue with that logic.

The baby whimpered, and she stuck a pacifier in his mouth.

The redheaded kid pushing the tire swing ran over and pulled at her arm.

Terri used sign language with the boy, speaking as she did. "What is it, Toby?"

He responded with his hands, and John adjusted his opinion of the woman. She might not be financially well off, but she seemed to care about the children under her charge. "Go on to the bathroom. I'll check on you in a minute."

"When did you first realize Ronnie was missing?"

"We had lunch, and I was cleaning up, but the kids were going stir crazy so I told them they could play outside for a few minutes. I put the baby down for a nap, then checked on the others. That's when I saw the backpack on the ground."

John narrowed his eyes. "The kids were left unattended outside?"

Anger flashed in the woman's eyes. "The yard is fenced in. I can see it from the window in the kitchen."

"But not from the baby's room?" John guessed.

She patted the baby's back as he started to fuss again. "No. But it only took a minute to put him down."

John grimaced. "A minute is all it takes for something to go terribly wrong."

———— , ————

Amelia had to talk to someone. And she didn't want to bother Sadie with her troubles. She'd been a burden to her sister all her life.

So she left Sadie and the baby and drove straight to see her therapist. She parked on the side of the road in front of the office, but just as she stepped out, a pickup raced by, swerving toward her.

Amelia screamed and jumped behind her car to avoid being hit. Icy sludge and snow splattered all over her.

Shivering, she wiped at the mess as the truck raced away.

She watched it disappear into the fog ahead, her heart pounding. The truck had nearly run her over.

She started trembling from the inside out. Had he done it intentionally?

Or was she being paranoid again?

Shaken, she turned and rushed up to the doctor's office. She glanced over her shoulder before she entered, searching to see if the truck had come back. But the street was quiet, almost deserted.

Inside, she greeted the receptionist, then knocked on Dr. Clover's door.

Dr. Clover arched a brow when she entered. "I didn't realize we had an appointment."

"We didn't. But I need to talk." She was desperate. And paranoid someone had just tried to kill her.

The ticking of the clock echoed in the silence, making her even more edgy.

Dr. Clover motioned for her to sit. "What's wrong, Amelia?"

Amelia sank onto the couch she'd grown to hate and love at the same time. The heater whirred, the blinds rattling.

"Outside a truck nearly ran me over."

Alarm sharpened Dr. Clover's features. "What?"

"When I parked and got out, a truck barreled by and nearly hit me."

"My God, some drivers are so careless."

"I'm not sure it was an accident," Amelia admitted as she shrugged off her wet coat.

"You think someone intentionally tried to hurt you?"

"I don't know," Amelia said, starting to doubt herself. The roads were icy. The driver could have hit a slick patch. "But I have felt like someone is following me lately."

"Are you taking your meds?"

Amelia startled, debating whether to tell the truth. She wasn't in the mood for a lecture. Finally, she sighed and shook her head. The doctor had insisted on honesty, saying it was the only way she could help Amelia. "I stopped the antidepressants. I couldn't paint while I was on them."

Dr. Clover made a low sound in her throat. "Is that why you came to see me? Because you think someone is following you?"

"Yes." She took a deep breath. "No. In short, my ob-gyn confirmed I gave birth. Then I talked to Ms. Lettie, the nurse who took care of me at the sanitarium, and she admitted I had a son."

Dr. Clover normally showed no reaction, but her eyes widened. "That must have been a shock."

"Yes, it was." Amelia fidgeted, wiping at a drop of mud on her coat. "There's more. Ms. Lettie said my baby was buried next to the Commander's daughter, but since he lied about that, I thought he might have lied about my baby, too."

Worry darkened Dr. Clover's eyes. "You had the grave exhumed?"

Amelia nodded, the image of the bear haunting her. "Yes, I went to Special Agent John Strong with the TBI, and he arranged it. But the grave was empty."

"Empty?"

"Yes. That is . . . except for a teddy bear like the one I had as a child." She picked at another piece of dirt caught in the fibers of her coat. "I mean, that Bessie had."

Dr. Clover crossed one leg over the other. "Why did you go to John Strong?"

Amelia bit back the truth about seeing John in her dreams. She didn't want to confess she was having strange dreams that she thought might be prophetic. The doctor might decide she was delusional again and force her back on the medication. Or worse, send her back to the sanitarium.

"I didn't want to worry my family right now. Besides, I saw him on the news. He's apparently one of the best when it comes to solving missing persons cases, especially involving children."

A heartbeat passed, and for some reason, Amelia sensed the doctor's disapproval.

"Agent Strong sent the stuffed animal and coffin to the lab to process it for evidence." Amelia shifted. "I have to know what happened to my child. If the Commander sent him somewhere to be in another one of his crazy experiments."

Dr. Clover studied Amelia for a long moment. "I'm not sure what to say, Amelia. The uncertainty has to be terrifying for you."

Amelia rubbed her arms to warm herself. The thought of her son suffering like she had chilled her to the bone. "It is."

She stood and paced. "Ms. Lettie said they stopped giving me the drugs when I was pregnant, but who knows what kind of long-term effects could have been caused by the years I did take them."

"So you're worried your baby might not be normal?"

"That's a possibility I have to consider," Amelia said.

Understanding flared in her eyes. She stood and gathered Amelia's hands in her own. "There is one technique we haven't tried that might help you recover memories of that time."

Hope budded inside Amelia's chest. "What technique?"

"It's called RMT, Recovered Memory Therapy. But . . . " Worry knitted her brow. "It could be dangerous, Amelia. It involves re-creating the circumstances in which the traumatic event occurred."

A cold sweat broke out across Amelia's neck. "You mean giving me the drugs again?"

Dr. Clover nodded. "Yes, and conducting the therapy in the sanitarium."

Amelia shook her head, fear seizing her. She'd do anything to find the truth.

Anything but that.

"I realize it only takes a minute for a child to disappear," Terri said sharply. "But we were at home and it was during the daytime."

"Child predators strike at all hours of the day and night."

"Listen, Agent Strong, I feel bad enough about this without you reprimanding me." Her shoulders sagged, and she suddenly looked exhausted, older than her age, which he'd have guessed was early thirties. "But I am honestly trying to help these kids, and I care about them. I grew up in foster care. I know what some of the homes are like."

The creak of the swing made John look across the yard. But the swing was empty, the wind pushing it back and forth as if a ghost was sitting on it.

"Have you noticed anyone watching the children?" John asked. "A strange car nearby or someone new in the neighborhood?"

The baby began to fuss, and she jiggled him up and down, trying to soothe him. "No."

"How about a car driving by often? Or maybe someone walking their dog? Oftentimes predators use animals or candy to lure children to come closer."

She rubbed at her temple with nails that had probably never seen a manicure. "I'm sorry. I can't think of anyone."

Coulter walked over, his dark eyes troubled. "The little girl said she saw a white van drive by after lunch. Said she noticed it because she thought it was an ice-cream truck."

Terri made a low sound of worry. "The ice-cream truck only comes to our neighborhood on Saturdays and not in the winter."

John silently cursed. "What else did she see?"

Coulter shook his head. "There was no snow cone on the side, but the van played music."

Fear and regret washed over Dr. Clover as she looked through the window and watched Amelia run to her car. Amelia kept looking over her shoulder, obviously terrified someone was after her.

She had good reason to be terrified.

Her phone buzzed, and she startled. Her hand shook as she picked up the receiver.

"She was just there?"

She closed her eyes, hating his voice. Hating what he made her do. "Yes."

"She's starting to remember things?"

"Yes. She knows about the baby."

Dr. Clover massaged the knot at the base of her neck. A stress headache beat against her temple. The nausea would follow.

She popped an antacid.

"Then do something," he snarled.

Dr. Clover closed her eyes, a war raging in her mind. She had always followed the code. Done as he'd ordered.

She couldn't refuse him now.

"June, you have to finish this."

Yes, she did. Her reputation depended on it.

Hell, her life depended on it.

She did not want to die.

Amelia wasn't paranoid. Someone was following her. She'd suggested RMT to Amelia, knowing it could help her recover the holes in her past.

But if she remembered everything, the memories could get her killed.

Chapter Eight

———————— o ————————

Amelia fretted about the doctor's suggestion of RMT as she drove back to her condo. If she agreed to it, it meant facing her demons again.

She'd barely survived once. Could she survive again?

If it meant finding out what happened to her baby . . .

No, not yet. She'd save RMT as a last resort. John would investigate and find answers just as he'd found Darby Wesley.

Besides, if the Commander or someone else at the hospital had taken her son immediately after his birth, and they drugged her afterward, she might not know anything more than what she already remembered.

Tugging her scarf around her, she climbed out of her car, her boots sinking into the icy snow as she trudged up to her condo.

But the moment she opened the door, she froze. Someone had been inside. What was that strange smell? A man's cologne?

She grabbed the umbrella in the stand by the door, pausing to listen for an intruder. But only the sound of the wind whistling echoed back.

The wind blowing through the open window in the kitchen.

She hadn't left it open.

Cold air engulfed her as she rushed to close it. But the hair on the back of her neck stood on end.

She glanced at her studio and saw her paints on the tray where she kept them. Except a new canvas stood in the easel, one splattered with dark lines of reds, grays, and blacks. She gaped at the vicious swirls and strokes, emotions pouring through the bleak colors and bold lines.

She hadn't painted that canvas.

Had she?

Her stomach quivered with nerves as fear washed over her. Could she possibly have blacked out and painted it? Had a new alter emerged?

The furnace squealed, and she startled, then remembered the open window and scent of the man's cologne. Gripping the umbrella in case she needed a weapon, she walked toward her bedroom.

Ting. Ting. Ting. The wind chimes tinkled outside.

Ticktock. The clock's noise sounded ominous, as if it were amplified.

Amelia fought the haunting memories the noises evoked, but when she saw the teddy bear, her legs buckled.

That was Bessie's bear.

Amelia clutched the wall for support. She hadn't seen that bear in months. She'd left it at Papaw's farmhouse and thought it burned in the fire.

Adrenaline surged through Amelia as she drove her Mini Cooper toward the old farmhouse where she'd spent her childhood.

She had to get away from the condo. Someone had been there.

She needed to go home, someplace safe. Back to Papaw's land, to the guesthouse he'd built as a studio for her when she was younger. It was her sanctuary.

The road curved and wound sharply around the mountain, the ridges jutting out like spikes, the bare tree branches stark against the gray sky. Dead leaves swirled across the road, the wind whistling shrilly as the last remnants of winter screamed that spring would have to wait.

When she'd been locked away in the sanitarium, she had missed the seasons, missed the spring blossoms bursting to life on the trees, the dogwoods and magnolias scenting the air with life and color, the wildflowers shooting up from the ground, damp with rain, and dancing in the breeze. She'd missed the blazing colors in the fall as the foliage changed, the summer sun clinging to the sky as summer bled into autumn.

Her hospital room had been sterile and cold, all white and metal, virtually a prison, chaining her to the dark loneliness.

She veered onto the dirt and gravel road leading to the farm, a sense of loss overwhelming her at the sight of the charred remains of her family home. The guesthouse remained, but the farmhouse lay in ruins.

Memories of her and Sadie running through the fields, riding horses, and climbing trees floated back into her mind.

Although the memories were peppered with the lost days of her youth, with the alters taking over, with the nowhere nights.

Her therapist had encouraged her to keep journals. The alters had destroyed them, though.

Something niggled at the back of her mind. Had they destroyed all of them? Could she have hidden some of them in a place the alters might not look?

She'd search again.

Hopefully she'd written something about her pregnancy in an entry. Something about the father of her baby.

She pulled to a stop in front of the guesthouse that had doubled as her studio, then sat and stared at the wind chimes swinging and clanging in the wind.

After her grandfather's death, she had moved to the condominium complex for therapy and to escape the past.

But she didn't feel safe there anymore. Someone had been inside the condo. She didn't want to stay there that night in case he came back.

Battling the wind ripping at her coat, she climbed from the car and walked up to the porch. In between hospital stays, when her medication had been stable, she'd been released to the care of Ms. Lettie, and she'd lived in the guesthouse. Maybe the answers to her lost years were there.

Nerves tingled along her spine, fear clawing at her.

But she summoned her courage, unlocked the door, and stepped inside.

The voices of the alters whispered through the house, reminding her she hadn't lived there alone.

The paintings she'd done during her most tumultuous years lined the walls, a sea of macabre renditions of being imprisoned, of the darkness that had consumed her life.

Of the fear that had nearly choked her as she'd begun to merge her alters and realized what some of them had done. That Skid, the teenage boy who'd vowed to protect her, had actually wanted to destroy her completely so he could take over.

She'd also painted side-by-side views of her and Sadie, the comparison stark. Sadie was light and she was dark.

"You're not all dark," she whispered to herself.

And she wouldn't let the demons win.

She walked through the rooms, searching the desk drawers and the closet for the journals or something, anything, Papaw could have left behind.

The old church hymnal that Papaw had loved so much sat on the end table by her bed alongside his Bible.

Papaw had believed in God and redemption. He'd always been close to the preacher and considered him a friend.

Hope spiked in her chest. If Papaw had known anything about her baby, the one person he would have turned to was Reverend Bartholomew. He told him everything.

———————— . ————————

John searched the computer database for missing boys with the same MO as his current case, five- to nine-year-olds, and noted they all had one thing in common.

They all came from troubled families or foster homes.

Other similarities in the MO—none of the kids had come from families with money, no ransom demands had been made, and there were no witnesses.

Which made the motive for the crimes even more chilling.

———————— . ————————

Zack scratched a picture of an airplane on the wall. The airplane would take him away one day. He would fly over the clouds and the ocean and the trees and find where he was supposed to be.

Far away from the banshees.

The door opened and the big man with the steel-colored eyes stared down at him.

"Where's Devon?" Zack asked.

The man's hand fell to the metal rod at his belt. Zack's legs shook. Was he going to use it on him?

"Devon is gone. And if you don't cooperate, the same thing will happen to you."

Zack straightened his shoulders. He wouldn't cry or scream.

They would punish him for that.

He had to fight them though. He wasn't meant to live there. He didn't fit.

He didn't know how he knew, but he did. It was just a feeling that something wasn't right.

That he was meant to be somewhere else. Like the little boy who talked to him in his head. He belonged with him. They could be friends.

But the big man jerked him by the arm and ordered him to walk. Zack did as he said, looking for a way to escape as he led him down the hall. Footsteps sounded outside.

Guns fired. A truck rumbled.

Metal screeched as the guard opened a heavy door and pushed Zack through it.

Chapter Nine

————— ⊙ —————

The small wooden church sat on a hill overlooking Angel's Ridge, its steeple rising toward the heavens. The ridge had been named for the folk legend claiming that parishioners had seen angels floating in the clouds above the church, their sweet voices echoing along the ridge.

The place should have brought peace, yet Amelia broke out in a cold sweat as she climbed the steps.

Papaw had loved this church. He'd confessed his sins weekly to the preacher. If he'd known about her baby, he could have told Reverend Bartholomew.

But the place brought back more dark memories for her. When she was small and the voices had emerged, Papaw had brought her to the church, hoping the preacher could save her soul.

"I'm at my wits end," he'd said. "The devil's done got in my little girl."

"We'll perform an exorcism," the reverend had said. "We'll purge those demons."

They'd tied her down, and the preacher had shouted and spoken to God. His hands had touched her, cold and icy, then he'd spoken in tongues, telling the devil to release her.

He'd even let snakes crawl over her body.

Then they'd stripped her and taken her to the river and immersed her below the water. All the time the preacher and her father had prayed and begged God to purge her of the demons.

Her screams had bounced off the mountain, yet no one had come to rescue her.

That night she'd lain shaking and frostbitten beneath Gran's blankets, alone and terrified. She had nightmares of hell for weeks afterward, certain she was going to burn like the Salem witches.

Shuddering at the fear that quaked through her once more, she almost turned and ran back to the safety of her car.

But a thunderous roar sounded, and she looked up to see a tree branch snap off and fly down toward her.

Amelia jumped to the side to dodge it, her body shaking. A nervous laugh bubbled in her throat.

"Is that you, God, telling me I don't belong here?"

"You don't," another voice whispered. Her alter Rachel, the religious zealot who'd tormented her when she'd dated Six.

Rachel had disappeared when Amelia turned Six in to the police. But she must have just lain dormant, waiting on another chance to surface.

Amelia straightened her shoulders and reached for the door. "I'm not here for redemption. But my baby didn't deserve to be hurt by Blackwood."

Determined, she entered the small church her papaw had loved, feeling like a foreigner. The door banged shut. An omen maybe?

No, she refused to let it deter her.

Although she expected lightning to strike any minute.

Crystals of light shimmered through the stained-glass windows, slanting a rainbow of colors across the whitewashed floors. Organ music chimed from speakers, dramatic and reminding her the church was a hellfire-and-damnation church with primitive Southern roots.

She ran her fingers along the smooth wood of the pews as she walked down the center aisle, her gaze focused on the cross at the top of the altar and the carving of Jesus below it, his hands folded in prayer, his eyes cast upward to heaven as if calling on his father to offer strength.

"Sadie?"

She spun around, bracing herself as she faced the reverend. "No, it's Amelia."

Understanding dawned, and he walked toward her, his robe with the gold sash draped around his neck billowing around him. "It's nice to see you here. How are you doing?" His once dark hair had grayed, wrinkles creating grooves beside his eyes. "Amelia?"

She was suddenly overcome by the idea the reverend might think she was still possessed by the devil. Panicked, she headed toward the side door. "I shouldn't have come." She didn't deserve to be there.

No one could love her. Not even God.

"No, wait." He crossed the room to her before she could flee. Amelia trembled, willing herself to be strong.

He gently touched her arm and beckoned her to look at him. "I owe you an apology for not believing you when you were younger. For not realizing what had happened to you. I'm so sorry, Amelia."

Emotions welled in her throat, making it difficult to speak. "It wasn't your fault."

"Maybe not, but someone should have seen what was happening in Slaughter Creek and stopped it."

"Papaw finally figured it out, and died because of it."

The reverend nodded, a pained expression pulling at his mouth. "Just as your mother and father did."

He coaxed her to a pew, and she sank onto it, her knees weak.

"Now, talk to me," the reverend murmured. "You obviously came here for a reason."

She lifted her chin. "I need answers."

He squeezed her hand, his age-spotted skin a sharp contrast to her smooth, pale complexion. "About what?"

"I'm having memories of the past," she began. "Father, I gave birth to a baby when I was locked in the sanitarium."

Surprise, then resignation, stretched across his face. "Come with me to my office. I have something for you."

"What?" Amelia asked.

"Something your grandfather left for you."

Amelia frowned, but followed him through the back to his office. He crossed the room, and lifted a painting of the Last Supper from the wall to reveal a hidden safe.

"Why do you have a safe?" Amelia asked, curious.

"I call it my safe of secrets," the reverend said with a smile. "My parishioners often tell me things in private, and they give me things to pass on to loved ones. Sometimes it's a confession of sorts."

He removed an envelope, closed the safe, then held it out toward her. "Your grandfather entrusted this to me before he died. He thought that one day you might come seeking answers, and he wanted me to pass this to you."

Amelia took the envelope, then walked back to the sanctuary to read it in private.

What was so important that her grandfather would have the reverend lock it away in his safe of secrets?

John met with Coulter and his chief to discuss the latest kidnapping. He gestured toward the whiteboard, where he had posted pictures and notes of the cases.

"It looks like a pattern began about six years ago. An eight-year-old boy was kidnapped from a home for children outside Slaughter Creek called The Gateway House. It's a home where children are temporarily placed when removed from troubled homes or bad situations.

"The house parents work with social workers to give the kids temporary care, but also to find them permanent homes."

"So others have gone missing from that place?"

"Some, yes, although there are other cases from different places. The kidnappings also spanned Georgia, North Carolina, and South Carolina. The one common factor—the kids all came from broken homes, foster homes, single-parent homes where there had been problems reported."

He pointed to the board and read off the information he'd collected.

"Case number one—Leonard Watts, an orphan, disappeared from The Gateway House six years ago, age eight at the time.

"Case number two—Bailey Samuels, disappeared from a foster home. Mother a drug addict. She ODed in prison.

"Case number three—Jim Bluster, seven when he went missing from a trailer park. Father deceased. Mother left him home alone while she went to a bar. He ended up in social services."

Then the more recent cases of older kids: Devon Ruggins, Regan Ludson, Corey Simms.

Darby Wesley was the only child recovered.

"And now Ronnie Tillman is missing," John added.

Coulter rubbed a hand down his chin. "Damn. You're right. It looks like we've got a serial kidnapper on our hands."

"One who hasn't been caught because he jumped states for a while. But think about it. He chose these kids because they might not be noticed right away."

His chief cursed. "And because there are no parents to push the police not to give up."

John snapped his fingers. "Exactly."

But Amelia's child had been taken as a baby.

Her case couldn't be related to the others.

"What's his motive?" Coulter asked.

"You think he's a pedophile?" the chief asked.

John exhaled. "Maybe. Although he could be taking them and setting up private adoptions to make money. The adoptive parents might or might not be aware the adoptions are illegal and that they're paying for kidnapped children. Either way, when or if they discover the truth, they're not likely to come forward for fear of losing the child or facing charges."

"That makes sense. And the man could be making big money," Coulter said. "But most families adopting want babies."

"True. Maybe he's working with a child-trafficking ring."

"I'll call my contact in Atlanta," Coulter said. "He's working undercover on a case now to break up one of the bigger rings."

Coulter and the chief left, and John plowed through the notes on the more recent kidnappings, searching for another connection.

His pulse spiked when he noted that neighbors of at least two of the missing boys had noticed a white van in their neighborhoods.

A white van that played the same music as an ice-cream truck.

———————— · ————————

Amelia's hand trembled as she tore open the sealed envelope from her grandfather.

A rosary fell out, surprising her. Her family wasn't Catholic, so why would Papaw have put a rosary inside?

Curious, she unfolded the letter and began to read.

Dear Amelia,

If you're reading this, it means I'm gone and I never got a chance to talk to you about what I learned.

I am so sorry, my darling little granddaughter, that I failed you. Even Sadie doesn't know what happened that night with Arthur Blackwood, and I prayed for years she'd never remember.

*I tried so hard to get you help, not realizing I'd
trusted the wrong people, the doctors at the sanitarium,
even Ms. Lettie. I take that blame and guilt with me to
my grave and have prayed for redemption, and that one
day you'll forgive me.*

Amelia wiped at the tears trickling down her cheek. "I never
blamed you, Papaw."

Because none of them had understood what was happening.
She rolled the rosary beads between her fingers and continued to read.

*I know now that Commander Blackwood survived
the night he attacked you at the guesthouse years ago,
then hid out and worked behind the scenes to keep his
project a secret. A few months ago when I discovered he
was still alive, I confronted him and told him I was going
to expose him for the monster he was.*

But he played a wild card, one I had no idea he had.

*He told me you'd had a child. A baby boy born on
July 4th.*

He threatened to kill the child if I came forward.

*Please know that I struggled with telling you, but I
feared for your life and your son's.*

*I don't know where he is, but one of the nurses at the
sanitarium, a fellow church member, came to me one
day and gave me this rosary. She was dying of cancer and
wanted to lift the burden from her soul—that burden
being she was at the sanitarium when you gave birth.*

She claimed a woman left your son at a church.

*These beads came from that church and should help
you find him. I had planned to track him down myself,
but Blackwood is onto me.*

*You may think you're weak, that you're not strong
like Sadie, but girl, you are the strongest one of us all.*

*Go find your little boy, and when you do, know that
Granny and I and your mama and daddy will be smiling
down on you and him from heaven.*

———————— , ————————

The dark, cold van rumbled around a turn, gears grinding, tires churning on the ice as it threw Ronnie against the side of the cab. It smelled like gas. So did the man.

He needed a bath. But Ronnie bit his tongue. Grown-ups didn't like to be told what to do. He'd had that beat into him over and over again.

Suddenly the vehicle roared to a stop, and Ronnie banged his shoulder. The man opened his door with a screech, then circled around to Ronnie's side and yanked the door.

"Get out, kid."

Ronnie started to shake. The man didn't seem so nice anymore. "Why?"

The man grabbed his arm and jerked him down from the seat. Ronnie stumbled, his sneaker hitting ice. He tried to stay on his feet, but the man dragged him to the back, shoved open the door, and threw him inside.

Ronnie hit the cold floor with a thud, his ankle twisting.

"I don't want to go with you anymore," Ronnie said. "Take me back to Ms. Terri."

A mean laugh rumbled from the man's belly. "Ms. Terri don't want you, kid. She gave you to me for five hundred dollars."

Ronnie's eyes blurred with tears. Ms. Terri had sold him?

Why? He'd tried to be good. Not to be trouble.

But he was sickly, and that inhaler was a problem.

"Now be quiet back here, boy. If you make noise, you'll be sorry."

Ronnie curled into a ball as the man slammed the door. Seconds later, the engine fired up, and jerked him as the man took off.

He didn't want to cry, but he couldn't help it. Ms. Terri didn't want him. But what was this man going to do to him?

He'd paid money for him? What did that mean?

Ronnie had heard stories on the streets about what boys had to do to earn their keep. His stomach pitched at the thought.

The truck bounced over a pothole, jarring his teeth, and he dragged himself up against the side. It was cold one minute and hot the next.

And the air smelled funny. Nasty, like someone had peed back there.

He suddenly couldn't breathe. Air was getting stuck in his throat. His nose felt funny. His head ached. He was gagging . . .

He crawled around, using his hands to search in the dark. He needed his medicine. But there was nothing on the floor of the van.

Terror ran through him. His inhaler—where was it?

In his backpack.

He heaved for a breath again. But that was in the yard.

Not in the van with him.

He gasped, leaning over on his hands and knees. It was his asthma. It was getting worse.

The truck bounced over a pothole, and he collapsed on the cold steel bed. He crawled toward the back door and hunted for a latch to open it from the inside. But it was too high and he couldn't reach it.

The asthma was getting worse. No air . . . no air . . .

He fell back onto the floor, straining for a breath. But he couldn't take one . . .

Chapter Ten

⊙

Amelia had thought about her grandfather's letter all night and had to talk to John.

She studied the slick stones of the rosary beads, then traced her fingers over the wooden cross as she battled her way through the sludge to his building.

She didn't know much about the Catholic religion, only that the beads symbolized a counting of prayers.

And that her grandfather had left them as a clue.

Gathering her composure, she hurried inside to his office, shaking snow off her hair. When she knocked, he called for her to come in.

He looked rumpled and tired as if he hadn't slept much the night before.

"Amelia," he said with an eyebrow raised. "What brings you here?"

Photographs of several boys were tacked on a whiteboard to the side of his desk. One was Darby Wesley. Notes were scattered across his desk, as if he'd been sifting through them.

"You've been working all night?"

"There was another kidnapping."

Panic mingled with worry for the missing child. No wonder he looked exhausted. "Another little boy?"

He nodded. "Ronnie Tillman. Mom's in prison, father's dead. The boy was abducted from his foster home."

"Do you think it was connected to the Wesley kidnapping?"

"It looks that way. All I know so far is that the kidnapper was driving a white van. The other kids in the yard heard music similar to that of an ice-cream truck."

"That's how he lured the boy to him," Amelia said with a shudder.

"Exactly." John went to the credenza and poured himself some coffee. He offered her a cup, but she declined.

"Now why did you come?"

She tensed at his irritated tone.

"I know you're busy," she said. "But this is important, John."

An awkward moment stretched between them. "I'm sorry, Amelia, but this case is a priority. It has to take precedence. A little boy's life depends on it."

"What about my little boy?" she asked, anger hardening her voice.

"I'm sorry but your son has been gone for years, and is probably in a home with another family. This child has asthma and doesn't have his inhaler with him. If he has an asthma attack, he could die."

John hadn't meant to make Amelia feel guilty. But he was worried sick about the Tillman boy. And every hour that passed lessened his chances of finding him alive.

Besides, something about the mere sight of her disturbed him on a level he had to deny.

He wanted her.

In spite of all the reasons he shouldn't, he ached to touch her. To remind himself that something beautiful existed in the midst of all the darkness and pain and violence in the world.

But that dark world was his. It was where he belonged. Not with someone special like Amelia.

Amelia rose from the chair, her mouth firmly set. "Then I'll leave you to work," she said. "I can take care of this myself."

Her tone raised a red flag. "Take care of what?"

"Nothing," she said, although disappointment flickered in her eyes as she turned away.

Dammit.

Knowing that Arthur Blackwood might have been involved meant that asking questions could endanger Amelia.

There was no telling how many minions he had working for him. One of them might try to silence her as they had before.

He bolted up from his chair and stopped her at the door with a light hand to her shoulder. That simple touch sparked a current of awareness in him that made him yank his hand back.

"All right, talk to me, Amelia," he said gruffly.

She angled her head, the orbs of her eyes filled with such deep anguish that he felt her pain in his soul.

"I spoke to Reverend Bartholomew. He was a friend of my grandfather's and his pastor for years."

She had to be going somewhere with this. "And?"

"Before he died, Papaw gave the preacher a letter for me."

"What did the letter say?"

Amelia wet her lips with her tongue, drawing his gaze to her mouth. A big mistake. He suddenly imagined kissing her, hunger jolting through him.

Not a good sign.

"That he was sorry for what the Commander did to me, and he was trying to make things right." She held the necklace in her hand. "Papaw discovered I'd had a baby boy. He left me these rosary beads."

A strong sense of déjà vu hit John as he looked at the cross. A faint memory of being inside a Catholic church.

A feeling of needing to pay penance.

"Was your family Catholic?"

Amelia shook her head. "No. But these came from the church where my baby was left. Papaw said he didn't have time to trace them, that Blackwood was onto him."

John frowned, details of the Catholic church playing in his head.

"Rosary means 'crown of roses,'" John said instinctively. "It refers to a series of prayers. The traditional fifteen mysteries of the rosary were standardized in the first century."

Amelia looked at him with an odd expression. "You're Catholic?"

"No." At least he didn't think he was. But there were all those lost years of his life.

A time he knew nothing about. And the distinctive sense he'd needed a confessional . . .

"May I look at them?"

She handed the beads to him, and he cradled them in his palm. Suddenly he saw himself as a small boy, ducking into a church. Organ music groaned from the front as people filed in and knelt, made the sign of the cross, and bowed their heads in prayer.

But he wasn't part of the service. He was hiding out.

Why?

"Do you think we can trace them to a specific church?" Amelia asked.

He narrowed his eyes. "You can buy rosary beads at dozens of places, and online."

"But these are old," Amelia said. "And look at the back of the cross. A symbol of a saint is etched on it."

John walked back to the computer and clicked some keys, searching for Catholic churches near Slaughter Creek.

A list appeared on the screen along with pictures of the churches and rosaries associated with them. Some rosaries were fashioned from wood, some from silver, with various combinations of saints and religious symbols on them.

"There it is, see the small 'SMHC,' " Amelia said, excitement marking her tone. "Saint Mary's Holy Church. It's about thirty miles from here. I have to go there. Someone at that church might know what happened to my baby."

John stood. "I'll check it out." The last thing he wanted was for her to go and be disappointed. Cold cases were difficult.

Witnesses forgot things, paperwork got lost, sometimes those connected with a crime had passed on.

And if the Commander had been involved, it might be dangerous.

Amelia had been mentally unstable at the time she gave birth. It wasn't a stretch to think she'd done something to the baby.

Something she didn't remember because it was too painful for her to face.

———————— . ————————

The ride to St. Mary's Holy Church dragged, compounded by the new storm moving in and slowing traffic. Wind and sleet battered the vehicle, turning the skies a blackish gray and making the woods seem even eerier. Debris from the latest hailstorm had torn branches from trees and tossed them across the road and forest.

"I'm sorry to pull you away from the kidnapping case," Amelia said.

John checked his watch. "It's all right. Coulter is researching other cases for a connection. He'll call me if we get a lead."

"Tell me about this missing boy," Amelia said.

John scraped a hand down his jaw, his beard stubble rasping in the silence. "The poor kid has been bounced around for years. His mother's in jail on drug charges. He was recently placed at his current foster home."

His phone buzzed and he snatched it up. "Yeah?" A pause. "Okay, keep me posted if anything comes in on the Amber Alert."

He ended the call. "Terri Eckerton, Ronnie's foster mother, wants to make a plea for Ronnie on TV."

"What about the real mother?" Amelia asked.

"She signed away all rights. She cared more about her next fix than her son."

Terrible. She could never abandon a child.

But Skid or Viola could have.

———————— , ————————

Helen Gray studied the picture of Ronnie Tillman on the news for any signs he might be the boy she was looking for.

She'd joined the social-work group months before in hopes of finding him and making things right. She'd tried so hard these past few years to atone for her mistakes.

But so far, she hadn't had any luck.

Her coworker Sara tapped Ronnie's photo with a grimace. "This kid is just one of a dozen who disappeared this week across the country. I'm so glad you decided to join our group. We need all the help we can get placing these children and following up to make sure they're taken care of."

Helen nodded, nerves on edge. "Ronnie Tillman has health issues. They need to find him fast."

"He's a sweet-looking kid," Sara said. "But he's had a tough life. No one wants a child with health problems and an attitude."

"He's spunky?"

"That was the last family's complaint."

But spunk could be a positive attribute. It could help him survive.

She studied his face again. Ronnie had dirty brown hair and was small, but he was the right age. Six.

For years she'd studied every little boy in a stroller, on the play-ground, at the park, inside a store, searching everywhere she went.

She'd failed as a mother. Had been lured into bed by a monster years ago, one who'd hooked his claws in her and held on tight, using whatever method of torment he could to keep her silent and at his beck and call.

Sara grabbed a stack of folders and waved as she left for a meeting.

Troubled, Helen walked outside the office onto the deck, her breath catching at the way the wood frame hung over the sharp ridge, leaving a half-mile drop into the canyon where anyone who fell over would meet certain death.

She'd been teetering on the edge for years. Daring herself to jump and end the guilt.

Daring herself to live and confess the truth about what she'd done.

———————— . ————————

"Holy fucking mother," he muttered as he opened the back of the van and found the boy on the floor, his body shaking like he was having a convulsion.

"What's wrong with you, kid?"

The boy didn't respond.

Cold terror shot through him, and he shook the kid. But the boy simply looked up at him with glassy eyes.

Shit. He'd been in a hurry and hadn't done his research on this one. He liked the healthy, strong ones.

But this kid's skin was ice cold, his lips turning blue.

He shook him again, but the boy's feet banged the metal floor of the van, and he was as limp as a dead snake.

Furious and scared the boy would die, he closed the door, jumped back in the van and drove like hell. Damn sleet drilled against the windshield, and fog blurred his view. He swerved to avoid a tree in the road, cursing.

The kid needed a doctor, but a hospital would ask questions, want insurance.

Call the police.

What a fucking mess.

Sweat beaded on his hands as he spun the van around and raced toward the little clinic he'd passed down the road. A doc-in-the-box.

They'd know what to do.

He tucked his gun in his jacket pocket, relieved when he spotted the clinic ahead. Only one car in the parking lot. Had to be the doc's.

Good.

Something about the boy reminded him of himself. He couldn't let him die. Besides, he wasn't a kid killer. He was saving these boys. Turning them into men. Giving them a purpose.

He threw the van into park, jumped out and retrieved the boy, throwing his own coat over him to keep the sleet from pummeling his face. The boy looked pale as milk, his breathing choppy.

Knowing he had to play it smart, he tucked his hat low on his head, then glanced around from inside his jacket, searching for security cameras.

One on the corner. He tucked his head low and ducked, averting his face to avoid being captured on camera.

Breathing hard, he ducked inside, took the jacket off while keeping his hat low, and raced to the receptionist behind the glass partition. She couldn't be more than twenty, her blond hair streaked with red and black, earrings in the shape of grizzlies swaying from her lobes. Her name tag read "Wynona."

"Help. He can't breathe."

Startled when she saw the way the boy lay in his arms, she jumped up and waved him back through the door.

"Dr. Ableman," the girl called. "Emergency!"

A wiry-haired man with bifocals rushed toward him, alarm slashing his face at the sight of the child.

"In here." The doctor motioned for him to place the boy on a table inside an exam room. "What's his name?"

Shit. If he told him the truth, the doc would run for the phone. "Timmy."

"He your son?"

"No, my sister's," he said. "I was driving him home and suddenly he couldn't breathe."

The doctor began to check his vitals. "He has asthma?"

Jesus, he didn't know. "I . . . his mama didn't say. She just dumped him on me 'cause she had to go to work."

The doctor frowned as if his story didn't quite fit.

"You have insurance?" the girl asked while the doctor went to work on the kid.

It was a routine question, but he spotted a local newspaper with Ronnie's picture on the front page and realized she and the doc most likely recognized the boy.

"Yeah, I do." He pulled the gun from his pocket and aimed it at the girl. "Here's my insurance."

The girl screamed and threw up her hands. He motioned for her to sit in the corner and waved the gun at the old man, who looked panicked.

"Just fix the kid and we'll be out of your way."

The doctor's graying eyebrows drew together. "There's no need to hurt us."

He smiled as if he agreed, but the two of them were already as good as dead.

It didn't matter how damn pretty the girl was. She'd have to die.

Chapter Eleven

———— o ————

Paintings of the saints adorned the church. Sunlight shimmered through the stained-glass windows, and a litany of candles filled an altar, some lit, others waiting for sinners and those in spiritual need to light them as they prayed.

Amelia hesitated before they made it to the altar.

"Is something wrong?" he asked.

She wrung her hands together. "I don't belong in church."

His mouth twisted into a frown. Good God, he understood that feeling. He felt as if the powers that be might strike him down any minute and the demons would carry away his soul.

But Amelia had been a victim. Somehow, he didn't think he had been one.

"Why not?" he asked.

"I . . . I've made too many mistakes."

"We've all made mistakes," he said, sure as hell he'd made plenty of them. "That's why people go to church, for salvation."

"Maybe I'm not worth saving," she said in such a troubled voice that his chest tightened.

"You were a victim, Amelia. Commander Blackwood is the

one who deserves to go to hell." He hoped the bastard was burning there.

"But what if my memory is all screwed up? What if one of my alters gave my baby away?"

John released a sigh at the uncertainty in her voice. He didn't totally understand the alters thing, except that they were part of Amelia. The part that couldn't cope.

Dammit, she'd had good reason to invent them. "I guess it's possible, but don't you think that would have come out in therapy?"

Amelia ran a finger along one of the pews. "Maybe, maybe not. Maybe I'm not as well as I thought."

He didn't know what she meant by that and didn't have time to ask. A priest appeared from the confessional booth, his robe billowing around him, his gold cross shining in the light, as he approached.

"Welcome to Saint Mary's. I'm Father Hallard."

"Thank you, Father." John introduced them and flashed his credentials.

Amelia removed the rosary from her neck and showed it to the priest. "My grandfather left these beads for me," she said, then explained about the son she'd given birth to.

"We believe someone brought the baby here," John said. "It would have been in July six years ago. Were you here at that time?"

Father Hallard shook his head. "No, I came to Saint Mary's about three years ago. Father Dennis was here, but I'm afraid he's gone on to glory."

Frustration splintered Amelia's face. "How about a nun or another priest who worked with him?"

Father Hallard scratched his head with a crooked finger. "Yes. Sister Grace was here."

"Can we talk to her?" John asked.

His white brows formed a straight line. "Of course."

The priest led them through a set of doors that opened to a greenhouse garden. Set in the midst of the snowy yard, it didn't look real.

Housing units sat to the left, ivy winding up and down the sides of the stone structure, although at this point everything was covered in a layer of white.

Two nuns sat chatting quietly by a fountain while an older nun knelt in front of a statue of Jesus with her head bowed.

Father Hallard gestured for them to wait until she finished her prayer, then he introduced them. "Sister Grace, this is Amelia Nettleton. She claims that her baby boy was stolen from her six years ago and believes someone dropped off the child here."

Sister Grace clutched the folds of her habit.

Amelia adjusted her shoulder bag. "I think Commander Arthur Blackwood took my son when he was born. Do you remember a man bringing a baby boy here around July fourth of that year?"

Wariness crossed her face, but she nodded. "Not a man. A woman."

Amelia sucked in a breath. "What was her name?"

Sister Grace frowned. "She didn't give her name."

"I know it was a long time ago, but this is important. Please. Can you at least describe her? I'm afraid for my son."

The nun's eyes widened. "All I can tell you is that she left a note asking us to take good care of the baby. And she left rosary beads with the infant."

———————— · ————————

The woman looked familiar to John, but he had no idea why. Maybe he'd been raised by nuns or attended a Catholic school.

"Did the woman say the baby was hers?"

The nun shook her head. "No, I got the impression he was a child she'd rescued. That she thought he was in danger."

"What was she afraid of?" John asked.

"She didn't say. She just asked us to find a loving, safe home for him."

Amelia gripped the woman's arm. "What happened to the baby?"

The nun's eyes darted sideways toward the priest.

"Go ahead," he murmured.

"I passed him through a team. An underground network that helps women and children escape bad situations."

John gritted his teeth. The underground networks prided themselves on secrecy. They had to.

"Can you give us the name of the person you handed the baby off to?"

She shook her head.

"She is bound to secrecy for the protection of the women and children she helps," Father Hallard said.

"Please," Amelia said to the nun. "My baby was taken against my will. I have to find him and make sure he's safe."

The priest and nun exchanged a look, then Father Hallard spoke up. "We can't give you a name or address. But I'll see what I can learn."

Underground networks sometimes used illegal means to hide women in trouble and help them escape. The fewer people who knew about the group, the safer the women and children would be.

John didn't like it, but he understood it was necessary to protect them.

Amelia shook his hand. "Thank you so much. This means a lot to me."

Amelia wrote her cell number on a piece of paper, then tore it off and handed it to the priest. "I'll be waiting."

John's phone buzzed. Coulter. He punched connect. "Yeah?"

"John, we just got a 911 call. A shooting at a doc-in-the-box. A witness claims he saw a white van leaving the place in a hurry. CSI is there now."

A white van. John sucked in a breath. "I'll meet you at the clinic."

"Make it the hospital," Coulter said. "The girl is hanging on by a thread. I'll stay at the clinic with CSI."

Adrenaline surged through John. If the kidnapper had taken Ronnie to the clinic, that meant the boy was hurt or ill. But he might still be alive.

And this woman might be able to tell them something.

He had to hurry.

———————— . ————————

John dropped Amelia off at her place, and raced to the hospital. A car accident, five cars in a chain reaction due to the black ice, slowed him down as other drivers decelerated to get past it.

An ambulance had just arrived, and he hurried to the emergency workers surrounding the patient on the stretcher.

The medic shouted vitals to the ER doctor in charge, one nurse held the IV pole as they pushed the woman inside, while another held pressure on her wound. Blood soaked the sheet and her clothes, and she looked so pale that John wondered if she'd survive.

"I'm Agent John Strong with the TBI," he said, addressing the triage group. "Is this the shooting victim?"

"Yes. Her name is Wynona Akers." The heavyset nurse at the foot of the bed shot him an irritated look.

"Wynona may know something about a missing child. She's our only lead right now to the kidnapper."

"She needs emergency surgery," the doctor said. "Your questions will have to wait."

"I understand," John said, "but the boy's life is in danger."

The young woman moaned, her eyes fluttering open. John rushed along beside the team as they pushed the gurney into an ER room.

Wynona reached for his hand, and he took it. "What happened, Wynona?"

The doctor shouted orders, a page for another doctor blared over the intercom, and the nurse tried to shove John away.

But Wynona clung to his hand as tears rolled down her cheeks. "Scared."

"Shh, it's going to be all right," John said, soothing her. "They're going to take good care of you here. But I need your help. Did the man who shot you have a boy with him?"

She gave a small nod.

John showed her a photo of Ronnie from his phone. "Is this the child?"

"Yes," she said, her voice cracking. "Couldn't breathe."

"He was having an asthma attack?"

She nodded, her eyes closing again.

"Was the boy alive when they left?"

The girl nodded slightly.

"What did the man look like?"

She tried to speak but a rasp came out instead. "Hang in there," he told her.

But a second later, alarms pealed and the nurse coaxed him out the door as they shoved a crash cart in the room to try to save the girl's life.

He watched through the glass partition, praying she'd make it.

But her body jerked and convulsed as they used the paddles on her, and the monitor flatlined.

———————— · ————————

The followers of the Commander were strong. He should know— he had been one of them.

They had united, and believed in his mission. They would carry on his legacy and continue to protect what he'd done.

But now he had his own plans. His own agenda.

"Amelia Nettleton hooked up with that agent John Strong, and they're asking questions about the baby."

He held the phone with a white-knuckle grip. He'd hired this man to do his bidding, and by God, he'd better perform. "They have to be stopped."

Tension vibrated over the line. "What do you want me to do?"

"Whatever it takes."

He ended the call, ditched the van at a junkyard, broke a window in the run-down garage, and lifted a set of keys for a beat-up gray sedan that had been left for repairs. He shoved the kid inside. The clipboard said the owner wouldn't be back for three days, and the mechanic had already fixed the engine and rotated the tires.

Perfect.

The car would help him and the kid get off the grid.

At least the boy was alive. The medicine had eased his breathing, and the kid had passed out. He hoped to fucking hell he slept all night.

That had been too damn close. He'd started the van, and by the time they were pulling out, a black Cadillac had rolled in and parked, an old man and lady getting out.

He'd almost killed them, but damn if the scrawny woman wasn't pushing a walker, the old man leaning on a cane, both of them wearing glasses and hearing aids.

Figuring they were on their last leg anyway, and they wouldn't make reliable witnesses, he let them live.

But any fool could have seen he was driving a white van.

Ditching it was the only thing to do, or else the cops would be all over his ass.

He turned off the main road and wound through the woods, crawling at a snail's pace as his tires skidded and clawed for control on the slick asphalt.

If he could just cross into the Great Smokies, he'd be all right for the night.

Then he could decide what to do with the kid. If he was worth training or if he should cut him loose and move on to the next recruit.

His boys had to earn their spots. Be worthy of becoming heroes for the cause.

Chapter Twelve

———— ○ ————

John called Coulter as he left the hospital. "The girl said the doc treated Ronnie for asthma and that he was alive."

"Did she give you a description?" Coulter asked.

"Afraid not. She . . . didn't make it." Damn, the girl was too young to die. "Anything from CSI?"

"They're still processing the place for prints. The medicine cabinet had been rummaged through so the unsub may have taken some meds for the boy. CSI is checking the doc's computer to see what might be missing."

"Tell them to look at Flovent. It's commonly used as a rescue inhaler as well as to treat asthma."

"Will do." Coulter paused. "At least the perp is trying to keep the boy alive. That's a good sign."

"Yeah, but for what reason?" John asked, on edge. He certainly hadn't left any witnesses behind, meaning he was a cold-blooded killer.

"Did the clinic have security cameras?" Coulter asked.

"Yeah. I took a look, but the unsub must have known the cameras were there and kept his face averted."

"Size? Hair color?"

"I could only make out that he was a big guy. Not fat, but wide like a linebacker." Coulter paused. "Looked like he had a bad leg. A limp."

"Maybe a military man," John said, honing in on the injury.

"Could be."

"What about the van?"

"A partial plate. I sent it to the lab and issued a BOLO."

"Who called in the shooting?"

"An older couple. They saw a white van racing from the parking lot, then found the doc dead."

"They give a description of the man?"

"No. They were pretty shook up. Said the van was going too fast for them to get a good look."

"What direction was the unsub headed?"

"He turned onto the highway leading toward the Smokies."

Jesus. That meant miles of forests and wilderness. Like a needle in a haystack.

"Listen, Strong. The foster mother is going ahead with that interview with Brenda Banks. She wants to make a public plea for the return of the boy."

John grimaced. Not that he blamed the woman. Her plea might bring witnesses out of the dark.

But it might also draw crazies out who'd clog the investigation with false leads.

And waste time they didn't have.

———————— , ————————

Amelia entered the guesthouse at the farm, her nerves in her throat as she glanced at her studio. She hoped the priest could help her. If not, she didn't know where to go from there.

The scent of cologne suffused her, sending her head spinning. She glanced around the room, and saw a dark painting—this one of the cemetery where her son was supposed to have been buried.

Bones and skeletal fingers clawed through the ground. Ghosts floated in the wind. Blood dripped from the monuments.

Her pulse quickened. The canvas had been blank when she'd left.

Angry that someone was trying to mess with her mind, she grabbed the umbrella for protection in case the intruder was still inside. When she stepped into her bedroom, her legs quivered.

Whore had been scrawled in red lipstick across her mirror. And Bessie's bear had been stabbed with a knife.

Another message on the wall said, "You can run, but I'll find you wherever you go."

God, she'd left the condo to escape whoever was doing this. And now he'd been at the farm, in the guesthouse.

Amelia's head hurt just thinking about it.

"You're not going to get to me or run me off again!" Amelia shouted. "You won't."

Furious, she rushed to the closet, and grabbed her cleaning supplies. But she hesitated—if she cleaned up, she would destroy evidence.

Then again, what if John didn't believe her? What if he thought her alters were responsible? It was just the kind of thing Skid might have done . . .

Shame washed over her. She didn't want him to see how ugly her life was, how ugly it had been.

Biting back tears, she scrubbed the mirror clean. Then she took Bessie's bear, wrapped it in a blanket, and stuffed it in the top of her closet.

When she went back to the studio, she grabbed a butcher knife and slashed the painting, shredding it. Then she stuffed the pieces in the trash and carried them outside.

Breathing out, relieved to be rid of it, she jumped at the sight of headlights on the road by the farm. She rushed back inside and locked the door, then peered out the window until the car passed.

Leaning against the window, she wiped at the sweat on her neck.

But another one of her paintings caught her eye. This one was a crude drawing Bessie had done. She'd drawn herself hiding beneath the bed.

Bessie was pushing at a loose board and had a book in her hand. No . . . not a book. One of Amelia's journals.

Adrenaline surging, she hurried to the bedroom, dropped to her knees, and felt under the bed. A board was loose.

She tugged at the board, ripping a nail in her haste, but ignored the pain and jerked the board free. She slid her hand beneath the floor and felt around.

There.

A stack of journals.

Hoping they held some answers, she carried them to the kitchen table and spread them out. Viola and Skid had had a tendency to burn them to keep her from discovering their activities. But she'd managed to salvage a few.

The handwriting was so distinctive she could easily tell which alter wrote an entry. Little Bessie had drawn childlike renditions of a monster, and pictures of her and Sadie together riding horses or playing in the creek.

Skid's entries were full of anger and violence. He'd ranted about how stupid Amelia was, that he had to be the strong one and save her. That he'd taken blows from the Commander for her. He told her he'd saved her life. But later she'd realized he'd told her that to win her trust, that he'd deceived her.

Then there was Viola—Viola spoke of raw sex and passion, of her need for physical intimacy, of her need to explore her sexuality. She described slipping out of the house to meet up with boys in high school, of drinking and engaging in a three-way with two men she'd met at a bar, of liking rough sex and to be tied up in bondage.

She skimmed a diary entry:

*I love the men. They touch me everywhere, fuck me
blind. Then I forget what a crazy fool Amelia is. And that
Skid is mean as a snake.*

*I'm the best part of Amelia. The woman inside her
waiting to find love.*

*If she lets me take over, I'll have us a different man
every night.*

Revulsion slid through her. Amelia hated what she read, but she had to face her past to find the truth.

She flipped the pages, searching for any indication of her pregnancy, and discovered several pages had been torn out.

Why? Because she'd talked about the baby she'd lost?

Her phone jangled, startling her, and she raced to answer it. "Hello."

"Sister Grace told me to call you."

Her heart stuttered. The voice was so muffled she thought it belonged to a woman but couldn't be sure. "Yes. I'm looking—"

"Not on the phone. Meet me at Fox Hole Gorge. Midnight."

Amelia glanced at the waning sunlight filtering through the shades. Midnight was still hours away and another storm was brewing.

But she couldn't say no. She had to go.

———————— , ————————

Cameras flashed, the lights blinding John as he stood beside Ronnie's foster mother Terri Eckerton. Reporters sat near the podium, notepads in hand, microphones ready for questions.

Terri spoke into the microphone. "Ronnie is a sweet boy who has health issues. He suffers from asthma, and trauma can drastically exacerbate his condition." She dabbed at her eyes. "I'm begging you to bring him back. I don't have money for a reward, but . I love him and he deserves to have a warm, safe home."

"Do the police have any leads?" asked Brenda Banks.

John stepped up. "We believe the boy was abducted by a man driving a white van that plays the same music as an ice-cream truck. Today the kidnapper carried Ronnie to a clinic for treatment for his asthma, so we do believe the boy is still alive. Although the man who kidnapped him is armed and considered dangerous. He shot and killed the doctor and receptionist at the clinic using a thirty-eight. We ask that if anyone has information about the man or the child, please call the police immediately." He swallowed. "We also advise you not to approach the kidnapper yourself as he is dangerous."

Brenda cleared her throat. "Do you think this abduction is related to the Wesley kidnapping?"

John shifted. Jesus. Saying yes meant alarming the public and indicating they had a serial kidnapper on the loose. But responding with a no would be lying to the public. "At this point, we suspect it is, although we do not have concrete evidence confirming that. However, we do advise parents to watch their children closely and to be on guard for anyone suspicious lurking around your neighborhood, local parks, and schools. Any place frequented by children."

"Is it true that the kidnapper is targeting single-parent households or children in foster homes?"

"At this point, I can't make that conclusion." He took Terri's elbow. "Again, please call the police with any information regarding the case."

His phone was buzzing as he hurried Terri away from the cameras.

"What do we do now?" Terri asked.

He checked the number on his phone. It was Helen Gray, the social worker Liz was supposed to contact. "We hope the BOLO and this public plea turn up something, and that a witness comes forward. This man must have been rattled at Ronnie's asthma attack. Taking him to a doctor wasn't in his plan. That means he's probably panicked and off his game right now. Hopefully he'll make a mistake and we'll catch him when he does."

―――――――――― , ――――――――――

Fresh snow and ice nearly blinded Amelia as she drove along the winding road, night sounds echoing from the woods as she delved deeper and deeper into the mountains. Thick, tall trees crowded together, creating a dark, sinister feel, making her struggle against her phobia of the dark.

So many days and nights she'd lived in darkness, trapped by her own mind, imprisoned by Blackwood's staff and what he'd done to her, that now she slept with a light on.

Devious eyes and sounds warred with the peacefulness others found in the isolated areas, the sharp ridges and drop-offs an invitation to death.

She veered down a gravel road leading to the gorge, the miles of river flowing through the hills and rippling over jagged rocks. The place had been dubbed Fox Hole Gorge after a folk legend that claimed a pack of foxes lived in the gorge and were known to attack humans, tearing them apart with their bare teeth.

Campers reported that at midnight they'd heard the ghosts of the dead screaming to be saved.

Why had the person who'd called wanted to meet at the gorge?

Were they familiar with the legend?

John's warning about not meeting anyone in an isolated area echoed in her head. He wouldn't approve of her driving Fox Hole alone.

But she didn't need his approval. This meeting might lead her to her son.

Still, she wasn't naive. She'd grabbed her grandfather's shotgun and brought it with her.

She wound around a curve, then rumbled down the road, scanning the woods for life. Ahead she spotted another turn and veered onto it. It led to a clearing in the gorge where the foxhole was supposed to be.

She parked beside a cluster of rocks along the riverbank, her nerves on edge as she looked around. Suddenly wondering if she had been setup and why Sister Grace would have deceived her, she gripped the shotgun and scanned the area. It was pitch dark, an eerie creepiness engulfing the area.

She strained for sounds of the rumored foxes, startling when leaves crunched outside and the door to the passenger side of her car opened.

Her breath caught in her throat.

"Sister Grace sent me," a low voice said. "Please, put the gun away."

"I'm sorry. I was just nervous." Amelia placed the shotgun on the backseat. She couldn't totally discern the woman's face, but thought she saw a scar along her jaw. She was slight, a hooded jacket shadowing her face.

"You have to understand how dangerous it is for me to meet you," the woman said. "Women's and children's lives depend on our discretion and cautionary tactics."

"I promise you no one will know we ever met," Amelia said. "Did Sister Grace explain what I wanted?"

"Yes." The woman dug her hands in the pockets of her hoodie, and Amelia wondered if she carried a weapon for protection. "I know who you are and what you want. But looking for your baby could be dangerous."

"I don't care," Amelia said firmly. "I've lost so much already. I don't want my little boy to think I didn't love or want him."

"Sister Grace told you a woman dropped him off?"

"Yes."

"Our network doesn't keep records. But there's a chance your son was taken to The Gateway House." She slipped a folded scrap of paper into Amelia's hand. "It's outside Slaughter Creek. I don't know what happened to him from there."

Amelia clutched the paper in her hand, her pulse pounding. "Thank you."

The woman slid from the car and disappeared into the darkness.

She heard a car door slam shut and realized her contact had been parked in the dark beneath a bed of trees, hiding as she'd waited for her to arrive. A second later, a sound exploded into the night.

Amelia froze, terrified when she realized the popping sound had been a gun.

———————— · ————————

Zack rolled over in the darkness, footsteps shuffling outside the door. He balled his hands into fists, wishing he was as strong and powerful as the super creatures he'd read about online when he was supposed to be working.

They seemed to think he was some kind of wizard brain.

He'd failed them time after time. Soon they would realize he was just a normal kid. Then maybe they'd leave him alone.

Or they'd get rid of him like they had the others.

He pictured them digging his grave and shuddered.

The footsteps paused by his door. Something rattled. Then voices.

"He's not working out. We have to move him now."

"Where to?"

"Don't ask. Just do as they say."

Zack's stomach twisted, and he grabbed the nail from the floor and slid it between his fingers. He had to be ready. He had to fight.

Metal rattled. The door squeaked.

A faint light spilled through the gray room. Heavy boots pounded in time with the rapid beating of his heart.

He started drumming his fingers on his leg. The nail dug in. Tap. Tap. Tap.

They reached for him, and he jabbed the nail at the big one's eyes. The guy cursed, and flung him against the wall.

Zack's body bounced off the cement with a thud. Pain shot through his shoulder. But he pushed up and tried to run. The other one lunged at him, and he ducked and tried to make it under his arm.

But a fist came out and slammed into his back.

Zack grunted and went down, face first on the concrete.

Then the big one hauled him over his shoulder. He tried to fight, pounded on the guy's back, but something sharp jabbed into his neck.

A needle.

Then everything went black.

Chapter Thirteen

---○---

Amelia grabbed the shotgun and slid from her Mini Cooper, terrified.

But she had to see if the woman was okay.

She eased through the edge of the woods toward the woman's car, tripping over tree limbs, her boots sinking into the snow as she scanned the area.

An animal howled nearby.

Were the legends true?

Leaves rustled. Trees shook sleet down, pelting her. Footsteps crunched the ice.

She ducked lower, her breathing strained as she rushed to the passenger side of the car. She eased it open.

"Miss?" Amelia peeked through the door opening. "Are you okay?"

No answer.

Her hands shook as she clenched the shotgun. "Talk to me, are you all right?"

A faint sliver of moonlight shimmered through the window, and Amelia gasped.

The woman was slumped against the seat, blood running down her forehead. Oh God.

Panic squeezed the air from her lungs. Footsteps sounded again. Coming closer.

Amelia bit her tongue to stifle a scream, then raised the shotgun and fired into the woods. She didn't care if she hit anyone. She just wanted whoever it was to know she was armed.

Trembling with fear, she jerked to the right and fired again. Another noise sounded like a gun cocking.

She didn't wait to find out. She ran for her car, shielding herself as she lunged from tree to tree. When she reached the Mini Cooper, she hurled herself into the front seat.

A gunshot blasted the air, pinging off the hood of her car.

She threw the gearshift into drive, pressed the accelerator, and roared down the gravel drive. Another shot rent the air, this time pinging off the rear bumper, and she gunned the engine, skimming bushes and bouncing over ruts and holes as she fled from the gorge.

She flew down the road, swerving to avoid trees, her heart pounding as she glanced over her shoulder to see if anyone was following her. She didn't see lights, but heard a motor in the distance, and when she reached a fork in the road, another car appeared out of nowhere and barreled toward her.

Amelia jerked the steering wheel to the right and plowed ahead. The first car raced up behind her, then fired a shot again. This one pinged off the passenger side near the window.

She screamed and swerved to the left, barely missing nose-diving into a ravine. The second car flew past her and raced on, while the first one behind her lost control and careened over the edge.

With a migraine hammering at his head, John didn't sleep. He rarely did. Something about lying down in the dark made the void in his past seem even more hollow.

What had he done in his life before he'd become John Strong?

That nagging feeling that he hadn't always been a good guy haunted him.

A snippet of the past flashed behind his eyes. *He was in the wilderness, his body in camouflage, his face blacked out with paint.*

Get down. The enemy is planning an ambush.

He hunkered behind the dry bushes, but a bomb exploded in the distance. Bodies flew in the air, parts tossed around like rag dolls. Blood splattered as an arm landed at his feet.

He clenched his automatic rifle, bracing to fire . . .

The memory that had come on so quickly left just as fast, and John gripped his handgun with sweaty fingers. He was under his desk, crouched in hiding.

They were dragging him into a hole. A dark pit. Dumping dirt on top of him and burying him alive.

Shaking at the vividness of the memory, he crawled from the floor and sank back into his chair. PTSD—was he remembering that he'd been a soldier?

His head was splitting, pounding as if it might explode. His hand shook as he reached for his pills. He popped one with some water, sank into his desk chair, and forced himself back to work.

Little Ronnie Tillman didn't care if he had amnesia or PTSD or a migraine. Ronnie Tillman was fighting for his own life.

He turned to the wall of pictures of the missing kids, still trying to piece together the facts. His phone buzzed, jolting him, and he tensed. Maybe Ronnie had been found.

But Amelia Nettleton's number appeared on the screen. He punched connect. Something had to be wrong.

"John, it's Amelia. You have to come now."

He automatically reached for his weapon and strode toward the door. "What happened? Where are you?"

"The woman with the underground group called, and I drove out to meet her, but someone must have followed her. He . . . shot her, John. She's . . . dead."

He silently cursed as he grabbed his coat, and hurried to his vehicle. "Is the shooter still there?"

"He came after me, but his car went over the ridge."

"Tell me where you are. I'll call for an ambulance on the way."

"Fox Hole Gorge," Amelia said.

Fear shot through John, making his pulse jump. "Dammit, you went out there by yourself? What were you thinking, Amelia? Do you have a death wish?"

———————— . ————————

Perspiration trickled down Amelia's neck and into her shirt. She was shaking so badly she had to lower her head against the steering wheel and take deep breaths. Seconds ticked into minutes as she waited for John to arrive. Branches and twigs snapped under the weight of the storm, crashing all around her.

John's voice reverberated in her ears. He was mad at her.

But what was she supposed to have done? Ignore the call?

The flames from the car shot into the darkness, smoke curling upward and creating a cloudy haze above the gorge.

She scanned the area, half expecting to see the Fox Hole ghosts floating in the haze.

Or to see the second car coming back for her. But the road was deserted.

A siren rent the air, the engine rumbling as it chugged over the icy road. She flashed her lights to alert John to her presence, relief filling her when he pulled up beside her and climbed out.

Oblivious to the cold, she threw the car door open, and stood on wobbly legs. John's jaw snapped tight as he strode over to her. His gaze shot to the ravine below, at the billowing smoke and flames, then back to her. "Are you all right?"

She nodded, but she wasn't all right at all. Someone had tried to kill her.

"That poor woman," she whispered brokenly. "She was murdered because she talked to me."

Guilt overcame her, making her voice sound as shaky as she felt.

John looked furious, but suddenly he drew her into his arms. "God, Amelia, you could have died out here."

Amelia collapsed against him, her legs buckling. His powerful muscles made her feel safe for the first time in her life, as if nothing could harm her as long as she was in his embrace.

"It's not your fault," John murmured against her ear.

"Yes it is," she whispered. "If I hadn't pushed Sister Grace to help me, this wouldn't have happened."

John stroked her back, soothing her, his voice so low and gruff that she clung to him. He was a savior for children, and she didn't deserve his comfort.

But she couldn't let go of him or pull away either.

"We can't be sure she died because you were asking questions," he said. "Remember, this woman worked with a network of others saving battered women and children. Someone from one of those cases could have been watching her."

True. But she didn't believe it, and neither did he.

He cupped her face in his big hands. "In fact, he could have tried to kill you just so he wouldn't leave any witnesses behind."

Another siren wailed in the distance, and John pulled away, then tilted her chin up with his thumb. "Are you sure you're all right?"

"I will be," she said, gathering her courage. "But I wish I could have saved that woman."

"We can't save everyone," he said. "She knew what she was doing was dangerous, Amelia."

Amelia still saw blood and closed her eyes, struggling for control.

"Did she tell you anything before she died?"

Amelia's chest tightened. In the wake of the shooting and explosion, she'd forgotten. She pulled the slip of paper from her pocket. "She gave me the name of a children's home where she thinks my baby might have been placed. It's called The Gateway House."

———————— , ————————

John introduced Lieutenant Marc Maddison and the CSI team to Amelia, and she explained the details of the shooting.

"Trouble follows you, doesn't it, Miss Nettleton?"

Amelia jutted up her chin. "Yes, it seems that way."

"What happened?"

"I met with this woman to get information about my little boy."

John explained about the underground network, and Maddison grimaced.

"This is the crime scene?" Lieutenant Maddison asked.

"There are two," John gestured toward the burning vehicle, then over his shoulder toward Fox Hole Gorge. "Amelia met the victim at the gorge, but someone shot and killed her. Amelia tried to escape in her car, but the shooter came after her."

"He lost control and went over the edge," Amelia explained.

"Did you see the shooter's face?" Maddison asked.

"No, it was too dark." Amelia twisted her hands together. "After I heard the shot, I ran to the woman's car to check on her and found her dead. Then he started shooting at me so I fired back."

Lieutenant Maddison raised a brow. "You have a weapon?"

"My grandfather's shotgun," Amelia said. "It's in my car."

"Did you hit the shooter?"

"No. I couldn't really see him, so I fired into the woods to scare him off."

"Who was the female victim?"

"I don't know her name."

"But you came out here in the middle of the night to meet her?" Lieutenant Maddison asked.

Amelia fidgeted under his scrutiny. "I talked to a nun earlier, and she told her to call me."

Lieutenant Maddison motioned toward one of the CSIs. "Stay here and call another team to process that vehicle when it stops burning."

The CSI nodded, and Maddison and the other two men followed John and Amelia to the clearing.

The woman's small black Toyota was hidden in the edge of the woods.

Flashlights shimmered as the CSI team began to comb the area.

"Stay here," John told Amelia. She'd already seen too much violence that night. Her look of gratitude made him realize just how rattled she really was.

He grabbed his flashlight and approached the car slowly in case the shooter hadn't been alone. Maddison directed his team to begin photographing the scene.

"Collect bullets and shotgun shells," Lieutenant Maddison said. "We'll need to compare them to the bullets from Miss Nettleton's gun."

The driver's door stood ajar, and John leaned in, frowning at the sight of the bullet hole in the woman's head. She'd been shot between the eyes. Clean. To the point. Immediate death.

Then the shooter had gone after Amelia . . .

His gut instinct suggested the murder was a professional hit, not the work of a raging, out-of-control ex-spouse or stalker.

Which meant he could have been targeting Amelia.

———— , ————

The dirt stuck to Zack's skin. Cold ate at his bones and toes where he had been stuffed below the ground. Water dripped from above, through the dirt. Cold. Icy. Making a puddle where he sat.

"This will make you strong. You must pass the test."

Pass it or die. The man hadn't said it, but Zack understood.

The banshees were screaming again. Singing their song of death. Laughing at the little boys who refused to give in.

The shrill sound was so loud, Zack thought his eardrums would explode.

Great loud shrieks that sounded as if the banshee was in pain.

Or was that her tearing out the heart of another lost one?

There were so many. The little boys wandered the endless halls in his mind. Crept in the side doors in the dark.

Turned into monsters before his eyes.

Just like the one who lived in his head.

"Help me," he whispered to the boy. "Please, help me."

But the boy was so far away he didn't know if it would do any good.

Chapter Fourteen

───────── ⊙ ─────────

Snow turned to sleet, slashing at John as he searched the woman's car and purse and found an ID. He brought it to Lieutenant Maddison. "The woman's name is Deanna Jayne. She was thirty-eight."

Maddison used his tablet and plugged her name into the databases. "She was a single mother of a fifteen-year-old girl. Her husband's in prison for spousal abuse."

"The reason she joined the network," John concluded.

"She has a sister," Maddison said. "Hopefully she'll take the daughter and raise her."

Amelia sighed, and tugged her hood over her head. Already snowflakes dotted her hair, and she was shivering from the cold. "Now her fifteen-year-old daughter is motherless. All because she tried to help me."

"Stop," John said softly. "The woman knew the dangers. She chose to join this group and chose to help you."

A CSI approached with the woman's cell phone. "I'll take this to the lab and see what we get off of it."

"This information has to remain confidential," John said.

"We don't want to endanger the women and children the group is trying to protect."

"I understand," Maddison said. "We'll analyze her phone records, incoming and outgoing, and I'll speak with Sister Grace to verify who's in the program before we step on any toes."

A CSI held up an evidence bag. "Looks like the shooter used a forty-five-caliber gun."

The type of weapon a professional might use, not a street gun.

"Any other forensics?" John asked.

"We're still looking," the CSI said. "So far the only prints on the car are the woman's."

Damn. He doubted they'd get much from the burned vehicle either.

"We found three shotgun slugs," another CSI said.

Maddison turned to Amelia. "I'll need that shotgun for comparison."

"I'll get it." John headed back to his SUV to drive Amelia to her car so he could retrieve the shotgun. His phone buzzed, and he frowned. It was almost one a.m.

Father Hallard's number appeared.

He quickly connected the call. "Father Hallard."

"Have you heard from Sister Grace?"

"No. Why?"

"Because she's gone."

"Are you sure?"

"Yes," Father Hallard said. "She left a note saying not to look for her, that it was safer if we let her go."

"She's on the run," John said. Which meant she might know more than she'd told them.

And she was afraid talking to them would get her killed.

———— , ————

Sleet hammered the trees and ground, stinging her cheeks. Amelia couldn't erase the image of the dead woman from her mind. The blood on her forehead . . .

Her poor daughter . . .

John looked troubled as he ended the call. "Sister Grace left town."

A sliver of fear trickled through Amelia. This other woman had been murdered, and now Sister Grace was gone . . . "Is she okay?"

"Father Hallard said she left a note saying not to look for her, that it was safer that way."

Amelia's heart pounded. "She's scared. She knew it was dangerous helping me."

"But she did it because she obviously believed you deserved to find your baby."

Still, emotions thickened Amelia's throat. Needing something to do with her hands, she fiddled with the buttons on her coat. "Then she thinks something bad happened to him."

John cut her a sideways look. "Maybe. Maybe not." They dodged falling twigs and hail as they rushed to his SUV. John drove to her car and retrieved her shotgun, then gave it to the CSI. Another team had shown up along with a tow truck to check out the burning vehicle and the driver before processing and clearing the wreckage.

"That gun belonged to my grandfather," Amelia said. She had very few things of his left. Most had burned in the house fire.

"I'll get it back for you after CSI finishes," John said.

John caught her hand, heat charging through her. "I'm going to follow you home and make sure you're safe."

Amelia swallowed hard. She wanted to argue that she was fine on her own, but she still hadn't told him about the intruder taunting her with her alters.

Besides, his gravelly low voice sent a shimmer of longing and awareness through her. She wanted to reach out and hold his hand, to hang on to him and ask him to stay the night with her.

But he was a professional working a case, not a man interested in her personally.

And she had too much baggage to expect any man to love her.

———————— , ————————

John followed Amelia back to the guesthouse on the farm listening to the news as he drove. The sleet storm was predicted to last through the next day.

"Roads are hazardous. Please stay home if you don't have to travel."

Right. He'd tuck in and make cocoa with Amelia and they'd stay in bed all day.

His chest clenched. Where had that thought come from?

The images that flashed in his head were so erotic and tender that his body hardened.

Dammit. Staying in bed and making love to Amelia was not an option.

The SUV churned through the layers of snow and ice on the drive, but he made it to the end and parked. The charred remains of the old farmhouse reminded him that danger had surrounded Amelia all her life.

He would make sure the danger ended.

She parked in front of the cottage, and he scanned the perimeter, searching for an intruder or someone who might be waiting to ambush her.

Hopefully CSI would pinpoint evidence on the shooter and find his motive.

Amelia rubbed her gloved hands together and ran up the path to her front door. She paused on the doorstep, her gaze searching the property.

His instincts climbed a notch, and he slogged through the sludge and met her on the stoop. The keys jangled in her shaking hands, and he took them from her. Her hands were shaking so badly he was tempted to cradle them between his own and rub them until they warmed.

But he couldn't touch her. If he did, he might forget his resolve to remain professional.

"Let me search inside," he said softly.

She nodded and let him open the door.

When he stepped inside and she flipped on a light, he immediately noticed the paintings against the wall. Dark, sinister canvases filled with blacks and reds, traumatic memories of what she'd endured at the sanitarium.

Some depicted Amelia and her twin as children who were close, yet in some instances so far apart that a canyon literally yawned between them.

One twin in the darkness, one twin in the light.

He quickly searched the interior for an intruder. The living area and kitchen were clear.

The homemade quilt on the bed made his chest tighten, and suddenly he saw the two of them tangled in the sheets together making love.

Heat speared him as the images continued. *He kissed Amelia, stripped her naked, and pounded himself inside her until they were both lost in each other.*

When he looked up at her, her eyes were luminous with emotions. Fear. Hunger. Desire.

Amelia was the most vulnerable-looking woman he'd ever met. Yet the strongest and most beautiful as well.

She had a depth to her eyes and spirit born from pain and loneliness and the will to survive.

A loneliness that called out to him from the far reaches of his own lost soul.

He could take lessons from her when it came to strength and courage. She had faced her demons, had undergone therapy to deal with them so she could be whole.

While he'd taken the coward's way out. Sure he was trying to redeem himself with good acts. But he hadn't faced his past, had been running from it, running from himself, too afraid of what he might find.

She lifted a hand and pressed it to his jaw, and his knees nearly caved. God, he wanted her.

Overcome with raw need, he pulled her into his arms and fused his mouth with hers. Hunger shot through him, making his body burn with desire as she parted her lips in invitation and threaded her fingers through his hair.

She tasted sweet and passionate and so lonely that she stirred his passion and filled the empty holes in his own troubled soul. She moaned and pulled him closer, rubbing her foot along his calf.

His body went rock hard, his cock pulsing with an ache to be inside her.

He groaned, hunger surging through him as she ran her hands down his back and over his ass.

Their tongues danced together, firing the raw desire raging through him, and he backed her toward the bed.

But just as he laid her down and her hair fanned across the pillow, another image interceded.

He was dressed in a military uniform, pacing beside a cell.

Children were crying somewhere, screaming that they needed help.

He had to get to them, save them. Then he looked down and he was holding a gun, guarding the place where they were being held.

———————— . ————————

The storm raged outside, but Amelia blocked it out as John's kiss swept her into a mindless world of pleasure. She raked her hands down his back, willing him closer, desperate to have him undress and to feel his naked skin against hers.

Her nipples beaded to stiff peaks, aching for his mouth, and titillating sensations skated through her as he probed her lips apart with his tongue. She yearned to run her tongue along his torso and down his abdomen to the sexual promises below his belt.

His hands, his touch, his mouth, his body—it all felt so familiar. So right.

Had they been together before? If so, why didn't she remember it? Why hadn't he mentioned it?

He growled low in his throat, then suddenly pushed away from her, his eyes flaring with emotions she didn't recognize. Their erratic breathing reverberated in the air between them, his eyes stormy with passion.

Yet his jaw was clamped shut, his mouth set in a grim line.

"That was a mistake."

Hurt speared her. "Why? Because you think I'm not stable?"

"I didn't say that."

She reached for him again, her body throbbing for release. "Then why is it wrong? You can't deny the heat between us."

"No, but it's just the moment. You could have been killed tonight," he said gruffly. "Adrenaline makes people reach out for comfort from whoever's closest."

Anger mounted on top of the hurt. "So you think I'd just jump in bed with anyone?"

He squeezed the bridge of his nose with two fingers, then cursed. "That's not what I meant. But I can't . . . I won't take advantage of you."

A cold hardness darkened his features, and he backed toward the door, boots clicking on the wood floor.

"Get some sleep. We'll visit The Gateway House tomorrow."

Pride made Amelia lash out. She'd been cast aside so many times in her life, rejected time and time again. Why couldn't he just love her?

Why couldn't anyone?

She jutted up her chin. "I can go by myself."

John shook his head firmly. "Not after what happened tonight." Without another word, he stalked out of the room. The door slammed behind him with a thud.

Amelia winced, feeling suddenly bereft and so alone she wanted to cry. She missed him already, missed the warmth of his hands and the strength she saw in his eyes.

Missed having him by her side giving her hope that she might one day have a normal life.

Was her memory playing tricks on her? He'd felt so familiar . . . Had they known each other before? Or was she simply fantasizing about something she could never have?

Too nervous to sleep, she slipped on her pajamas and skimmed through more journal entries, searching for any clue about her child and the baby's father.

Her frenetic sex with Six taunted her. Had she given birth to Six's son?

No . . . Dear God, she didn't want to believe her son's father was a serial killer.

———————— . ————————

The night looked dark and bleak as he stared across the mountains. Cold air swirled around him, making his leg throb. He rubbed it, the sleet banging against the roof taking him back to his childhood. To that bat swinging down toward him.

He heard the bone crack. He screamed, pain knifing through him.
The bat came down again.

He had tried to run but collapsed onto the icy ground and screamed in agony. The sleet pelted him, stinging like sharp needles, the moisture soaking him and chilling him from the inside out.

Tears ran down his face, freezing on his cheeks. He lifted his head and spotted a cave a few feet away. It would be warmer inside.

If he could make it inside . . .

But the few feet might as well have been miles.

He clawed at the ground, dragging himself across the ice. By the time he reached the entrance, he was out of breath, writhing in pain. He dropped his face into the snow and tasted blood and dirt and ice.

The memory faded, and he gritted his teeth to banish it. He had survived. And he was stronger now.

A man because of the harsh lessons he'd learned. Just as he would turn his own boys into men.

They had to be taught the hard way, too.

Now he had to get rid of Ronnie Tillman. The kid was trouble all the way around.

He would never meet the criteria.

But he would find another to take his place. And they would soldier on.

Chapter Fifteen

———— o ————

The ticking of the clock bellowed in the room and woke Amelia. Winter raged on outside, painting the sky a steel gray, the bare limbs rattling in the wind.

Still shaken by the shooting the night before, she forced herself to start her day. She brewed some coffee, then settled on the couch to study the journal entries. Outside more snow fell, huge flakes clinging to the tree limbs, making the backyard and woods a winter wonderland.

Yet nothing looked beautiful today because she kept seeing that woman's blood everywhere.

Desperate to banish the images, she turned back to the journal and found vignettes of Viola's sexual escapades with strangers.

Sex with men she hooked up with at bars. Men on the street. At a coffee shop. With orderlies at the hospital.

Viola had been extremely promiscuous. Some of the sex bordered on S and M. Viola liked bondage, liked to be spanked, liked it rough.

But one entry caught her attention:

Fuck me, fuck me, fuck me.

I whispered the words in the man's ear, begging him to take me harder and faster.

He shoved my skirt up, pushed me against the alley wall, and slammed himself inside me. I wrapped my legs around him and groaned as sensations rocked through me.

"You are all sweetness," the man murmured as he tore my shirt off, tugged one nipple into his mouth, and sucked me hard. Need spiraled down to my womb. Erotic sensations pummeled me, and I pulled him tighter, gripping his ass with my hands as he drove me crazy with his cock.

As soon as he finished, he adjusted his clothing and went his way.

That was fine with me. No attachments. No fuss. No demands.

Now if only I could keep Amelia from showing up and ruining it all. I don't think she likes men.

Except for that weirdo she hung out with at the sanitarium. Six.

Loser.

And when she was locked up, she flirted with one of the guards. He was supposed to keep her in line, make sure she didn't escape, that she obeyed.

I tried to hook up with him, but Amelia pushed me away.

I don't know his name, but one night she snuck out of her room and screwed him in the closet. Then the Commander caught them . . .

Shame and guilt choked Amelia. Maybe one of the men Viola had bedded had gotten her pregnant . . .

Or . . . the guard Amelia had had an affair with.

Who was he?

She rubbed her temple and closed her eyes, struggling to remember, but those days were a blur.

She flipped a few more pages and found an entry by Bessie, the little girl who represented the innocent child she'd been before the Commander had traumatized her.

Instead of words, Bessie had drawn a picture of her and Amelia, and Amelia had a belly bulge. Bessie had captured Amelia during the pregnancy.

Did she know who the father of her baby was?

Dr. Clover had said RMT might help her. Through it, she might learn the father's name.

A cold sweat broke out over her, and she struggled to breathe as a panic attack threatened. No . . . she didn't need to know the baby's father's name.

All she needed to know was that she had a son, and when she found him, she'd make sure he knew she loved him.

———————— , ————————

When John got up the next morning, he was still shaken by his reaction to Amelia. In the past six years, he'd shut himself off from getting involved with a woman, rationalizing he couldn't have a relationship because of his job and his fears of what he'd done.

So why did he feel so damned drawn to Amelia Nettleton? A woman with a history of mental problems? One who could have invented her story about a baby out of envy for her sister and her child?

He had no proof she'd had a baby.

Except for the rosary beads and the letter from her grandfather. And the nurse who'd cared for her for years had admitted that she'd given birth.

Worse, someone had killed the woman who'd tried to give her information about the baby.

Which meant someone didn't want Amelia to discover the truth.

They needed a list of all the women Deanna Jayne had helped—which would be nearly impossible to get with the network's secrecy.

His phone buzzed, and he snatched it up, worried the shooter might have come after Amelia.

"Agent Strong, it's Nick Blackwood."

"What's going on, Nick?"

"There was another bombing, this time at a DFACS, Department of Family and Children's Services, office in Chattanooga."

John groaned. "How many casualties?"

"Five. We've identified the bomber as a young man, fourteen."

"God. A teenage bully story like the school shootings?"

"Not from what I've learned so far. Turns out no one knew the kid. And when I looked into his past, it appears he disappeared from a foster home a few years back."

The hairs on the back of John's neck rose. "You think his disappearance might be related to the missing children case Coulter and I have been working?"

"We have to consider it. When I was searching for the Commander, I stumbled upon a group called SFTF, Soldiers for the Future. They were training and programming boys to be guerilla soldiers."

"I don't understand the connection."

"Just think about it. The kidnapper is only abducting boys. If his motive isn't sexual, perhaps he's taking them to train in his own army."

John ground his molars. Nick could be right. What if SFTF was building an army by abducting kids who had no family driving the police to keep searching for them?

Nick cleared his throat. "I'm on my way to talk to one of the members who's in prison now. Chet Roper."

"I'll meet you there."

A loud knock on the door startled Amelia. Maybe it was John with some answers.

She rushed to answer, but when she opened the door, she was surprised to see Sadie on the other side. The sleet had slacked off, but Sadie's teeth chattered, and little Ben lay curled against her chest in an infant harness.

"What are you doing here?" Amelia asked.

"Let us in, Sis, it's freezing."

Amelia waved her in. "I'm sorry." She helped Sadie out of her coat.

Still, Sadie's frown suggested something was wrong. "Jake finally told me what you said when you came to the hospital after I delivered. We need to talk."

Amelia started to argue, but her sister elbowed her way farther inside toward the kitchen and dropped something wrapped in aluminum foil on the table.

"What's that?"

"Cinnamon rolls Gigi baked." Sadie sank into the chair. "Now get us some coffee and tell me what's going on."

Amelia studied her sister for a moment, the connection between them so strong she should have realized Sadie would pick up on her anxiety. Maybe the time had come to fill Sadie in.

She poured them both coffee and took the chair across from her.

Her sister looked tired, but radiant. "Are you getting any sleep?"

"A little." Sadie stroked the baby's fine soft hair. "But he's worth it. Being this tired won't last long. So I've heard."

Amelia nodded and sipped her coffee, stalling for time.

Sadie drummed her fingers on the table. "Come on, Amelia, we've been through too much together for you to hold back anything. Spill it."

"Jake didn't want me to ruin your homecoming."

Sadie rolled her eyes. "Listen, you know how much I love Jake." She reached over the table and squeezed Amelia's hand. "But I love you just as much. And if you need to talk about anything, I'm always here for you."

Tears burned the backs of Amelia's eyelids, but she blinked them back.

"Oh, Sadie . . . "

Her sister looked her in the eyes. "If there's any way I can help, I will."

Amelia nodded, then told her about the dream, the doctor's visit confirming the truth, the rosary beads she'd found with their grandfather's letter, the death of the woman who'd given her the name of The Gateway House, and the Sister's disappearance.

"My God, Amelia, I can't believe this. Jake should have told me." Sadie rubbed little Ben's back as he squirmed. It seemed to soothe her as much as it did the infant, and made Amelia's arms feel even emptier. It was all she could do not to reach for him.

Amelia tapped her leg. "He loves you. The two of you deserved to have your special day with Ben. I've already put you through so much, Sadie."

"You didn't do anything wrong," Sadie said vehemently. "God, I hate Arthur Blackwood. I'm glad he's dead."

So was she. Except he'd taken her son's whereabouts with him to his grave.

———————— , ————————

Prisoners clanged on the metal bars as John and Nick passed by, yelling obscenities and making crude gestures.

The guard led them to an interrogation room, a small space with a metal table and two chairs. Roper shuffled in, shackled, his beefy face bruised and swollen, his lip cut, fresh scars on his forearms.

Chet Roper, aka number ten in the Slaughter Creek experimental program, had stuck by the Commander until the very end, protecting him.

Nick and Jake had arrested him for helping their father escape prison, and tortured him until he'd given up Blackwood's plan to leave the country, leading them to the helipad where their father's helicopter had exploded in midair.

John gestured toward Roper's black eyes. "Looks like you're making friends in here."

"Fuck you," Roper snarled. "You should see the other guys."

"We need your help," Nick said matter-of-factly.

"Fuck you," Roper said again.

John kept a steely control on his temper. Unfortunately prison didn't allow them to use torture as Nick and his brother had before.

Nick laid the photos from the DFACS bombing that day on the table, spreading the gruesome pictures of the dead bodies and carnage in front of Roper.

"What do you know about this?"

Roper's eyes remained flat, showing no reaction to the bloody, burned bodies. "Why do you think I know anything about it?"

"Because a teenager did this," Nick said. "And we think he might have belonged to SFTF."

A tiny twitch of Roper's mouth was his only reaction. "What makes you think that?"

"Because you and your militia group were teaching boys to be guerilla soldiers," Nick said bluntly.

Another shrug from Roper, his lips thinning into a straight line. "Soldiers, yes. Not terrorists."

John crossed his arms. "There's a difference with your group?"

Roper slanted a devious look toward him. "There's a difference."

Nick made a cynical sound. "Enlighten us."

Roper blew air between his teeth. "Soldiers protect and defend our country. Terrorists attack, killing targeted groups and innocents to make a point."

"And your teams were strictly trained to defend and protect?" Nick asked, a note of derision in his voice.

Roper leaned forward, the tattoo on his forearm snaking down to his wrist. "Yes." He gestured toward the photograph of a college kid with his leg blown off, the medics working to keep him alive. "We don't support terrorists."

Nick traded skeptical looks with John. To hear Roper talk, you'd think he'd been doing his country a service, which meant he really believed the crap spewing from his mouth.

"How did you recruit your soldiers?"

Roper smirked. "Each member solicited his own recruits. Friends. Family. Everyone had to be read in and agree."

"Or be brainwashed by your group."

Roper didn't respond.

John displayed pictures of the missing boys he and Coulter had been looking for, going back six years. "Have you seen any of these kids?"

Roper's thick brows bunched together in a scowl as he examined them. "Don't think so. Why?"

"All of them are missing. All from troubled homes and foster families. Kids no one might look for very hard."

Roper rolled his shoulders. "You think I had something to do with kidnapping them?"

"Did you?"

"No, I didn't have to steal kids."

"Then how did SFTF build its army?" John asked.

"I told you. Each man recruited his own followers."

John's lips curled into a snarl. "Who is abducting these boys?"

Roper shot daggers at him. "Are you deaf? I said I don't know."

John yanked the man by his shirt collar. "If you don't give

me something, I'll spread word in this prison that you kidnapped children and used them for yourself."

Hell, they all knew pedophiles were the lowest vermin in prison.

"You wouldn't," Roper said through clenched teeth.

John snatched the pictures and crammed them back in the envelope. "Watch me."

Roper shot up from his seat, chains clanging. Nick glared at him. "Talk, Roper. Tell us what you know."

Roper spit out a string of curse words, then dropped his big body into the chair like a rock. "I told you we didn't kidnap kids or make terrorists out of them."

"Then who does?" John asked. "Because we suspect this teenager wasn't acting alone."

Roper flattened his scarred hands on the table, then pounded it with one fist. "Look in the foothills of the Smokies. Word is there's a crazy son of a bitch who might be doing what you said."

"His name?" John asked.

"I don't know and that's the damn truth."

"What about their camp?" Nick asked.

Roper hissed between his teeth. "I can draw you a map."

John removed a pad from inside his jacket and shoved it at Roper along with a pen. "Get started. And if you're lying or setting us up to be ambushed, you'll be sorry."

———————— , ————————

Ice from the trees pinged off the roof, startling Amelia. Then her phone buzzed, indicating a text from John.

Be there in ten minutes to go to The Gateway House.

Amelia cleaned up the kitchen table from her visit with Sadie. Anxious to visit the children's home, she tugged on her coat and gloves, then her boots, preparing for the bad weather.

Her doorbell buzzed, the wind chimes tinkling from the front porch. She grabbed her purse and hurried to meet John. He looked so handsome and strong that for a second she could barely breathe.

His dark look locked with hers, the memory of their heated kiss making her body hot with need and desire.

But his rejection stung, a reminder that she didn't belong with him. Not with anyone.

"Let's go," he said in a gruff tone.

He didn't bother to wait on her, but turned and strode toward his SUV, the wind whipping his hair into a mess.

"What's wrong?" Amelia asked as she settled into the passenger side.

He shot her an irritated look. "Nick Blackwood called earlier about that suicide bombing. There was another one."

Amelia's heart hammered. She'd faintly heard the story on the news. "Another teenage bomber?"

"Yeah." He started the engine, flipped on the defrost, and cranked up the heat, then pulled down the drive. "Nick has a theory that there's a group behind these bombings similar to SFTF."

Amelia's mind raced. "Did the teens know each other?"

He exhaled. "I don't know yet. The coroner is working on IDs, then we can determine if they were connected."

They lapsed into silence as the storm kicked up. The black ice forced John to drive slower. Abandoned cars had been left on the side of the road, obviously from drivers who'd been caught in the mess overnight.

Amelia wanted to broach the subject of the kiss again, but now didn't seem like the best time. How could she ask for love when she had nothing to offer John?

John was focused on the road, clutching the steering wheel with a white-knuckle grip. A sigh rumbled from him, fraught with emotions Amelia didn't understand.

Still, need and hunger taunted her every time she looked at his strong face. She desperately wanted him to hold her again. It was almost as if she knew his touch, as if her body had learned it a long time ago and had been deprived of it for years.

As if she'd never really forgotten, as if she'd only stored those memories away so she wouldn't have to miss him so much while he was gone.

Good heavens, if she told him that, he would think she was insane.

John veered onto the turn that led to The Gateway House.

The wind swirled leaves and twigs across the road, gray skies creating a haze on the mountain, a thick fog swelling over the creek.

John swerved around a tree branch that had fallen, then veered onto a side road.

But just as they rounded a curve, Amelia saw thick plumes of smoke swirling in the air and flames shooting into the sky.

"Oh my God, John. The Gateway House is on fire."

Chapter Sixteen

———— o ————

Amelia threw the SUV door open, jumped out, and ran toward the burning building, her feet digging into the sludge.

John chased her and caught her around the waist to keep her from charging inside. "Wait, Amelia, it's too dangerous."

Amelia pushed at him, trying to get away. "But there could be children inside!"

John gripped her tighter, and turned her to face him. "I'll check. Stay here and call 911." He shoved his phone into her hands and rushed toward the building.

Wind beat at her as Amelia fumbled with the phone, her fingers trembling as she punched the emergency number. The wind could make the fire spread, though hopefully the snow and ice would stop it from reaching the trees.

"911 operator speaking. What's your emergency?"

"A fire at The Gateway House on Old Salter Road. Hurry!"

"I'll dispatch the fire department. Is anyone hurt, ma'am?"

"I don't know," Amelia said, choking on the words. "Just hurry!"

She jammed the phone in her pocket and approached the building. Heat seared her face and hands, the flames inching higher into the sky, the smoke so thick she could barely see the doorway or windows.

She ran to the side of the house where John had gone, hoping it wasn't completely engulfed. But flames were eating the walls. Wood crackled and popped, splintering, as the blaze consumed it. She headed around back, searching for John, but he was nowhere to be found.

She screamed his name just as a board sailed toward her. She ducked sideways to avoid getting hit.

A noise sounded, and flames burst from the windows, glass exploding and flying. Then the roof crackled as it began to cave in.

Terror seized her, and she tried to move closer, but the heat was too intense and she doubled over, choking on the smoke.

———————— , ————————

John beat at the flames licking at him as he ran through the house. He covered his mouth with a handkerchief as he leapt over patches of fire and burning wood.

Smoke thickened the air as the roof caved in.

He ducked into the hallway to miss being hit, then looked toward the stairs. Half of them were on fire.

Heart pumping, he jumped over a burning step and climbed the staircase, praying they lasted long enough for him to make it back down. Flames crawled along the walls in the hall upstairs and slipped into the bedrooms. He dodged more debris, heat scalding his arms as he checked the rooms.

They were empty. Thank God.

Another crashing sound, more wood splintering, glass shattering. He had to get out.

He exhaled into the handkerchief and made it back to the staircase, but it was engulfed. Dammit.

He glanced around for another way out. Not the window . . . the drapes . . . they were just starting to catch at the bottom.

He ran the other way and found a second staircase. The flames were starting to move up them, but he raced down anyway, dodging falling debris.

Sweat poured down his back and neck as he dove through the back door. He dropped to the ground and rolled in the snow to extinguish the fire.

"John! Where are you?"

Amelia's voice sounded far away, distant, terrified.

"John!"

"I'm here," he shouted, hoping she heard him over the thunderous roar of the house collapsing. Heat scalded the back of his neck and hands, the flames shooting outward from the burning wood.

The fog lifted slightly, and he spotted Amelia running toward him. He pushed to his feet and jogged toward her.

She fell against him with a sob.

"The children?"

His throat was so dry he had to swallow twice to make his voice work. "The house was empty," he whispered against her ear.

A siren wailed, and seconds later the fire truck squealed down the drive. The truck screeched to a stop, and firefighters jumped down, springing into action.

Amelia extracted herself from John's embrace as one of the firemen sprinted over to him. But her hopes of finding her baby crumbled with the destruction of The Gateway House. The place lay in ruins, the burning embers snapping and popping.

If her son had been there at one time, she might never know. All the records had likely burned in the blaze.

The head firefighter approached them.

John identified himself. "The house was on fire when we arrived."

"Anyone inside?" the fireman asked.

John shook his head. "No."

The firefighter ordered them to stay put, then hurried to join the crew, who'd rolled out hoses and were working to extinguish the blaze.

Amelia clutched John's arm. "John, if the kids weren't in the house, where are they?"

"I have no idea. But I don't like this. It seems awfully suspicious that The Gateway House burned down the day we came to ask about your son."

The flames looked bright against the dark clouds. The house collapsed in a deafening roar, embers glowing orange as they hit the pristine white, burnt wood scraps dotting the ground.

"Let's get you out of the cold," John told Amelia. He took her arm and gently led her to the SUV. She slid inside, a look of despair on her face.

"We're not giving up, Amelia. This is just a setback."

She nodded, although her eyes looked glazed, pained, shocked as she watched the firemen hosing the blaze.

Damn. It looked like someone wanted to cover up the past and would do whatever was necessary to keep them from finding the truth.

He checked his messages, hoping to hear that Nick had located the group Roper had mentioned.

And he wanted news about Ronnie Tillman. Nothing there either. But he did have a message from the social worker Liz Lucas had contacted.

He punched the social worker's number. On the third ring, a woman answered.

"Helen Gray."

John explained the reason for his call.

"Yes. Sorry I didn't get back to you sooner, but it took a while to look into your request about male infants born on July fourth."

"You have something for me?"

"A couple of names. The first is a couple from Chattanooga. They adopted a baby boy through a private agency shortly after July fourth of that year. The other couple lives near Slaughter Creek. They were foster parents who agreed to foster a baby, then later decided they wanted to keep him."

"I thought there were rules against that."

"There are, but this child has special needs, and the family argued that he most likely wouldn't be adopted so the judge agreed."

A special-needs child? If Amelia had been drugged during the pregnancy, her child could have been born with complications.

"Agent Strong, I must caution you though. Both of these families have raised these children since birth. And this information is confidential."

"I understand. But you also know that since the missing child may be related to the Arthur Blackwood case, a judge will issue a warrant to obtain that information."

Anxiety stretched between them. "All right, please use discretion. These people haven't done anything wrong. They love their sons and consider them their children. Tearing apart their lives and the security of the boys' lives could be a mistake."

"I'm aware of that," John said, his defenses rising. "But Miss Nettleton did not willingly give up her baby, and she deserves to know whether he's alive and if he's being taken care of."

"Are you sure she's stable enough to handle it if this is a dead end? Or if the adoptive parents refuse to let her see the boy?"

John gritted his teeth. He hoped to hell she was. Because from what he'd uncovered so far, she might not find the happy ending she wanted.

"One more thing," John said. "Have you ever worked with The Gateway House?"

A pause. "Yes. They do a good job of providing temporary homes for children until adoptive parents can be found."

"Do you know the house parents?"

"The Ellingtons? Yes, a nice couple. They care about what they're doing."

John rubbed his temple. A migraine was starting, gripping him at the base of his skull as if a jackhammer were starting to beat inside. "I'm at the house now. It just burned down."

"Oh my heavens! Was anyone hurt?"

"No one was inside. Do you know if they moved?"

"Not that I know of." Helen's voice broke off. "But I'll see what I can find out."

———— , ————

The stench of rotting garbage and urine clogged the air as he shoved the kid into the alley by the dumpster. He tossed the bag with his inhaler in it into the kid's lap. By God, he'd considered just leaving the boy in the Smokies, but he wasn't a kid killer.

He saved unwanted boys and gave them brothers. He made them heroes.

At least the boy would probably be found.

Yanking his ski cap down over his ears, he climbed back into the sedan he'd stolen an hour before, having ditched the other vehicle to throw the cops off his trail. The news said police were looking for his white van, but he was smarter than they'd thought. He'd traded cars twice now.

No one knew what he was driving or where he was going. Or that he'd been building his group for years. Plotting and planning, biding his time until the boys were ready. Committed to making a stand.

Leaving the kid behind, he wove through the small town of Slaughter Creek, smiling to himself. He was right under their noses and they'd never know.

But another boy had to take Ronnie's place.

He drove past the clinic where the poor kids got dental treatment. He'd gone there himself when he was little.

Had hated the stigma attached to being poor. Not just poor—poor white trash.

That damn dentist didn't give a shit about the poor kids, either. His laugh said he enjoyed causing them pain. Most of the time he hadn't even used Novocain. Said it cost too damn much.

Poor kids deserved what they got.

The last time he'd stepped in that place and the bastard had pulled three of his teeth, he'd vowed to come back and kill him.

Maybe he still would.

The door opened, and a little girl stepped outside with a woman holding her hand. A girl wouldn't do.

Had to be a boy.

If he waited long enough, he'd find one. He saw the bench where he used to sit and wait for the bus to take him back to school after he'd been drilled on and got a filling. So many fillings.

He hated that motherfucker dentist. Once a little girl had cried because she was scared and the dentist had slapped her across the face.

She never cried again.

The door squeaked open, and a boy emerged, his threadbare clothes hanging on his bony body. Bruises darkened his arms, but the boy tugged his sleeves down to cover them.

He remembered doing that, too. Hide and lie. Make up an excuse.

He'd fallen. Ran into a door. Stumbled down the steps because he was a klutz.

But that had taught him to be strong. To be a survivor.

He would do that for these boys. Teach them the same way.

The boy slumped down on the bench, head down, mouth drooling from the numbness of the Novocain.

He parked, got out, dug his hands into his pockets, and strolled up to the kid, careful to keep his head shielded by the ski cap. It wasn't holiday time, but he felt like he was Santa about to give the boy a present.

A way out of his miserable life.

A way to make changes in the world.

He stooped down and held out his hand. The boy's eyes lit up at the prize in his palm

Without a word, he stood and followed him back to the car.

Zack blinked, his head foggy, the room twirling like he was on a merry-go-round.

Not that he'd ever been on one, but he'd dreamed about it from the videos he'd seen.

But then there were colors and darkness and sickening sounds, swallowing him up in a dizzying rush.

Finally they'd moved him from the underground hole to another building. The rehabilitation center.

His last-chance stop. If he didn't follow orders, he'd end up in the ground again. This time for good.

That other boy was there, too. He heard his voice all the time.

Only the guard said Zack was alone.

Colors began swirling in his mind, flowing and running together. There were dragons that breathed fire and man-eating machines and noises that sounded like teeth crunching bone.

He tried to yell for help, but he couldn't move his tongue.

A howling sounded outside.

Were the colors and monsters and banshees all in his mind?

Or were the demons chasing him, trying to claw the skin off his back and drag him back to that dark hole where he'd never be seen again?

Chapter Seventeen

———— o ————

The embers of the fire glowed orange against the darkness as night fell, and the firemen finally started pulling in their equipment.

The lead fire investigator, Ian Wainwright, assured John he'd contact him with any forensics they found at the scene.

"I just talked to a social worker, Helen Gray," John said as he and Amelia drove away. "She said a couple named the Ellingtons managed The Gateway House. She's going to see what she can find out about their whereabouts."

The defrost whirred in the car. Amelia rubbed her hands together to warm them. Behind them, smoke still clogged the night sky. "I don't understand why someone would try to hurt the kids and couple who live there."

John twisted his mouth in thought. "Unless there was something going on with the house."

"What do you mean?"

"Maybe the couple was involved in some illegal adoptions. Or trafficking kids themselves."

"You think they could have sold my baby?"

John laid his hand over hers. "I'm just speculating out loud. We have to consider all possibilities."

Amelia felt sick inside.

"Helen also gave me the names of two families who adopted about the time your son was born."

Amelia's heart picked up a beat. "They might have him?"

"It's a long shot, Amelia. And these folks may not want to cooperate."

"I understand that." Amelia watched the trees fly past, gnarled branches bowing beneath the weight of the snow and ice. "I suppose if I were in their shoes, I'd feel the same way."

John drove onto the main road leading back into town. "One of the families lives near Slaughter Creek. I probably should get a court order, so we'll have to tread lightly, but I thought we might stop by there now."

Amelia's breath caught. So soon? Was she ready? What would she do if the child was hers? Should she tell him?

No, she'd work that out with his adopted family. If he had a safe, secure home and was happy, she didn't want to traumatize him by suddenly appearing in his life.

And if he wasn't her son . . .

She would keep looking.

John's expression looked grim. "Amelia, I have to warn you that this child has special needs."

Amelia's chest constricted. "Do you think that would matter to me?"

John's gaze met hers. "I don't know. Would it?"

Anger surged through her. Maybe she'd been wrong about the two of them being involved before. If they had been, surely he'd instinctively understand her.

"No," Amelia said firmly. "If he's my son, I'd love him no matter what."

The quarter moon peeked through the clouds over the mountain, adding a sliver of light to the treetops, but the forests seemed thick with darkness and there were very few stars shining. An indication winter wasn't ready to leave them.

And when it did, tornado season would roll in on its heels.

While they made a quick stop at Amelia's to change out of their smoke-filled clothes, John debated on calling the couple before they showed up. They might feel ambushed and totally shut down when they realized the nature of their questions.

But if he warned them, they might run.

Amelia lapsed into silence, her fingers moving up and down, tapping her leg. He watched her for a second and realized it was some kind of pattern that she repeated over and over again. He wondered what it meant, but refrained from asking.

It was most likely a nervous tic she'd developed due to PTSD.

"Tell me about this family," Amelia said. "How they adopted the boy."

He relayed the information Helen had texted him. "The Millers, Bonnie and Ralph, are foster parents. They've had at least a dozen children stay with them at different times."

"Any complaints about them?" Amelia asked.

"No," John said. "Six years ago they took in this little boy named Davie. He was small for his age and had vision problems as well as seizures. He's on medication."

They reached the couple's street. The family lived on the outskirts of town in a small brick house nestled among other similar homes. Most were dated-looking, but judging from the tricycles, bikes, and other toys scattered in the yards, and the snowmen, it was a family-friendly neighborhood.

He parked, and they walked up the sidewalk together. Amelia's quick intake of breath relayed her nerves. He rang the doorbell, then heard a woman yell that she was coming.

When she opened the door, he offered her a smile. She was

middle aged and pudgy with short curly hair and kind eyes. Behind them, he heard children laughing and chattering.

He introduced the two of them, bringing a frown to her face. "You're with the TBI? I recognize you from the news when you rescued that Wesley boy."

"Yes, I work with a task force looking for missing children."

A frown pinched her face. "I don't understand. Why are you here?"

"Please let us in and we'll explain," Amelia interjected softly.

Bonnie Miller motioned for them to enter. "Let me check on the children."

They followed her to the kitchen, a cozy room painted a soft green with a butcher-block table where three children sat. One girl, who looked to be about twelve, was working on math homework, a freckle-faced toddler boy was drawing a spiderweb, and another child of about six with wavy brown hair held a book of some kind. In fact, he was running his hands over the pages, which John realized were in braille.

He had to be Davie.

Bonnie introduced each of the kids by name. The girl offered a tentative smile, but the toddler didn't bother to look up. He was busy adding dozens of bugs caught in the spiderweb.

Davie seemed totally absorbed in his book although he was tapping his leg as he read.

"Kids, I'll be in the other room for a minute." She touched the girl's shoulder. "Come and get me if you need me."

The girl nodded. "Sure, Miss Bonnie."

John relaxed slightly, relieved that this foster home appeared to be loving, not like some he'd encountered through his job.

Bonnie led them to a small living room off the kitchen. A comfortable sofa and armchair filled one corner and faced a TV. Bins with toys were stacked against the wall.

"Now, why are you here?" Bonnie said, her voice concerned.

"We need to talk to you about Davie."

Bonnie's frown deepened. "What about him?"

"Do you know who his mother was?" Amelia asked.

Bonnie picked at a thread on her shirt. "No. He was dropped off at The Gateway House early one morning."

John tensed. "Did he have anything with him when he was found? A note? Blanket? Toy?"

Bonnie narrowed her eyes. "He was wrapped in a blue blanket and left in a laundry basket. Whoever abandoned him left a note saying she couldn't take care of him and to please find him a good home."

John glanced at Amelia, but her face was pale.

Could she have actually left the baby there herself when she was in one of her fugue states? Or could Davie be the baby the nun said had been left with at the church?

Amelia's heart melted at the sight of the children. The toddler was adorable, but the little boy practicing his braille had stolen her heart. He looked small for his age, and she couldn't help but wonder if he had other issues besides the seizures and his vision impairment.

"Now, Agent Strong," Bonnie said. "I've answered your questions. Tell me why you're interested in Davie."

John started to answer her, but Amelia gestured to let her explain. "Because of me, Bonnie. I'm looking for my son."

Bonnie turned to Amelia, her expression guarded. "You think Davie is yours?"

Amelia shifted. "I don't know. It's possible."

Bonnie leaned forward. "I don't understand."

Amelia took a deep breath. "I'm sure you heard about the CHIMES project that took place in Slaughter Creek?"

Recognition dawned in Bonnie's eyes. "You were part of it?"

Amelia nodded. "During that time, I was drugged and brainwashed. For a long time, I suffered from mental problems, but I've been undergoing therapy. Lately, I've recovered memories of giving birth."

"Amelia's grandfather left her a letter to be opened after he passed away telling her he'd discovered she'd had a son," John cut in. "He also left her some rosary beads, which led us to another contact, who referred us to The Gateway House."

Bonnie picked up a stuffed dinosaur from the sofa and began to rub it. "How old would the child be now?"

"Six," Amelia said. "And we know Davie is that age and you got him through The Gateway House."

A wary look darkened Bonnie's eyes. "So you gave him up and now you want him back?"

"My baby was stolen from me." Anguish clogged Amelia's throat. It was obvious that Bonnie loved the little boy and he seemed happy. "I know this may be upsetting, but if he is my son, I'd like to get to know him." And be a mother to him.

Although Bonnie had already filled that role.

Bonnie folded her arms. "Davie has had a hard go of it, Amelia. He's small for his age, gets teased, and he's completely blind in one eye with a very low percentage of sight in the other. It took him a long time to adapt here and to feel secure. My husband and I love him very much and don't want anything to impede the progress he's made."

"I wouldn't want that either," Amelia said. "But please know that I didn't willingly give up my child. He was taken from me."

Silence descended, deafening with unanswered questions.

"Mrs. Miller," John finally said. "Davie may not be Amelia's son. We have another family to talk to about this. But there's one way to find out for sure."

"You want to test his DNA?" Bonnie asked, her voice dropping a decibel.

"Yes," John said. "That way you'll know the truth and so will Amelia."

Bonnie gave Amelia a look that cut her to the core. "And what if he is your son, Amelia? Would you take him from the only family he's ever known?"

Amelia stood. She understood the woman's reservations. But at the same time, her child had been stolen from her, and she deserved to know him.

Tamping down her emotions, she squared her shoulders. "Please just agree to the test and then we'll talk."

"You said you had mental problems," Bonnie reminded her. "I read about you, you know. What makes you think you're well enough to take care of a handicapped child?"

———— . ————

John had asked the same question, but still he hated the doubt flickering in Amelia's eyes.

"I've worked very hard on my recovery," Amelia said. "And if Davie is my son, I'd like for us to work together so I can get to know him. I think it would be damaging to a child to grow up thinking his mother didn't want him, wouldn't you?"

Bonnie looked taken aback for a moment, then her expression softened. "Yes, I wouldn't want that for any child."

"I'm sorry if I upset you," Amelia said gently. "I don't want to tear up your family. Let's wait and see about the DNA and then we'll talk." She squeezed Bonnie's hand. "I honestly don't want to hurt anyone and will do whatever's best for my son."

The girl appeared in the doorway. "Miss Bonnie, Davie needs help. Freddy's throwing crayons, and Davie wants to make the cookies."

"I did promise them we'd make sugar cookies." Mrs. Miller stood. "All right, honey, tell the boys I'll be right there."

John knew Mrs. Miller would be on the phone to her husband the moment they left. Probably even to an attorney. "Can we get that DNA sample before we go?"

She looked hesitant for a moment, but gave a conciliatory nod.

Bonnie led them back to the kitchen and explained to Davie that they were going to take a swab from his mouth.

John's cell phone buzzed, and he snatched it from his belt just as he finished. "Agent Strong."

"It's Coulter. Someone just found Ronnie Tillman."

John's breath stalled in his chest. "Where?"

"By a dumpster in an alley."

"Is he alive?"

"I don't know. Medics picked him up and are on their way to the hospital. I'll have CSI process the scene and canvass the area, and I'll head to the hospital."

John waved to Amelia that they needed to go. They said good-bye to the family and rushed to the car.

Another childhood rhyme played in his head . . .

This little piggy went to market . . .
This little piggy stayed home . . .
This little piggy cried wee wee wee all the way home.

Crying did no good. He'd learned that the hard way.

Just like disobeying didn't get him anywhere except in the hole.

The hole was dark and scary.

These boys had to learn just like he had.

The boy, Danny, would do just fine. He was quiet. Meek. A follower.

He wouldn't give them any trouble like some of the others had.

But if he did, he'd be punished. And he'd learn fast.

If not, they'd ship him to another place. A place none of the boys wanted to go.

A place that made the farm look like a party and the things they had to do there fun.

Chapter Eighteen

———— ◦ ————

What's wrong?" Amelia asked as John maneuvered around a truck driving too slow and headed toward the hospital.

"Ronnie Tillman was found in an alley. The medics are transporting him to the hospital."

The image of the poor little boy lying in a bed of trash brought tears to Amelia's eyes. She could practically smell the stench of rotting food and wet cardboard. Plus the temperature was so frigid, he could've developed hypothermia in a short time. Who would do such a thing? "Then he's alive?"

"My partner didn't know any details. We'll find out when we get there."

Amelia started the tapping routine on her leg again, and John frowned, remembering the little boy had a similar habit. Was Davie Amelia's little boy?

She lapsed into silence until they arrived at the hospital. "You can stay here if you want or I can get you a cab home."

"I'll go in with you," Amelia said.

He didn't have time to argue. Little Ronnie might be fighting for his life. And if he could tell them anything about his kidnapper, he might be the key to cracking this case.

Amelia followed beside him as they entered the hospital, her hands jammed in the pockets of her coat, cheeks pink from the cold. Machines beeped, two paramedics rushed through the automatic doors pushing a stretcher, and doctors and nurses bustled around.

Coulter met him at the door. John quickly introduced Amelia, and he shook her hand.

"I called Ronnie's foster mother. She's on her way."

"How is he?"

"I don't know. The staff won't allow me back with him."

Damn.

A harried-looking man wheeled a pregnant lady inside. She gripped her belly and moaned, "I'm going to have this baby here if we don't hurry!"

A nurse ran toward her, soothing the couple and directing them where to go. John stared after them, something about the scenario striking a familiar chord.

He thought back to prior cases, but he'd never helped with a delivery on the job.

Maybe he'd been a fireman or paramedic before he lost his memory.

It still seemed odd to him that the police hadn't uncovered his identity. But apparently his prints weren't in the system, and for some reason, they hadn't found a driver's license with his photo and name on it either.

He'd even run them himself after he'd joined the Bureau but hit a dead end as well. Which led him to believe he'd changed his name, taken on a new identity for some reason. Because he was running from something?

But what?

The sound of doors opening behind him, then the elevator dinging, dragged his attention back to the moment. Amelia was fidgeting, glancing around the sterile walls as if they might close in on her.

Terri Eckerton raced in, her face etched in fear.

"Where is he? Is he all right?"

"We don't know yet," John said.

Coulter joined them. "They took him back to an ER room and are examining him now. But they wouldn't let me go with him."

She pulled away from them and ran to the nurse's desk. "Please let me see my boy. His name is Ronnie Tillman. He was just brought in."

The nurse checked a computer display, then stood. "The doctors are still examining him. Come on, follow me."

"We'd like to go with her," John said.

The nurse's brows pinched together. "Who are you?"

"We're with the TBI," Coulter said, clearly irritated. "This boy was a kidnap victim. It's urgent that we speak to him as soon as possible."

The woman cut her eyes toward Ronnie's foster mother. "You okay with them in there?"

She nodded. "Yes, just let me see him. Please. He has to be scared."

The nurse waved for them to follow.

They hurried through a set of double doors, then they wove through several curtained-off cubes until they reached one marked "Ten."

The nurse pushed the curtain aside to let them in.

——————— . ———————

Amelia's heart twisted when she saw the little boy in the hospital bed. His face was pale, his eyes too big in his narrow face, his body quivering as if he was still cold.

Terri rushed to him and gave him a hug. "Oh, Ronnie, I'm so glad they found you. I've been worried sick."

The little boy looked up at her with a frown and tears in his eyes.

Amelia's phone vibrated in her pocket, and she checked the caller ID. An unknown number appeared. She nudged John. "Let me get this."

He nodded, and she stepped into the hall. Curious, she pressed answer.

"Hello, Viola."

Amelia jerked her head around, suddenly nervous at the gruff voice. A male voice. And he was calling her by one of her alter's names. "Who is this?"

"You're a whore, you know that. But I don't mind. Neither did the other men you whored around with."

Amelia jerked her head around, searching the hospital waiting room to see if the caller was watching her.

"Who is this?"

"Meet me tonight."

Perspiration broke out on Amelia's forehead, and she stepped into the corner of the waiting room and backed against the wall. Viola had taken a lot of lovers, men Amelia didn't even know.

Amelia struggled for a calm voice. "What do you want?"

"I told you, I want to hook up with you again."

"I'm not Viola."

"Yes, you are. I've been watching you and I want my hands on you. All over you." He made a humming sound. "I want to strip you and put my tongue between your legs."

"Stop it!" Amelia said between clenched teeth.

"I know what you're doing," he murmured.

"What do you mean?"

"Looking for your baby. Who is the father, Viola? Me or one of the other men you screwed?" A sinister laugh echoed over the line. "Or do you even know?"

Shame washed over her. Whoever the bastard was, he was right.

She didn't know who'd fathered her son.

"You wanna know what happened to your baby?" he whispered. "You threw him away. That's the kind of mama you are."

Tears clogged Amelia's throat, and she shook her head.

But she'd had no control over herself years ago. What if he was telling the truth?

——————— . ———————

John stood aside as Ronnie's foster mother clasped Ronnie's tiny hand in hers. "I'm here, little man," she said softly. "You're going to be okay now."

John turned to the doctor, a woman with auburn hair and square glasses. "What did the kidnapper do to him?"

She fiddled with the pockets on her lab coat. "No sign of sexual abuse," she said in a low voice. "And surprisingly, no visible bruising."

John exhaled in relief. "So he didn't hurt him?"

"Not physically," she said. "But the boy is traumatized. He was also suffering from a major asthma attack and was dehydrated. If he gets upset, you have to leave."

"I understand." John crossed the room and touched Terri's elbow. Thankfully, the boy's breathing was steady, and the color was returning to his cheeks. "We need to ask him about what happened."

Terri looked worried but agreed. She gently brushed her fingers across Ronnie's cheek. "Ronnie, sweetie. When you were missing, this nice man here Agent Strong was looking for you." She gestured toward John, and he offered the kid an encouraging smile.

"You're a brave boy," John told Ronnie. "I don't want to upset you, but I need you to tell me what happened."

Ronnie glanced at Terri, and she squeezed his shoulder. "Agent Strong wants to find the man who took you and make sure he doesn't hurt any other children."

Ronnie coughed, and Terri handed him some water, tilting the straw for him to drink. When he finished, he looked back at John.

"He was big and had bushy eyes."

"You mean bushy eyebrows?" Terri said gently.

He bobbed his head up and down.

"What else can you tell me about him?" John asked. "What color was his hair?"

Ronnie bit his lip. "Brown. It was shaggy like he forgot to comb it. And he smelled like sweat and cigarettes."

"That's good, Ronnie," John said. "Did he have hair on his face? A beard or a mustache?"

Ronnie touched his chin. "A little bit down here."

"Good. How about scars?"

The boy's eyes widened, and he pointed to his cheek. "Yeah. I think it was above his eye."

So the kidnapper hadn't hidden his face from Ronnie. "Anything else? How about a tattoo?"

"Yeah. But I couldn't tell what it was."

"Where were you?"

Fear darkened his face. "He put me in the back of a van."

"A white van?" John said, wanting confirmation for one of their best leads.

Ronnie nodded and his chin quivered. "But then I got sick, and he took me to a doctor." The boy's face paled again and he began to tremble.

Terri shot John a concerned look, then sat down on the bed beside Ronnie and rubbed slow circles over his chest. "That must have been scary."

"He shot that lady and man, and they bleeded everywhere."

"I know, buddy, I'm so sorry you saw that," Terri said, soothing Ronnie.

The doctor cleared her throat. "That's enough for now."

John touched the kid's shoulder. "You did good, Ronnie. Just another couple of questions. Were there other boys where you went?"

He shook his head.

"Did the man say where he was taking you?"

"No. He just said I wasn't any good. That he shouldn't have picked me 'cause I was weak."

John turned that comment over in his head. That was the reason he'd dumped Ronnie in the alley.

But what was Ronnie too weak to do?

Dammit. If it was the same unsub behind the Wesley boy's abduction, he was probably already looking for another kid.

Helen Gray shuffled the papers on her desk, worried about the Ellingtons. Amelia Nettleton wanted answers about her baby.

Helen looked through the files she'd pulled up. She wanted answers, too.

But she had to keep her reasons to herself. No one knew why she was there.

No one ever would.

Her coworker flipped on the television. "There's a newscast about that missing boy Ronnie Tillman. He's been found."

Helen turned her attention to the set.

Brenda Banks, the same reporter who'd covered the story about the Slaughter Creek experiments, stood beside Agent John Strong.

"We have recovered six-year-old Ronnie Tillman," Agent Strong said. "He was abducted from his foster home, and was found in an abandoned alley tonight. He is in stable condition at the hospital and has been reunited with his foster family."

"Was he able to tell you who abducted him?" Brenda asked.

"No," Agent Strong said. "But we do believe the kidnapper left him because he suffered from asthma, and that this may not be the first child he's abducted. Parents should be vigilant about watching their children."

Helen's coworker took a call and left the office, and Helen studied the agent's face, his intense brown eyes, the square jaw, his high cheekbones—she'd read about him on the Internet. Knew finding missing children was his cause.

That he had been in a terrible accident, and head trauma had caused him to have amnesia. That he remembered nothing about his life before a few years ago.

It was best he didn't remember. Not her or what happened before his accident.

Safer for her.

Safer for him.

Chapter Nineteen

———— o ————

After he left the press conference, John drove Amelia home, then drove to the lab to drop off little Davie's DNA sample.

Ronnie's words disturbed him. The kidnapper had gotten rid of him because he wasn't any good, because he was weak.

What had he meant by that?

If the kidnapper wanted strong, healthy boys, there had to be a reason.

He didn't like any of the possibilities that came to mind.

Had the kidnapper wanted boys with no health risk because it decreased their value to human traffickers?

Disgust soured his mouth. Child labor, sex slaves, he'd heard and seen it all.

Images of the SFTF camp where boys were being trained for military combat taunted him. Roper had claimed the members recruited their soldiers through family members and friends, and that the boys weren't forced to join.

But what if one of the members had found an alternative way of recruiting? He would want strong, healthy boys and Ronnie wouldn't have fit.

An image of himself as a preteen flashed behind his eyes, and he squeezed the steering wheel. *He stood by an older man wearing a military uniform. They were deep in the woods somewhere. The area was desolate. A barbed-wire fence surrounded the area, thick trees lining the edges, creating a fortress.*

Other teenage boys marched in tandem to their leader's commands, weapons angled over their soldiers as if preparing for war.

The leader called John over and ordered him to the firing line. He placed a hand on John's shoulder.

"Shooting takes great concentration, but you're ready for it. Look through the sight finder and line up your target. When you shoot, shoot to kill."

John aimed the gun at the target. Cardboard cutouts of men and women, some dressed like soldiers, some like civilians.

Somewhere in the distance, he heard a cry. Not just one, but several cries and screams for help.

When he looked up, he saw children passing by. Children chained together. A tiny girl with huge sad eyes was watching him, a haunted look on her face.

"Shoot," the leader commanded.

The girl mouthed the word help.

He froze, heart hammering. What was wrong with the girl? Why did she need help?

Then he looked at the other children. They looked washed out, eyes vacant, complexions pasty white, limbs battered and scarred.

Suddenly the leader pushed the end of his gun at John's temple.

"Do not disobey me," the voice ordered.

John's hand shook slightly as he dragged his gaze from the little girl and pulled the trigger. He hit the target dead on, and the cardboard cutout of the man exploded, shattered pieces floating to the ground like ashes.

_____ , _____

Black clouds hovered above the guesthouse, threatening to unleash more hail any second as Amelia climbed her porch. She'd decided to stay on the farm instead of her condo. Maybe being there would jog her memories.

She hadn't told John about the phone call. She was too ashamed of what the caller had said.

Because there was some truth to it. One thing she'd learned in therapy was that she had to own up to her actions. That the alters had been part of her. And she had to come to terms with that before she could heal.

It was another reason she didn't belong with a man like John. He was a hero, while she had let so many people down, had such a fragmented life that she was still learning secrets about herself.

She checked over her shoulder a dozen times, the sense someone was watching making her skin crawl. A tree had fallen in the drive, and dead limbs littered the yard. The wind hurled twigs and snow across the ground, icicles cracking and breaking in the storm.

She fumbled with her keys, but managed to unlock the door, then rushed inside.

Her stomach dropped when she saw the canvas she'd left blank smeared with red, the word *WHORE* scrawled across it, the paint dripping as if it were blood.

For a moment she couldn't breathe as the phone conversation echoed in her head. Someone was trying to either scare her or make her crazy by forcing her to remember the past.

But if she told John that, would he think she was crying wolf? That she might be doing these things herself?

A year ago, one of her alters *would* have done this.

Shivering at the thought, she glanced toward her bedroom and saw her underwear strewn across the floor. Her panties had been slashed to shreds, black and red lace dotting the floor like a bed of dead roses.

The journals she'd been reading had been torn apart, pages ripped from the binder and shredded like confetti, destroying the words on the page as if to say none of what she'd written had happened.

Or one of her alters had returned to torment her and make her think she was losing her mind.

A sob caught in her throat. Her lungs squeezed for air, but she forced herself to step to the edge of the room. On the mirror in her bathroom, there was another message.

Jagged letters written in red.

Time for you to die.

Amelia's stomach pitched. Enough was enough. She couldn't hide this from John anymore. She'd have to convince him that she wasn't crazy. That she hadn't relapsed.

She wanted to find whoever was doing this and make them stop.

Furious, she dug her phone from her purse and punched John's number.

———— , ————

Wind beat at John's SUV as he drove from the lab toward his place. His phone buzzed, and Amelia's number flashed on the screen. He pushed connect, wishing he had answers for her, but his head was filled with questions about The Gateway House and Ronnie Tillman.

"Amelia?"

"John, someone's been in my house."

John's chest clenched. "Is the intruder still there?"

"No," her voice cracked. "But he left me a threatening message."

"Lock the door. I'll be right there."

He jammed his phone in his pocket and made a U-turn at the next intersection, pushing the gas to the floor, even though black, icy patches appeared out of nowhere.

A black sedan had skidded off the road, the driver waving for help, but John didn't have time to stop. He phoned it into the sheriff's office instead and gave the deputy the location.

Frustrated at the sudden traffic, he blew his horn, anxious to get to Amelia. When the two-lane road suddenly became four for a few feet, he sped past the pickup in front of him, grateful for four-wheel drive.

An eighteen-wheeler coming toward him on the curve was going too fast and sludge spewed from his tires, splattering John's window.

Dammit to hell. He flipped on the wipers, blinking, the white lane lines nearly invisible on the dark mountain road.

He rounded the next curve, then veered into the drive for Amelia's, cursing again at the tree that had fallen. He swung the SUV to the right around it, bouncing over the uneven pastureland until he maneuvered back onto the driveway.

Amelia's car was parked in front, the lights on inside the guesthouse. He searched the perimeter, but the woods behind her house were so dark all he could see were the trees, thick and ominous.

He threw the SUV into park, jumped out, and jogged to her front door. He raised his fist to knock, but Amelia swung the door open.

One look into her ashen face and terrified eyes, and he pulled her up against him and held her tight.

Amelia collapsed into John's arms, trembling all over, tears leaking from her eyes. She was trying so hard to be strong, to prove she wasn't crazy anymore.

But even she didn't know if she was sane.

Who would torment her like that?

John stroked her back, gently soothing her with his hands. "It's okay, Amelia. I'm here."

The words she ached to hear. That she wasn't alone.

Was she so desperate for love that she'd let a new alter emerge?

He feathered her hair back from her face with such gentle fingers that it felt erotic and made her body instantly warm. Her breathing rasped in the air.

John dropped tender kisses into her hair, making her want to cry again, but this time because no one had ever been so tender and loving with her.

She fought back a sob, knowing he wouldn't understand. No one did. She'd lived her whole life feeling unwanted, like an oddity, like no one could ever love her.

Yet John hadn't questioned her when she'd called. He'd come to her, and now he was holding her as if she wasn't an outcast.

"Shh, it's okay, I'm here," John murmured. "You're not alone."

More words that made her want to cling to him and never let him go.

Words that somehow felt familiar, as if he'd said them before.

She stilled, her body craving more of him, her mind filled with questions.

"You need to show me what the intruder did," John said next to her ear.

She nodded against his chest, then lifted her head, her fingers still holding on to his arms.

His gaze met hers, his dark eyes filled with the kind of heat that made a woman want to tear off her clothes and bare her soul.

"Amelia, show me," he said, his professional manner back intact.

She inhaled a sharp breath, then let go of him, reminding herself that when he left—and he would leave—that she would have to stand on her own.

———————— ————————

John forced himself to pull away from Amelia before he did something stupid as hell like kiss her and take her to bed.

For God's sake, he knew better than to fall for a woman on a case.

But something about Amelia was so damn sweet and vulnerable and . . . sexy . . . that he couldn't resist.

She had been abused so much of her life that she deserved something good to happen to her. He wanted to give her that happy ending more than he'd ever wanted anything in his life.

But what the hell did he have to offer?

He pulled away from her. "Show me what he did." He said "he" although the intruder could have been a woman.

The deep longing and need in her eyes tore at him, but she nodded and released him as if she knew she had to gather her courage.

She let him in the entryway, both of them shaking off the cold as the wind slammed the door shut on its own.

"There, the canvas in my studio," Amelia said, a slight quiver to her voice. "It was blank when I left earlier."

He swallowed, tempering his reaction when he saw the word *WHORE* written in red paint, dripping like blood.

"I got a phone call earlier when we were at the hospital. A man's voice. He called me Viola, called me a whore."

Shock slammed into John. "Why didn't you tell me?"

Her expression crumpled with pain. "Because I was ashamed."

His heart clenched. "Amelia—"

"You don't understand. Viola was one of my alters, the promiscuous one. What he called me . . . it was true about her."

John steeled himself against the anguish in her eyes. "You're not that person," he said, knowing it was true.

Amelia sighed wearily. "But I was, John. Viola was part of me and I can't forget that."

He gritted his teeth. She seemed to be accepting what she'd done in the past. He wished he had the courage to face whatever he'd done. "Is there anything else?"

She nodded, her eyes flickering again with disgust. "In my bedroom and bath."

He followed her, anger surging through him at the sight of her underwear shredded across the room.

"The paper—"

"My journals," Amelia explained. "I kept them for years for therapy. I've been looking through them, hoping to find some answers, to learn more about my pregnancy. About the baby's father."

She pointed to the bathroom, and he saw the message on her mirror.

Fury railed through him. Amelia did not deserve this.

"I'm going to get a security system installed here right away," John said. "It may take a couple of days to get my guy out here, but trust me, once it's in, no one will get past it."

There was no way he'd let the bastard who'd done this get away with hurting Amelia.

Amelia fought the humiliation washing over her. She'd told John the truth. She had to because she was done with lies and pretending to be something she wasn't.

If he thought less of her, then she'd accept it. After all, she'd dealt with rejection and ridicule all her life.

He angled his head toward her, his eyes seething, brows furrowed. "Who else knew about your alters?"

Amelia shrugged. "Everyone. My story's been in the news."

That meant any lunatic out there could be taunting her.

But the timing had to be important. "Has this happened before?"

She averted her gaze, worrying her lip with her teeth.

John cleared his throat. "Amelia?"

"The other night, I found a teddy bear." She moved to the closet, stood on tiptoe and raked her hand along the top shelf.

Confusion mingled with fear when she found the shelf empty. Agitated, she rushed past him into the studio and began to look through the canvases stacked against the wall.

"I don't understand," she said, her voice strained.

John followed her, his face contorting into a frown. "What?"

She looked up at him, fear seizing her that he wouldn't believe her.

"Tell me," he urged.

She twisted her hands together. "The other night someone left a painting of the cemetery where we looked for my son. There were bones and ghosts floating in the cemetery. It was . . . dark."

"You didn't paint it."

"No." Her pulse clamored. "I also found a teddy bear on my bed, one that was just like the bear we found in the coffin. Except this one was Bessie's bear, my child alter, and it had a knife stuck in its chest."

"But it's not here now?"

She shook her head, knowing she sounded crazy.

But she had found that bear and the painting just like she'd found the one that night. Hadn't she?

John phoned Lieutenant Maddison to come to Amelia's, and his security-specialist buddy to install a system in her house the next day.

While he waited, he took some photographs of the painting, the shredded journals and underwear, and the message on her mirror.

Amelia was visibly shaken and retreated to the kitchen to stare out the window at the unforgiving mountain ridges while Maddison processed her house.

Maddison surveyed the message and the shredded pages. "She kept journals?"

"Yes."

Maddison arched a brow. "You know her history. Do you think it's possible she did all this herself?"

John chewed the inside of his cheek. He had to consider the possibility. "I don't think she did."

A heartbeat passed, the silence thick with doubt. She'd claimed an intruder had done something like this before, that he'd left a teddy bear.

But it was missing.

"Then you believe her story?" Maddison asked.

He wanted to, more than anything. "Like you said, I know her history and so does everyone in town and half the people across the country. Someone could have done this to make us think she's unstable so we wouldn't believe her and I'd stop looking for her son."

Maddison finished bagging the pieces of the journal along with her underwear. Maybe he'd find some forensics on it to tell them who had broken into Amelia's.

As soon as Maddison left, Amelia walked back into the bedroom and looked at him, her eyes troubled. "He thinks I did this, doesn't he?"

John's gaze met hers. "He's just doing his job."

"But that's what he thinks," Amelia said. "Do you believe that, too, John?"

He glanced at her hands. There was no paint on them. Of course, she could have written the message or painted that canvas and cleaned up before calling him.

Her weary sigh reverberated in the air. "If you don't believe me, then why are you looking for my baby?"

Because she needed someone to believe her and help her.

"I do believe you," he said instead. "And I won't give up, Amelia, not until we know the truth."

Gratitude flashed across her face, making her look so damn beautiful that his lungs tightened and his body hardened. He wanted to hold her again.

To kiss her and lie her down and make love to her.

Hunger and need darkened her eyes, their gazes locking for a long moment. Neither one of them had slept, and morning was starting to break the sky, the sun battling through more storm clouds and losing as the grayness swept it away.

"There's another couple I want to interview this morning," John said. "They adopted a little boy named Eddie. Let me take you someplace safe while I go talk to them."

"He said he'll find me wherever I go. I don't want you to be in danger, too."

"Don't worry about me, Amelia. I'm a professional."

Amelia's breath rushed out. "Let me grab a quick shower and I'll go with you to talk to the family."

He nodded, then waited in the other room while she ducked into the bathroom. But he had to step outside in the frigid air to cool the heat in his body and keep himself from asking her if he could join her.

Silence thickened in the car as John drove toward the Sweenys'. Amelia looked out the window at the trees swaying in the wind. Ice and snow rained down from the limbs, splattering the windshield, the road slick with ice.

Amelia's past was shady, but questions about his own nagged at him. Where had he been when she was locked in the sanitarium?

Dammit, that endless void loomed like a pit he'd fallen into, one he couldn't find his way out of.

The first few months of his amnesia he'd searched for the truth. Had hoped his memory would return on its own.

Was he single? Married? Did he have a family out there looking for him? Did he have children?

What kind of job had he worked before?

And why was there no information about him? How could he be in his early thirties with virtually no footprint in the world?

The only answers that made sense disturbed him even more. Someone had intentionally erased his identity. Maybe he was in Witness Protection, but if so, federal marshals would have been looking for him.

Maybe he was a criminal who'd covered his identity? Or an undercover agent in a secret government unit?

Maybe a unit that trained hit men?

His gut tightened. Emanuel Giogardi, one of the Commander's subjects, had been trained to be a hired killer.

But if John had been a killer, why would he be so drawn to finding missing children?

He parked at the suburban home belonging to the Sweeny family, hoping to catch them before they left for work.

Mrs. Sweeny was a schoolteacher. Her husband owned his own garage and repaired foreign cars.

Amelia hadn't said ten words the entire ride. She looked nervous. Hell, he didn't blame her. Every time she looked at a six-year-old boy, she must wonder if he was her son.

"Are you sure you're up to this?" he asked as they made their way to the front door.

Amelia exhaled slowly, and straightened her spine. "Yes, I'm fine."

She might look vulnerable and fragile, but she was a gutsy woman. Any kid would be lucky to have her as their mother.

He punched the doorbell, and a woman dressed in a pantsuit with short blond hair opened the door. "Yes?"

"Mrs. Sweeny?"

"That's right."

John identified himself, then Amelia. "We'd like to talk to you about the little boy you adopted."

The woman's face drained of color. A second later, anger flashed in her eyes. "What about Eddie?"

"We don't mean to upset you, Mrs. Sweeny, but it is important that we talk. Is Eddie here?"

Tears gathered at the corners of the woman's eyes. "No, my son passed away a month ago."

———————— , ————————

Amelia's heart shattered, both for the child and the woman in front of her. "I'm so sorry, Mrs. Sweeny," she said softly. "We had no idea he was gone."

"It's still so painful," she said. "We . . . loved him so much."

"I'm sure you did." Sorrow assailed Amelia. If this child was her son, she'd missed any chance of ever getting to know him.

John pressed a hand to Amelia's back as if to offer comfort. "I'm sorry, too. Is it okay if we ask you some questions?"

Mrs. Sweeny crossed her arms. "Why would the TBI possibly want to talk to me about Eddie?"

John spoke in a low voice. "It's about his adoption, Mrs. Sweeny."

Her eyes widened. "We went through legal channels."

"We don't believe you did anything wrong," Amelia said quickly.

"What happened to Eddie?" John asked.

The woman brushed angrily at her tears. "He had a genetic disorder, a chromosome abnormality."

"Did you know about his health issues when you adopted him?" John asked.

The woman shook her head. "Not at first. He was diagnosed a few months after we got him."

"But you kept him anyway?" Amelia said.

"Of course," Mrs. Sweeny said with no hesitation. "We loved him. From the first moment we held him, he was our son."

Amelia fought tears. "I'm so sorry about his illness, but he was very lucky to have you."

Mrs. Sweeny relaxed slightly. "Thank you for saying that. A lot of people didn't understand." She took a deep breath. "Now, I still don't see why the TBI is interested in Eddie."

Amelia cleared her throat. "We're here because of me. I had some emotional problems six years ago because I was one of the subjects of the Slaughter Creek experiments, but now I remember—I *know*—that I gave birth to a little boy. And the hospital staff took my baby away from me." Pain tinged her voice. "I didn't give him away, Mrs. Sweeny, not willingly. All I want to do now is find out what happened to my son."

A strangled sound came from Mrs. Sweeny's throat. "My Lord, you think Eddie was your baby?"

———————— , ————————

John gritted his teeth. Obviously the woman had loved the little boy.

But if this child was Amelia's, then her search had come to an end. The fact that he'd inherited a genetic abnormality could fit with drug use during gestation.

One more life Arthur Blackwood had ruined.

He hoped the bastard was rotting in hell.

"What do you know about Eddie's birth parents?" John asked.

Mrs. Sweeny bit her lip. "Not much. He was only a day old when we got the call."

Amelia exhaled, a sound filled with anxiety.

John willed her to be strong. "Do you remember the name of the social worker you worked with?"

Mrs. Sweeny looked at Amelia, her expression torn. "Her name was Rusty Lintell."

John grimaced. Rusty Lintell was dead. She had been murdered two years ago by one of the CHIMES subjects.

He pushed Danny into the dark room, knowing the first twenty-four hours meant he had to teach the boy to do as he said.

After all, he was offering him a chance to make a statement to the world. To change things.

But he had to toughen him up first.

"Where are we?" Danny asked, shivering as a tree branch scraped the windowpane.

"A layover place for a while. " Hell, he'd been awake the entire night. Hadn't slept for the adrenaline pumping through his body. He had to get some rest. Laying low during the day was best. They'd travel again come dark.

Danny's thin body suddenly looked frail as he sank down and leaned against the wall. A spider crawled across the floor and Danny held out a finger and let it crawl into his hand.

His own past returned in a blinding sea of darkness, his face transposed over Danny's. Except instead of a spider, the rats in the cellar had crawled all over him.

His mother's cruel lessons were ingrained in his brain.

"Take your punishment like a man," she'd told him.

He had fought at first. Until he was too weak to fight back. Until he'd learned to tolerate her hands on him and the cold that swallowed him in the box where she locked him at night.

Hidden from sight. Away from other children.

Away from the men she brought into the house.

Forgotten, sometimes for days at a time.

Just like the kids he was taking. Forgotten. Neglected. Abused.

Danny was one of them.

"I'm going to make you important, son. One day everyone will know who you are, Danny. Would you like that?"

Danny nodded, then drew his knees up to his chest, and wrapped his arms around them.

Yes, he was saving him. Danny was overlooked at that damn foster home. Lost. Passed by as if he didn't exist.

With the Brotherhood, Danny would shine.

Chapter Twenty

———— ◦ ————

The pain radiating from the Sweeny woman was so intense that her grief made Amelia's heart ache. She touched John's arm. "Maybe we should go, John."

"Amelia, we've come this far. You deserve to know the truth."

Unfortunately, whether or not Rusty Lintell was working for Arthur Blackwood was a question left unanswered by her death.

But if she had taken Amelia's baby from Blackwood, she could have given him to the Sweeny family.

And now he was gone.

John cleared his throat. "Mrs. Sweeny, there's one way we can determine if your little boy was Amelia's son. She deserves closure."

Amelia sighed. "If Eddie was my baby, it won't change anything for you, Mrs. Sweeny. But I'll know, and I can stop looking and move on."

Resignation snapped in the woman's eyes. "What do you want me to do?"

"Do you have a comb or brush, even a toothbrush, anything that might have his DNA on it?"

The woman closed her eyes for a moment as if torn over what to do, then opened them and murmured for them to wait. She disappeared for a moment, and returned carrying a hairbrush. "This was his."

John removed a bag from his pocket and bagged it. "We can test his hair for DNA and then we'll know the truth."

Mrs. Sweeny caught his arm before they could leave. "Please, can I have the brush back when you're finished?"

"Of course."

They turned to leave, but Mrs. Sweeny called Amelia's name. "I hope you find what you're looking for. I do understand what it's like to lose a child. I don't wish that on anyone."

Amelia thanked her, but the deep sadness that had pervaded her eyes when John had first met her returned. Like him, she knew that if Eddie was her little boy, she would never get to meet him.

It was unforgiveable. And one more thing Arthur Blackwood had stolen from her.

John's cell phone buzzed that he had a text from Helen Gray. *I have information regarding The Gateway House. Meet me at my office.*

―――――― . ――――――

Amelia struggled not to give in to despair as John drove to the lab. There was still the possibility that Davie was her son.

But it could be Eddie. Which meant she'd lost any chance of ever knowing her own child.

She waited in the car while John dropped off the hairbrush. When he returned, he looked frustrated.

"Any news?"

"DNA takes time. Lieutenant Maddison will call us as soon as he gets the results." They started the drive toward Slaughter Creek. "Helen Gray sent me a text saying she has information about The Gateway House."

"They know who set the fire?"

"Not yet."

"How about where the children and house parents are?"

"I don't know. We'll find out when we talk to her."

They lapsed into silence until they arrived, the windshield wipers scraping freshly fallen sleet as they drove. Bundling up in her coat and scarf, Amelia followed John up to Helen's office, an older colonial-style house that had been converted into a business on the main street of Slaughter Creek.

Helen greeted them at the door with a smile. The social worker was probably in her early fifties, but attractive with dark hair and brown eyes. Eyes that looked kind but worried.

"Come on in, Agent Strong, Miss Nettleton."

"Thank you for texting," John said. "Any word on the Ellingtons?"

A frown pulled at Helen's mouth. "No, I'm afraid not." She gestured for them to take seats. "I did some research, though, after we last talked regarding the adoptions that occurred through The Gateway House."

John leaned forward. "And?"

Helen pushed a printout toward John. "I followed up on a few of the cases to see how the families and children were adjusting and found something disturbing."

"What do you mean?"

Helen tapped the printout with her finger. "Three of the families I spoke with confirmed that everything was fine with their adoptions. But there were four other families I couldn't locate."

"They moved?" John asked.

Helen sighed. "No. The addresses listed as their homes were fake."

———— . ————

John contemplated the implications of the social worker's statement. Had the Ellingtons been working a child-trafficking ring?

Had Blackwood started another project by using subjects from The Gateway House?

Or was he jumping to conclusions that the cases were even related?

"Can I have a list of those names?" John asked.

Helen nodded, tapped some keys, hit print, then handed him the list.

John's cell phone buzzed, Coulter calling. He stepped out of Helen's office into the hallway to answer.

"Yeah?"

"Another boy was kidnapped. Name is Danny Kritz."

John dropped his head forward and rubbed his eyes. Dammit. This was his fault. If he'd stopped this kidnapper earlier, Danny Kritz wouldn't have had to suffer. "Where was he taken from?"

"A dental clinic."

"Text me the address and I'll meet you at the clinic."

He disconnected and motioned to Amelia, who'd followed him into the hallway. "Another child was kidnapped. I have to go. Can you get a cab home?"

Amelia nodded, and he tugged his coat up over his neck and hurried to his SUV. A little boy's life was in danger.

——————————— · ———————————

Amelia waited until John drove away before going back inside to talk to Helen. Helen stood in front of a whiteboard where dozens of photographs of children had been attached with magnets.

Her eyes widened in surprise when she saw Amelia, and she flipped the board around, looking nervous. "Did you forget something?"

Amelia tapped her fingers up and down her sides. "Thank you for helping us. Can you tell me about the three families who said their adoptions went smoothly?"

Helen frowned. "That information is confidential."

"If they agree to talk to me, you can come with me," Amelia said. "But they might be able to tell me something about the people at The Gateway House."

Helen gnawed on her lower lip for a moment. "All right. I'll set it up. But we'll meet here."

"That's fine," Amelia said. "I appreciate it."

"I'll call you after I speak with them."

Amelia thanked her again, then stepped outside and phoned for a cab. Cars crawled by in the sludgy street. The snow capping the mountain peaks looked ethereal, but the wind was pounding the trees and there was nothing peaceful about the way she felt.

By the time she reached her guesthouse, she was antsy, wondering how soon Helen could set up the meeting.

Maybe one of the other families had seen her baby. Or maybe they'd kept in contact with the Ellingtons.

It was a long shot, but she couldn't ignore any lead.

The cab driver let her out in front of her guesthouse, and she rushed to the door. But nerves fluttered in her stomach. Would she find more damage inside?

Hand shaking, she opened the door and took a quick glance around. Her canvases were stacked against the wall just as she'd left them that morning. She peeked in the bedroom. Bed still made, no more underwear or scraps of her journal lying around.

She breathed a sigh of relief, but suddenly the sound of a baby's cry echoed through the walls.

"Mommy," the voice cried. "Mommy, where are you?"

Amelia whirled around, searching the studio for the source of the sound.

"Mommy . . . help me . . . "

A sob caught in Amelia's throat. That voice . . . the little boy's cry . . . it sounded so real.

But it couldn't be . . .

Perspiration beaded on her neck. *Was* she losing her mind again?

"This is Mrs. Kritz," Coulter said as John entered the clapboard house at the edge of Slaughter Creek.

One look told him the family had little money. The wood was rotting on the house, the porch was falling in, a few window-panes were broken out, and out the backdoor window he spotted an outhouse down a trail in the back.

A single fuel oil heater burned in the small living room, probably the only heat in the shack.

The mother sat in a rocking chair, a tissue wadded in her hands, her eyes red-rimmed and swollen. On the other side of a grimy window, three boys ranging from three to five were play-ing in the snow, building a snowman, their clothes tattered and dirty, their bodies thin and bony.

"The school was supposed to pick him up, then he was to ride the bus home," she cried. "But he didn't show up."

John checked his watch. "Isn't it a little early for school to be getting out?"

"Early-release days, they send 'em home so parents can go in for conferences."

"And the school took him to the dentist?"

She nodded. "First, I thought the stinker just missed the bus, that maybe he snuck off with a friend and was lollygagging around. So I called the school and they said they thought I picked him up at the dentist."

"Do you pick him up sometimes?"

"No, sir. My car ain't been running right."

"So why did the school think you picked him up?"

"They said I called 'em and told 'em I'd get him, but I didn't do no such thing."

John gritted his teeth. "What was Danny wearing, Mrs. Kritz?"

She rubbed at her forehead. "I dunno, a T-shirt and jeans. He gets himself dressed on account of I been up all night with Baby

Boy and then got to feed the other little ones and the phone was ringing, goddamned bill collectors." She threw her hands up. "I do the best I can."

"Do you have a picture of Danny?" Coulter asked.

She spit snuff into a tin can, then waved one hand toward the kitchen. "They took his picture at school. I didn't have no money to buy 'em, but Danny's teacher sent home the proofs and said we could keep 'em."

"I want to put it on the news and in the National Center for Missing and Exploited Children's database," Coulter said.

She motioned that it was okay, and Coulter stepped inside to retrieve the picture.

The baby started fussing, and she handed him a cracker. "Shh, boy, it'll be all right."

But it wasn't all right. One of her children was missing, and John wanted to promise her they'd bring him back.

"Mrs. Kritz, where is Danny's father?"

"He skipped out on us right after Baby Boy was born. Said he didn't sign up for this." Her face fell. "I told him I didn't either, but we play the cards we're dealt. And Danny was his kid anyway, not mine."

God, he'd heard this story before. People clueless about birth control or too lazy or irresponsible to use it. A vicious cycle that was often repeated.

"So you don't think he would have taken Danny, maybe for a visit?"

A mat of stringy brown hair fell across her forehead as she shook her head. "No. Heard he took a job on an oil rig somewhere. Ain't been home for over a year."

"Have you seen anyone strange lurking around your house? Someone watching Danny?"

The baby fussed again, and she scooped him up, opened her blouse, and began to nurse him. John dragged his gaze from the sight, uncomfortable with her lack of modesty.

"Ain't seen anyone."

"How about a white van? One that looks similar to an ice-cream truck?"

She scrunched her nose. "Maybe. Seems like I saw one the other day. Come to think of it, it was the same day that nosy social worker stopped by. That's how Danny got into that free dental clinic."

"What's her name?" John asked.

"She's a he," Mrs. Kritz said. "Name's Sonny Jones. He say my Danny need fillin's or his teeth gonna fall out."

"What did Mr. Jones look like?" John asked.

Mrs. Kritz shrugged. "Had a goatee. Wore a hat, couldn't see his eyes."

John tensed. Was it the same man Ronnie described? Could he have worn a disguise? "Do you have a card with his contact information on it?"

The baby finished eating and she adjusted her blouse, then patted his back. "No, he just showed up one day, said he worked with the school."

"Slaughter Creek Elementary?"

"Yeah." One of the other kids stumbled, scraped his knee, and began to cry.

She stood to go to him at the same time Coulter walked out with the photograph.

"I promise we'll do everything we can to find Danny," John said.

She murmured okay, but had her hands full with the crying toddler, whose ear-piercing wails had started the baby crying as well. A metal can rattled as he stepped outside, and he looked over and saw a scraggly dog scrounging through the woman's garbage.

John and Coulter walked back to their vehicles. "I'll get this into the system, issue an Amber Alert, and verify the story about the father."

John pulled his phone from his pocket. "I'm going to call the school and set up a meeting with the social worker, then drop by the clinic."

John climbed in his SUV and cranked the engine and heater as he pressed the number for Slaughter Creek Elementary. Seconds later, a female voice answered.

He identified himself and explained he was looking into Danny's disappearance.

"Oh my goodness, we heard about that. What happened?"

"He was last seen at the free dental clinic. That's the reason I'm calling," John said. "I need contact information for Sonny Jones, the social worker who arranged for him to attend the clinic."

"Agent Strong, I'm afraid I don't know what you're talking about."

"What do you mean?"

"There is no one named Sonny Jones working with the school system."

John pulled onto the road, bouncing over the ruts. "Are you sure?"

"I'm positive. The only social worker we work with is a woman by the name of Helen Gray."

Dammit. This man who called himself Sonny Jones must have made up his story to get close to the Kritz family.

He'd been watching Danny for a reason.

Chapter Twenty-One

———————— o ————————

Mrs. Kritz would be overwhelmed with guilt when she realized she'd been duped by this man who called himself Sonny Jones.

John wanted more information before he dropped that bombshell on her.

He punched the number for the lab as he parked in front of the dental clinic.

"This is Agent Strong. Do you have the DNA results on those samples I dropped off?"

Lieutenant Maddison cleared his throat. "Not yet, the lab is backed up."

"Call me when you get something," John said. If one of them matched Amelia's DNA, he could close that case, and Amelia would have her answer.

It would be up to her what she did with that information.

"We did pull two calls off Deanna Jayne's phone," Maddison said. "Both traced back to burner phones, so it was a dead end."

"Probably victims covering their tracks," John muttered, frustrated. He understood the need for the underground organization and their tactics, but when one of their own was killed, it made it damn near impossible to find the killer.

Unless someone else came forward. Which had yet to happen.

He thanked Maddison, then on a whim called Brenda Banks and filled her in. "I respect what this woman did, Ms. Banks, but maybe if you ran a piece on her death, it might prompt someone to phone in a tip."

"I doubt it," Brenda said. "These women survive because they remain in the dark."

"I understand that. But even an anonymous tip would help."

Of course they'd have to weed out the pranks and crazies.

"I'll see what I can do," Brenda agreed. "I know Sheriff Black-wood is looking for her killer."

"Good. Keep me posted." John ended the call, rubbing his gloved hands together as he strode up the path to the dental clinic. The building was weathered and old, the threadbare carpet musty smelling. Faded paint was chipping off the walls, and a waiting room filled with what looked like hand-me-down toys sat to the right. Three children were playing with blocks on the floor, while two women in chairs thumbed through magazines.

He approached the receptionist window and identified himself.

The gray-haired woman fluttered her fingers through her short curls. "Oh my, you're here about poor little Danny."

"Yes, ma'am," John said. "I spoke with his mother, and she said a social worker named Sonny Jones arranged for Danny to receive treatment here."

A frown puckered between her eyes. "Usually that's the way it works."

"But the school said they had no record of Mr. Jones working with them."

Another frown accentuated the fine lines around her mouth, and she clicked a few keys on the computer, then looked back up at him, a perplexed look on her face. "That's odd. There's no mention of Sonny Jones in the file, and no referral letter."

"So you never met this man?"

She shook her head. "No, usually the school-assigned social worker, or sometimes the counselor, brings the children in. Danny came with a group from Slaughter Creek Elementary, but yesterday we received a call saying his mother was picking him up."

"Mrs. Kritz said she thought he was riding the bus home," John said.

"I know, I don't understand what happened. We did check. The school counselor said she received the same call. So we didn't think anything of it."

"But you realize now you were tricked," John said.

Regret flickered on the woman's face. "Apparently so. I've been worried sick about that boy."

She should be worried. "I need copies of your phone records," John told her.

She folded her hands on the desk. "We have rules. I'll have to talk to someone—"

"Forget your rules, a child's life is on the line. Besides, I'll have a warrant in an hour."

He didn't bother to wait for a response. He dialed the judge to request a warrant for both the school and clinic's phone records, then phoned their computer analyst to get him on the job.

She was checking in another patient when he hung up.

"Do you have security cameras outside the building?"

"Yes. We installed them last year because we had a theft. Some teenagers stealing drugs."

"Can I see the tapes from when Danny was here?"

She nodded, rose, and waved him through the door to the back. She showed him into an office and set up the camera feed, then left to tend to the front desk.

He heard a child crying in the back, then the sound of a drill.

The camera feed came on, drawing his attention to the screen. For a few minutes, he watched as patients arrived on a small school bus. Danny was one of them. He recognized him from the photograph. He was quiet and kept to himself.

Another group climbed the same bus to go back to school. A little girl of about five clung to a woman's hand as they entered.

He searched the street for someone watching the children, for the white van, scrutinizing the cars that passed, but the angle of the camera focused on the door, limiting his visibility.

Eventually Danny moped out the door and slumped down on the bench in front of the clinic. The kid was wearing a thin jacket two sizes too small and looked cold and miserable.

Then a shadow appeared beside Danny, a thick bulky coat camouflaging his body. But he could tell he was tall, slightly hunched. A man's build. John strained to see his face, but the figure remained just on the edge of the camera as if he knew it was there.

Then the man leaned closer and said something to Danny, and the boy stood. Danny's expression looked troubled, his eyes big in his narrow face. But he gave a nod, then followed the shadow, quickly disappearing out of sight.

The child's voice wouldn't stop.

"Help me, Mommy. Help . . . "

Ting. Ting. Ting. There went the wind chimes again.

Amelia covered her ears with her hands as she combed the rooms of the guesthouse, searching for a radio or a recorder, something that would explain the child's cries.

Were they in her head?

God knows, she'd heard voices before.

She checked the medicine cabinet and found the bottle of Lithium the doctors had given her. She'd stopped taking it long ago.

Although the bottle was nearly empty . . .

Had she taken some and forgotten? But the Lithium was supposed to control her psychosis, not make her hear voices . . .

A cold sweat broke out on her brow. Had she backtracked with her treatment and allowed another alter to emerge?

Terrified, she hurried to her phone to call her therapist, but her cell buzzed before she reached it. She snagged the phone, frightened it was the man who'd called Viola.

But Helen Gray's number showed on the caller ID.

"Hello."

"Amelia, I convinced two of the families to come in and meet you. The other family refused."

"What time?"

"They're on their way now."

"I'll be right there."

Amelia grabbed her keys and purse, tugged on her coat and gloves, and raced outside to her car. The mountain roads were treacherous, desperately in need of snowplows as cars crawled along.

Fifteen minutes later, she was seated in Helen's office.

A heavyset man and his plump wife sat across from her, both looking nervous, while a couple around her age held hands, their faces wary.

Helen introduced the first couple as the Harolds, the second as the Irwins.

"I don't understand why we're here," Mr. Harold said in a terse voice.

"There's nothing wrong with our adoptions, is there?" Mrs. Irwin said in a tiny voice.

"We went through proper legal channels," Mr. Irwin said before she or Helen could respond.

Helen held up her hand to quiet them. "As I explained on the phone, I simply needed to ask you some questions about The Gateway House and the Ellingtons."

"Why?" Mr. Harold asked abruptly.

Amelia spoke up. "Because of me. Six years ago I gave birth to a baby boy, but he was taken from me against my will. I need to know what happened to him."

"We adopted a girl," Mr. and Mrs. Harold said at once.

"So did we," the Irwins said, voices filled with relief.

"We understand that," Helen interjected. "But you adopted children around the same time Amelia's son was adopted."

"When a TBI agent and I went to The Gateway House to talk to the Ellingtons," Amelia explained, "The Gateway House had burned down and the Ellingtons were gone."

"What about the children?" Mrs. Irwin asked.

"They were gone, too," Amelia replied. "That's why I wanted to talk to you. Have you heard from the Ellingtons?"

Mr. Harold pulled at his mustache. "We haven't talked to them in years."

Mrs. Irwin rubbed at a stain on her slacks. "Not since the adoption was final."

"Did you notice anything strange about the couple when you worked with them?" Amelia asked.

"What do you mean, strange?" Mrs. Harold asked.

Amelia hesitated. She didn't really know what to ask. "Like they were hiding something? Were they upfront about the details of the children you adopted?"

Mrs. Harold stood. "I knew you were getting at something. You want to try to take our kids away from us."

Mrs. Irwin jumped up and grabbed her husband's arm, her expression panicked. "Oh no, Stanley, don't let her do that. She can't take Marie from us."

"That's not the reason I'm here," Amelia said.

"We need a lawyer before we answer any more questions." Mr. Harold took his wife's hand and rushed toward the door.

The Irwins followed, the couples speaking in harsh tones as they exited. Helen hurried after them trying to calm them down.

The fact that the couples had bolted suggested they suspected something shady about the Ellingtons and The Gateway House.

But they weren't talking.

Amelia twisted her hands together, antsy to know more about the couple who hadn't shown. She glanced through the door and saw Helen talking in low voices to the couples, so she tiptoed around to Helen's desk and checked her computer.

The other couple's name was Bayler. She scribbled their address on a sticky note, then jammed it in her pocket, and waited until Helen wasn't looking and snuck out.

She'd talk to this other couple herself.

They hadn't shown for a reason, and she wanted to know what it was.

———————— , ————————

John's fingers tightened around his phone as he left the lab. He hoped to hell the tech could isolate an image and give him a description of the man who'd abducted Danny.

"We've got another bomb," Agent Nick Blackwood said over the line.

Good God. Another kidnapping, and now another bomb? "Where?"

"A social-work conference in Nashville."

Jesus. He'd missed the news this morning. "Number dead?"

"Thirteen, but it could have been more."

"This group is escalating. Tell me about the bomb."

"Another suicide bomber, boy, age twelve."

"Twelve. God."

"These have got to be connected," Nick said. "Since the bombers all came from different areas, we're searching their computers to see if they connected online."

"Good point," John said.

"Could be these are practice, test rounds, and the group is gearing up for something bigger."

John scrubbed his hand over the back of his neck. "Did you locate the group Roper pointed you to?"

"The map led to an empty campsite. Someone may have warned them we were coming," Nick said. "I'll continue looking and keep you posted."

"Send me a list of the bombers' identities and backgrounds."

"I'll send you what I've got so far." John waited on the info to come through, then phoned the tech department. He spoke with Arianna, one of their best techs, and explained his theory. "Run an analysis on children who disappeared in the state of Tennessee and surrounding states, specifically boys who disappeared between the ages of five and nine." He contemplated the age of the bombers. "Go back about fifteen years."

"I'm on it," Arianna said.

Dread balled in his gut as he hung up. If what he suspected was true, if these teen bombers were kidnap victims, the unsub had been abducting children for over a decade.

Which meant he'd already escaped detection for years and knew how to cover his tracks.

And John wouldn't stop until they caught him.

——————— . ———————

Amelia studied the house where the Baylers lived. It was a well-kept gray Victorian set on an acre of land with a pond and dozens of live oaks to the right. The snowy ground made it look like a postcard, yet something about the sharp turrets and angles and the tiny attic window reminded her of a horror movie.

For a brief second, she thought she saw a little boy's face pressed to the glass. His hands pounded the glass in a silent scream as if he were trapped.

According to the file Helen had found, the couple was in their midthirties. They had tried for two years to have a baby before finally turning to adoption.

They had a six-year-old son named Mark.

When no one answered her knock, she rang the doorbell. Wind battered her with ice pellets as she waited in the eerie quiet.

Finally she stepped to the side and peered into the garage. A black sedan was parked inside, although there was a second space that was empty.

She moved to the right and peeked through the front window, but the lights were off. Still, she could see that the house looked as if it had been ransacked.

A lamp was overturned, magazines were strewn on the floor, and the desk drawer stood askew. Deciding no one was at home, she descended the porch steps and walked around to the back of the house, her teeth chattering. A small stoop led to the back door, snow piled a foot high.

She looked inside and noticed dishes piled in the sink. A pantry was open, and it appeared that the items inside had been rummaged through.

Had someone broken inside? Were the Baylers all right?

Nerves on edge, she jiggled the door. It was locked, but she pulled a hairpin from her hair and picked it, a skill she'd picked up from Skid. The floor squeaked as she stepped into the kitchen. The rooms were drafty, ice cold.

Slowly, she moved past the kitchen table, then through the hall, pausing to note the photographs of the family on the wall. An attractive blond woman, a handsome dark-haired man, a small boy with big brown eyes and brown hair. They looked like a happy family.

Amelia's heart tugged. If this boy was her son, his adopted parents obviously adored him.

She climbed the steps, found the little boy's room first, and quickly assessed the contents.

A set of bunk beds. Toy dinosaurs, a football, action figures, books, and a child's table loaded down with Legos. A photograph of the boy in a soccer uniform hung on the wall, making her heart swell with longing.

Judging from the posters on the wall and the books, he liked fantasy stories and supernatural creatures.

Slightly unsettling for a six-year-old.

She checked the closet and noticed the drawers to his dresser were opened. It looked as if clothes had been removed.

Frowning, she hurried to the next bedroom. The parents' room. Nicely decorated, but just like the boy's room, the dresser drawers stood open and so did the closet door. There was a space on the floor that was empty but held the imprint of a suitcase.

The truth hit her—after Helen had called the couple, they decided to take the little boy and run.

A noise sounded. The floor squeaked. Amelia turned to see if someone was in the house and thought she saw a woman. Mrs. Bayler?

Then something hard slammed against the back of her head, and she collapsed.

———————————

He removed the prosthetic leg, cursing at the throbbing that constantly gnawed at him. Phantom limb syndrome, that's what they called it.

Damn fools. It felt real as hell to him. Not like a phantom limb.

He'd lost it years ago. Lost it to that fucking beating.

"You good-for-nothing lowlife. You have to be taught a lesson."

Gut-wrenching pain had riddled his maimed body, and an endless sea of blood had pooled around him.

He had been the same age as the boys he was training.

Danny watched him from the corner, his eyes glued to the mangled leftovers of his leg, but he showed no reaction.

The kid was a real trooper. Hadn't complained or whined. Hadn't asked any questions. Had accepted his fate and the promise of becoming someone important.

Maybe because he was so small and the other children picked on him.

Yes, he'd chosen well this time.

Danny wasn't sick like the Tillman kid. He would thrive where he was taking him.

Chapter Twenty-Two

———— o ————

The sound of computers and voices echoed through the halls as John entered the forensics lab.

Coulter was already there, waiting on him, eyebrows furrowed. "What's this about?"

"I think these kidnappings may be related to another investigation. Agent Blackwood faxed photos he found on surveillance cameras of the most recent bomber as well as a picture someone snapped on their cell phone of the first bomber."

"And?"

"I've got a hunch."

Arianna tapped her tablet. "I pulled up that list you wanted."

John gave her a quick thanks. "Let's see if the pics of these bombers match."

Coulter propped his hip against a nearby desk while Arianna went to work. John watched the computer system scroll through pictures searching for a match. Five minutes later when they hadn't found one, John drummed his fingers on the desk.

"Arianna, let's use facial recognition software with age progression and compare the images."

"Can you narrow the parameters?"

"Focus on boys who disappeared from foster homes, The Gateway House, or single-parent homes."

"Okay." She tapped a few keys, and the computer program began to run, flashing photo after photo on the screen, comparing them.

"You really think this kidnapper has something to do with these bombings?" Coulter asked.

"Think about it. He could have kidnapped these two boys, held them for years, and brainwashed them to become suicide bombers."

John explained that The Gateway House had burned down, and that the Ellingtons were missing along with the children who'd been living with them. "There are unaccounted-for adoptions of children who passed through The Gateway House. It could be a front for trafficking kids or—"

"Or for someone building their own terrorist group." Coulter's eyes lit up at the possibility of connecting the cases.

John nodded. "Commander Blackwood tried something similar, except he was working on perfecting soldiers, not terrorists. And he drew kids from a free clinic. It also would explain the reason the abductor released Ronnie Tillman. He wanted strong boys who he could shape into what he wanted."

The computer program beeped that it had a match. "Look," Arianna said. "Your first bomber's name is Allen Crone. He disappeared from a government-funded daycare center in Nashville when he was five. Mother lived in the projects. Teacher said one minute he was on the playground, and the next he was just gone."

"Did the police have any leads?" Coulter asked.

Arianna accessed the file. "They suspected the stepfather because of abuse allegations. But he had an alibi, and so did the mother. The police questioned neighbors, other teachers and workers at the daycare, even the children, but came up with nothing. The case eventually went cold."

Except that missing children's cases were never closed.

A dinging sound, and the program found the latest bomber. "His name is Larry Romberg. Lived in Cleveland, Tennessee, with an ailing grandmother after his mother abandoned him. Apparently she was a drug addict. Larry disappeared from a Laundromat where the grandmother forgot him. Later she was diagnosed with Alzheimer's."

Another boy who had no one to push the police to find him.

John looked over Arianna's shoulder as she scrolled through the police reports and photos of the crime scenes.

"Wait," John said. He pointed to a picture of a snowy playground where Ronnie Tillman had gone missing. "Enlarge that photo."

She tapped some keys and enhanced the picture.

John narrowed his eyes. "Looks like odd foot impressions. One is heavier than the other. It could mean he wears a special shoe of some kind. Or that he has a handicap."

"And that you're right. We have a serial kidnapper on our hands."

John grimaced. "Nick discovered a website that Blackwood's followers frequent. That's how he found Roper."

"I'll look at it again," Coulter said. "Maybe there's something that will lead us to this unsub."

John's phone buzzed. Helen Gray. "I need to take this." He stepped outside Arianna's office and connected the call. "Agent Strong."

"Are you with Miss Nettleton?"

"No, why?"

A second passed. "We met with two of the families who adopted from The Gateway House, but one couple refused to come in. I stepped out of my office for a moment, then Amelia left in a hurry. I think she may have stolen some information from my computer about the other couple. I'm afraid she might have gone to see them. I don't have to tell you that I could get in trouble for this—"

"You won't," John assured her. "Just give me that address. I'll find Miss Nettleton and make certain to smooth things over with the couple."

Another pause riddled with anxiety.

"I promise I'll use discretion," John said.

"I'm texting you their name and address now."

John disconnected, explained to Coulter and Arianna he needed to go, and headed down the hall to the elevator as he read the text. Five minutes later his tires squealed, grinding the sand the snowplows had poured on the roads as he raced from the parking lot.

He tried Amelia's cell, but she didn't answer. Damn.

As he pulled down the Baylers' street, he saw Amelia's Mini Cooper parked in front of the Victorian house. Icicles dripped from the roof, and crystals of ice were plastered to the window-panes, giving them the appearance of broken glass.

He screeched to a stop, threw his SUV into park, jogged up the steps, and pounded on the door.

When no one answered, his instincts kicked in. He peered through the front window. The house looked as if it had been torn apart.

His instincts roared to life, and he pulled out his gun and crept around the outside of the house, checking the windows and perimeter in case someone was lurking around.

But the house was eerily quiet. Dark. No movement inside.

Palms sweating, he made it to the back door. The fact that it was ajar made him grip his gun tighter. He stepped inside, sweeping the kitchen, then hallway and living room, for Amelia.

Or someone lying in wait.

But he didn't see or hear anyone. Instead, silence cloaked the rooms. The only sounds were his breathing and the squeaking of the wood floors as he climbed the stairs.

The first room on the right, a child's, was empty, although toys and clothes were scattered as if someone had left in a hurry.

The wind outside whistled, rattling windowpanes, and he rushed to the next room. Dark. He paused, watching for an intruder waiting to attack.

The curtains fluttered by the window, drawing his gaze to the corner. Dammit.

Amelia was lying on the floor, unconscious.

————————— . —————————

Amelia roused from unconsciousness, her head spinning, the world a blur. What had happened?

She'd come in looking for the Baylers. She'd thought she saw Mrs. Bayler . . . then someone had hit her.

"Lie still," a voice murmured. "I've called an ambulance."

The man's voice registered, gruff and soothing. His hand stroked the hair from her face so gently that tears burned her eyes as she struggled to look at him.

John was there. Saving her. Always saving her.

She lifted one hand and pressed it against his cheek. "John?"

"I'm here," he said. "What happened?"

A barrage of other images pummeled her. *She was in the hospital, drugged, disoriented. White coats rushed by in a blur. Some strong chemical odor permeated the air. Machines beeped, shrill and loud. The orderlies were holding her down, injecting her with yet another narcotic.*

Locking her in that room.

A guard stood at the door, armed. He would shoot if she tried to escape.

————————— . —————————

John's chest constricted at the sudden sliver of fear in Amelia's eyes. For a second, she looked as if she was afraid of him.

He had seen that look before.

The realization made his anxiety mount. How could he have seen it when he'd only known her a few days?

Another memory teased at his subconscious. *A woman looked up at him with trusting eyes. Needy eyes.*

Her lips whispered his name . . . his body heated. He wanted to touch her, but doing so was forbidden.

The image quickly disappeared, leaving him confused and with more questions. Who was the woman? Someone he'd been involved with before he'd met Amelia? Someone waiting for him to come back?

The truth was buried somewhere in his lost past.

Secrets that would confirm he hadn't been a good guy before his accident.

Secrets he would have to face before he could be whole again, to maybe have a real life. A life that involved more than chasing kidnappers and predators and going to bed alone at night.

The siren wailed closer, jerking him back to the moment. "The ambulance is almost here. What happened, Amelia?"

She clutched his arm. "I came here to talk to the family, but they were gone. At least I thought they were."

"You didn't see anyone when you arrived?"

"No. The house . . . was empty. But then I thought I saw Mrs. Bayler."

John spoke through gritted teeth. "She must have knocked you out to give them time to get away."

Amelia tried to sit up, but she swayed, and he caught her.

"You probably have a concussion," he said. "Just lie still."

She touched the back of her head, wincing. "We have to hurry and find them, John."

"We will," John said.

The possibilities raced through his mind. Ones he didn't like. The Ellingtons had disappeared when they'd learned John was investigating The Gateway House, and now this couple had run, too.

What were they hiding?

The paramedics arrived, and John hurried to let them in. While they examined Amelia, he searched the house for signs of foul play or that the child was hiding somewhere.

But he didn't see blood or signs of violence. He did find the little boy's room disturbing. Several books on dark, paranormal creatures were jammed in the bookshelf. He flipped through the sketchpad on the kid-sized table and saw sinister outlines of a monster.

Then a drawing of a boy locked in a tiny room, the narrow window at the top the only light source. More creatures circled the outside as if trying to scratch their way inside the room.

He searched the closet but found nothing except a few T-shirts and jeans left. Questions needling him, he jogged back to the kitchen, then checked the kitchen desk, but he didn't find a checkbook or computer. There were no suitcases in the house either, indicating they packed and left willingly.

He searched for an address book or notepad with information on family or a friend they might have called, but found nothing.

It was most likely they'd disappeared out of fear that Amelia would press for custody if they'd adopted her child, but they also could be in trouble. Maybe the adoption was illegal? Maybe they knew they had adopted a kidnapped child?

Maybe they were accomplices in something much bigger . . .

He phoned Arianna. "I need a search warrant for the Ellingtons' phone records at The Gateway House and for files at the adoption agency."

"I'll get right on it."

"Also, run a background check for me on Eugene and Dana Bayler."

John drummed his foot on the floor as he heard the keys tapping. A minute later, Arianna returned. "Eugene Bayler is a lawyer. He focuses on adoptions."

Dammit, that made sense.

"Looks like he was financially set."

"Probably made his fortune charging hefty fees for private adoptions."

"His wife Dana was a stay-at-home mother. Volunteered at the church, at the preschool. No record of any trouble on either one of them."

"No complaints against Mr. Bayler?"

"None that I see. I'll let you know if I find anything on their phone records."

John hung up and found Amelia sitting up, looking flustered and arguing with the EMT.

"I'm not going to the hospital," she said firmly. "I'm fine."

The young man looked at John. "Her vitals are good, but she could have a concussion. I suggested we hospitalize her overnight for observation."

"I can't be locked up in a hospital again." Her voice quivered. "I spent half my life in one, John. I'm not going back."

Considering her history, he understood her paranoia of hospitals. He couldn't blame her. "I'll stay with her and make sure she's all right tonight."

The medics traded concerned looks, then one of them shoved a clipboard toward Amelia. "If you refuse, you have to sign a waiver."

Amelia snatched the papers, scribbled her name, and handed them back to the guy.

He and the other medic grabbed their kits and left. John touched Amelia's arm.

"Come on, I'll drive you back to your place."

Amelia jutted her chin into the air. "I'm perfectly capable of driving myself."

John frowned. She was both beautiful and stubborn. "You have a head injury, Amelia. I'm driving you. The crime team is on their way. I'll have one of the patrols drop off your car later."

Amelia bit her lip. "Fine."

The crime van rolled up seconds later, and John showed them where Amelia had been assaulted.

"Comb the place for forensics," John said. "In the boy's room, look for a hairbrush or toothbrush, something with his DNA. I want it processed and a comparison run to Ms. Nettleton's."

"What's going on?" Lieutenant Maddison asked.

"It's possible the couple ran because they adopted Amelia's baby."

"You think the couple attacked her?"

John shrugged. "Maybe. They love the child, they don't want to lose him." John paused. "And Mr. Bayler is a lawyer who handles adoptions."

Understanding registered on Maddison's face. "Definitely could be a motive."

"Yeah." He handed a photo of the couple to Maddison. "Alert officers to report their location if they spot the couple."

———————— , ————————

Sometimes when Zack closed his eyes at night, he saw things. The monsters. The banshees.

And sometimes he saw himself.

Only he wasn't locked up in this place where metal bars banged shut and kept him prisoner.

He was in a nice warm bed with a mom and a dad who fed him ice cream and didn't make him do tests. Painful tests.

They had started a few months ago.

He had failed them all.

He closed his eyes and turned toward the concrete wall. The cold swallowed him, and he hunched beneath the scratchy blanket. The image came again.

His face.

The boy was in his mind again. Only this time he was wearing different clothes. Jeans and a T-shirt. And he was riding in a car.

But he was scared.

Zack couldn't see his face, but he heard his breathing. Loud, uneven sharp sounds like a death rattle.

Zack's heart raced. He could feel the boy's fear as if it were his own. Hear the boy's heart pounding just like his own.

Where were they taking him? What was the boy scared of?

He struggled to see more. Tall trees rushed by as the car took the boy deeper into the mountains. The car swerved and slid on the ice. Sharp ridges reached out as if to grab the boy.

Then the boy screamed.

Footsteps pounded outside his door. Zack jumped. The boy's face disappeared.

Men's harsh voices echoed in the hall. Keys jangled. The metal door screeched open.

"Stand up," the man ordered.

Zack sucked in a breath and faced the man. The shiny buttons on the man's uniform glinted in the dark.

"We have to move you again," the man said, his voice bitter.

Zack braced himself for a blow. He felt like he might wet his pants.

And that would mean more punishments.

Then the man jerked his arm and dragged him from the cell.

"Where are you taking me?" Zack cried.

"Shut up," the man snapped.

His big, cold fingers cut into Zack's arm. He dragged him down a long hall. The cold dankness made him shake. He dragged his feet, but the man jerked him harder, then threw him into the back of a van.

More darkness, then he closed his eyes and let himself go someplace far away. Someplace the banshees couldn't find him.

Finally the van stopped, and the man hauled him outside. He dragged him toward a long dock where a small boat was waiting. The dock rocked back and forth below him. Wind tossed and beat at the boat.

The man hurled Zack onto the deck, then tossed him down some steps into a hole.

A motor fired up. The boat began to rock.

Zack clawed at the floor. Where was he taking him? Out into the ocean to kill him and dump his body where no one would find him?

Chapter Twenty-Three

———— o ————

A trucker passed John, slinging muddy sludge against his SUV as it passed him on the mountain road.

Amelia was resting her head against the seat and had closed her eyes, but she startled when he jerked the wheel to the right. The guardrail neared his side, but he managed to right the vehicle just in time to keep from hitting it, and slowed on the black ice.

By the time they reached Amelia's, more clouds had rolled in. Amelia dropped her purse on the table by the door, and his gaze was drawn to a painting in the studio. A beautiful painting of her holding a baby boy.

"Did you paint that from your memories?"

Amelia folded her hands together. "No, that's my twin sister Sadie and her newborn."

John studied the painting again. The features of the woman looked so much like Amelia that it was startling. Yet on closer examination, he saw the differences. Subtle but there.

Sadie looked content, relaxed, happy.

Amelia looked restless, tormented, sad, as if she was searching for a way to find the love and peace her sister had found.

He wished he could give it to her. But the only thing he had to offer was more questions and secrets.

"Your sister's baby . . . that's when your dreams started?"

Annoyance flashed in Amelia's eyes. "Yes. And before you say anything, at first I thought my dream meant I was envious. That's the reason I went to the doctor and the prison to see Ms. Lettie before I came to you."

Amelia rubbed at her forehead.

"Headache?"

She nodded.

"Lie down, Amelia. You need to rest."

"But we still don't know where the Baylers are, or where the Ellingtons took the other kids at The Gateway House."

"We're doing everything we can to find them," he said gently. "If something comes up, I'll tell you. I promise."

"Thank you for bringing me home."

She looked so vulnerable and lost that John wanted to solve all her problems. "I'm not leaving you alone tonight."

Her eyes widened.

"Not with a head injury. And not after what happened."

"I'm fine, John. That's not necessary."

Her stubborn independence both annoyed him and tugged at his heart. He couldn't resist. He reached up and stroked a strand of hair behind her ear. "Someone attacked you earlier. And someone has been inside, you know that. Someone who obviously doesn't want us digging into the past."

"I won't give up. I have to know what happened to my son."

"I know." He trailed his fingers down her cheek, her lips beckoning him to kiss her.

"John?"

Her soft whispery voice made him forget any reservations. Amelia had suffered so much. He wanted to take away that pain.

Her lips parted on a sigh, a sound filled with need and loneliness.

A loneliness that he felt deep in his own soul.

And he lowered his head and claimed her mouth with his.

——————— , ———————

Amelia sank into the kiss, savoring the comfort of John's strong arms as he slid them around her. The trembling she'd struggled to control subsided in his embrace, yet another kind of trembling rippled through her.

He teased her lips open with his tongue, and probed her mouth with his, eliciting a moan from her. She closed her eyes, images of the two of them entwined in bed together titillating.

She wanted him in her bed now.

Passion and need drove her to pull him closer. She threaded her fingers in his dark hair and stroked his calf with her foot. He groaned, tugging her against him so she felt his thick sex pressed against her belly.

Erotic sensations flooded her. His touch felt gentle yet commanding. Hungry yet tentative.

Raw, passionate.

Nothing like Six's.

It felt so wonderful that she coaxed him toward her bedroom. John's fingers trailed down her shoulders to her back and to her waist, then he slowly lifted her blouse and pulled it over her head. His hungry gaze met hers, fire flashing in the depths of his eyes.

A fiery passion that made her tug at the buttons of his shirt until she raked it over his shoulders, and he tossed it off with a grunt. Hers fell beside his, and he kissed her again, walking her backward toward her bed.

She kissed him greedily, tracing her hands over his back, then down to his belt.

He reached for his belt and shucked it off, but instead of stripping his jeans, he slipped her skirt down over her legs and dropped it to the floor.

Cool air brushed her nipples, the tips hardening as his gaze raked over her. She felt naked and wanton in her bra and lacy panties.

She'd had raw sex with other men, allowed Six to treat her roughly, and no telling what Viola had done with men. She shuddered to think about it.

But this was different. Instinctively, she knew that John's big body would somehow complete her. That it wasn't simply about sex.

They were making love.

Her breath caught at the thought, and she tore at his jeans. He yanked them off, then crawled above her in his boxers, his hard length teasing the sensitive area between her thighs.

She parted her legs, welcoming him, wanting him desperately, urging him to join his body with hers.

His beard stubble tickled her neck as he kissed her behind the ear and planted sweet tongue lashes along her throat. She moaned and thrust her hips upward, splaying her hands on his bare back.

Her fingers touched something jagged, puckered skin. A scar.

He stiffened, and looked into her eyes. "It's ugly."

"We all have scars," she whispered. God knows hers were on the inside, but they were there.

"But most people know how they got theirs." He dropped his head forward.

"What do you mean, John?"

He hesitated, stroked her hair. "I don't want to talk about it now, but there are things I've done that I'm not proud of."

He looked as if he wanted to say more, but she pressed her finger to his lips.

"I don't care what you did or who you were, only that you're here now," she whispered.

Indecision played in his eyes, but his hunger must have snuffed out the voice telling him no, and he kissed her again. Need and desire built between them as he fused his mouth with hers, then he ripped it away and licked his way to her breasts. He laved one, then the other, suckling her so hard that sensations rippled through her, building to the brink of an orgasm.

Just when she thought she might explode with pleasure, he dropped his head lower and trailed kisses down to her inner thighs. With one quick yank, he peeled off her panties. She groaned as he nudged her legs apart and teased her clit with his tongue.

Her body quivered, lost in the sensation of his mouth on her and the urgent stroke of his tongue against her flesh. She clawed at the bed covers, trembling as her release splintered through her.

She cried out his name as pleasure consumed her. Images of John thrusting inside her, filling her as he moaned her name, flooded her.

———————— · ————————

The sweetness and hunger in Amelia's lovemaking made John's body rage with need. He wanted her more than he'd ever wanted another woman.

But other disturbing images bombarded him. Images of him holding a gun. Fighting. A woman screaming. She was hurt and he needed to help her.

But he didn't . . . he couldn't . . .

He'd failed . . . what had happened to her? Had he caused her pain? Her death?

Conflicting emotions pummeled him, and he looked into Amelia's eyes. Hers glazed with passion and raw desire.

But a sliver of fear also shined, dark and unforgiving.

He'd seen snippets in his mind over the last few months, moments where he was almost certain he'd been a soldier. That maybe the scar on his back had come from combat. He had another one on his abdomen and a long jagged one on his upper thigh. All consistent with military injuries—or his accident . . .

"John?" Amelia said softly. "What's wrong?"

Self-recriminations shouted in his head. He wanted to assuage the uncertainty in Amelia's voice.

But what kind of bastard was he? He was taking advantage of her vulnerable state.

Another voice whispered to him. *Maybe he had been a terrible man, had been responsible for a woman's death.*

But he wasn't that person anymore.

He grabbed his jeans and yanked them on. How could he be sure he wasn't that man? That he hadn't killed that woman? "You need to rest."

Amelia crawled toward him, her breasts swaying, drawing his gaze to her naked body. God, he wanted to thrust his cock inside her.

Amelia took his hand and pressed it to her cheek. "But I want to be with you."

He pressed his mouth into a thin line. "I shouldn't have touched you, Amelia. You have a head injury."

"My head is fine," Amelia said. "But I don't understand why you're pulling away."

Hating himself for starting something he should have never started, he shook off her hand. "Go to sleep."

He grabbed his shirt and shoes and strode from the room. When he reached the studio, he glanced at the picture of Sadie and her baby, and knew Amelia wanted that in her life.

But he wasn't the man to give her that love or happily-ever-after.

Not when he didn't know who he was or what he'd done in his past. If she knew the truth, she wouldn't want to be with him.

———————— , ————————

Amelia tossed and turned for hours, willing John to return to her bed. But he'd made his decision and stayed away all night, leaving her alone and aching for his arms again.

John had just proven what she'd thought all along. That he couldn't love her. That she wasn't worthy of anyone's love.

Eventually she fell into an exhausted sleep, but instead of dreaming about him, she dreamed a baby was crying in the house.

Then a child's voice called to her for help.

She jerked awake, disoriented and wondering about that child's voice.

Should she consult her therapist and confide that she was hearing voices again?

If she did, the doctor would medicate her . . .

The medication numbed her, made her feel disoriented, dazed, and confused.

She needed a clear head in case she found her son.

No . . . *when* she found him. She wouldn't stop until she did.

The strong scent of coffee wafted toward her. She dragged on her robe and tiptoed into the kitchen. The room was empty, but she looked through the front window and saw John sitting on the porch with a cup of coffee in one hand, his phone in the other.

Fresh snow dotted his hair, the dark strands beckoning her fingers to embed themselves in the thick depths.

Needing to be near him, she dragged on her coat, poured herself a mug of coffee, and walked outside. Just the sight of him made her heart stutter and her body ache again.

John glanced up, turmoil on his face. His eyes were slightly bloodshot as if he hadn't slept either. His hair stood in disarray as if he'd raked his hand through it a dozen times, and he needed a shave.

But that dark beard stubble and his unkempt look only made him sexier.

"Thanks. I'll meet you there."

He ended the call and stood. "How's your head this morning?"

"Fine." Amelia reached up to touch his hair, to smooth down the rumpled ends, but he pulled away.

She dropped her hand. "You didn't sleep?"

"I don't need much sleep." His gaze met hers, and she saw something there. Need. Lust. His own brand of pain.

But something else tainted his eyes. Some emotion she couldn't define. A cold hardness that made her wonder if he wasn't the man she thought he was.

He jerked his gaze away first. "I have to go. We have a lead on the suicide bomber case."

John parked at the convenience store on the mountain road, noting the signs for the pumpkin farm nearby and others advertising the camp where tourists panned for gold. Too late in the winter for either. Instead, the places were deserted, like a ghost town.

With every mile he'd driven, he'd regretted bringing Amelia along with him.

But leaving her alone would have put her at the mercy of the person who'd attacked her two nights before.

Dammit, he was letting his feelings for her cloud his judgment. Back there when she'd nearly touched him, he'd almost given in. Almost let her.

But that would have been his undoing.

Because it had taken every ounce of his restraint and several walks in the cold during the night to keep him away from her bed.

Amelia opened her car door, not bothering to wait on him, and he quickly followed her, squashing images of her between the sheets with him on top of her. A black pickup was parked in front of the store, a beagle poking his head out the front passenger-side window.

Signs for fresh produce pointed to a small stand beside the station where steam oozed from a big black cauldron. An old-timer was stirring what he assumed was a pot of boiled peanuts. But the vegetable bins were empty, coated in ice.

Wind swirled dead leaves around their feet, the sky nothing but black clouds. He held the door open for Amelia, instinctively scanning the store as they entered.

A rail-thin man in overalls stood at the register to pay for his beer and cigarettes. He gave cash to the cashier, a scruffy-looking man who was as big around as he was tall. The buttons on his shirt looked like they might pop, revealing a wifebeater undershirt, and his jaw bulged with chewing tobacco, his teeth black.

John waited until the man left, then approached the cashier. "Are you the person who called in the tip about the Ellingtons?"

The man spit a string of tobacco into a Styrofoam cup. "Yeah. Name's Wally. You the police?"

"TBI." John flashed his ID, then showed the man a picture of the couple. "Is this the man and woman you saw?"

"Yeah."

"Were they alone?" John asked.

"Naw. They had a couple of kids with 'em. Two boys about five or six."

Amelia gave him a concerned look.

"Were the children hurt?"

"Not that I could tell. They was real quiet. One of 'em had to pee so the man took him to the bathroom while the lady stocked up on snacks."

Danny Kritz was the latest to be taken. Could he be with the Ellingtons? Were they working with the kidnapping ring? "Did they call the boys by name?"

"Didn't hear it if they did. They weren't here long, seemed like they were in a hurry, like they were nervous."

He supposed they were. "Did they say where they were going?"

He pulled at his chin with stubby fingers. "The man was looking at a map. Said he was hunting for some campground."

"Where?"

"There's one about twenty miles from here."

"What were they driving?" John asked.

"An RV."

John glanced around the store for security cameras but didn't see any. "Did you get the license plate?"

"Tag was missing. Had one of them handmade signs saying they'd ordered it."

"Can you give me directions to that campground?"

"Sure enough." The man took a map from the stand by the register, opened it, and drew a line with a red marker outlining the route. "What did these folks do?" the man asked.

John took Amelia's elbow to escort her to the door. "They may be involved in a kidnapping ring," John said over his shoulder.

The man looked surprised, but John and Amelia hurried to the car. If the Ellingtons were involved in the kidnappings, maybe they would lead him to the person behind the abductions.

John wound around the mountain, driving deeper into the ridges. The Ellingtons were obviously looking for a place to hide and planned to use the isolation of the woods to cover their whereabouts.

What did they plan to do with those boys?

Trees hugged the embankment, making it shadowy and dark as he followed the road along the creek until he spotted the sign for the campground. It was a tourist spot, but off the grid, and this was the off-season. Campers parked and hiked the five miles up to the waterfalls. Here they enjoyed peace and quiet and nature.

Here they could camp for days or weeks and no one except another tourist or hunter might see them.

Now it was virtually empty. Desolate-looking with winter and cold.

He approached the campsite, slowing as he searched the shadows. Even though it was daylight, the heavy, thick trees and storm clouds added a dismal gray cast.

The perfect place to hide.

Chapter Twenty-Four

———— o ————

John swung the SUV to the side, parked, and opened his door. An RV was parked at the edge of the creek. An animal moved through the woods, brush crackling. Creek water raced over jagged rocks.

The area was isolated, no other people or campers around. People usually didn't come in winter.

Another indication the couple was running from something.

Suddenly a man emerged from the RV, holding a shotgun aimed at them. John started to reach for his own weapon, but the man raised the gun higher, his finger on the trigger. "Don't come any closer, Mister."

"Mr. Ellington, put the gun down!" John shouted. "I'm with the TBI."

"How do I know you're not lying?" Ellington yelled.

John flashed his badge. "I tried to see you at The Gateway House, but when we arrived, it was on fire."

"Please, we just want to talk to you," Amelia shouted as she stepped from the passenger side. "Think about the children with you."

"I'm trying to protect them," the man said.

"Then talk to us," John shouted. "We don't want anyone to get hurt."

Seconds stretched into minutes. Mrs. Ellington appeared, looking frightened, and the two of them spoke in low voices. Finally Ellington lowered his shotgun to his side. "All right. We'll talk."

John motioned to Amelia to stay behind him as he stepped from behind the SUV. "Put the gun down first," he ordered.

Ellington laid the shotgun on the ground, and John lowered his own weapon and stowed it into the holster beneath his jacket. Amelia's sigh of relief mirrored his own.

He approached Ellington slowly, noting that his wife gripped his arm as if she was holding him back.

"Is there a place we can sit down and talk?" John asked.

Mrs. Ellington pointed to some lawn chairs situated by a campfire and led the way to them. John spotted the boys peeking from the camper door. At least they were safe.

"What's this about?" Mr. Ellington asked.

"I think you know," John said. "We were coming to talk to you the day The Gateway House burned down. Why did you run?"

"Who said we ran?" Ellington muttered.

"It's obvious," John said. "You're hiding out here now."

"We had to," Mrs. Ellington said in a broken voice. "We were scared."

"Scared of what?"

The couple exchanged worried looks. "Tell him everything," Mrs. Ellington said to her husband.

The man patted his chest. "First of all, I don't want me and the wife to get in trouble."

John's instincts kicked in. "Why would you be in trouble?"

"It's about the adoptions," Mrs. Ellington said. "We think that's why someone set fire to the house. They wanted to get rid of us so we wouldn't talk."

"Then you have to tell us what's going on," Amelia cut in.

"What do you have to do with this?" Mr. Ellington asked.

Amelia squared her shoulders. "Commander Arthur Blackwood took my baby when he was born. Then a woman dropped him off at a church. I think he was sent to The Gateway House from there. It would have been around July fourth six years ago."

Mrs. Ellington pulled a shawl around her shoulders. "We did get a little boy about that time," she said. "A woman left the infant all bundled up in a blue blanket with a note asking us to find a good home for him."

Amelia exhaled. "What happened to him?"

"A nice couple adopted him just a couple of days later."

"Do you remember their names?" John asked.

"Adoptions are confidential," Mrs. Ellington said. "We have to protect the adopted parents' rights."

"What about my rights?" Amelia said. "I didn't give my son up. He was stolen from me."

John wanted to comfort her, but he forced himself not to touch her. "She's right," John said. "This is a kidnapping case. I can get a subpoena—"

"Our records burned in the fire," Mr. Ellington said.

"But you remember the name of the couple?" Amelia asked.

Another look of fear passed between the couple. "A nice couple named the Baylers."

Amelia gasped softly. "That's the reason the Baylers left town," Amelia said. "They must have known we were onto them."

"Do you think they set fire to The Gateway House?" John asked.

Mr. Ellington shook his head. "No. We think it was the man who arranged the adoptions. He called and told us someone was asking questions, and that we'd better not talk to anyone."

John folded his arms. "Who is he?"

"His name is Axelrod," Mr. Ellington said. "He has his own agency that places children. He's found homes for several of the boys who've come through The Gateway House."

John grimaced. "I take it these are private adoptions and he charges a hefty fee."

The couple nodded.

"And Mr. Bayler handled the legal work?"

Mrs. Ellington tightened the grip on her shawl. "That's right. But everything was legal."

"Not if they were selling stolen kids," John said.

The couple's eyes widened. "We don't know anything about that," Mr. Ellington said. "I swear. We just tried to give the children who needed it a temporary home."

Sincerity laced his tone, but John reserved his opinion. "Did you follow up on the placement of these children?"

"No," Mrs. Ellington said. "The adoptions were private."

"What made you run?" John asked.

Mr. Ellington ran a shaky hand through his white hair. "Like I said, Mr. Axelrod told us not to talk if anyone asked questions. That threw up a red flag. Then we saw the stories about those boys being kidnapped, and we got worried."

Mr. Ellington talked with his hands, "You see, Axelrod specialized in finding homes for boys around the age of the kidnapped victims."

John gritted his teeth. It sounded as if he was filling orders. Which could mean child trafficking. Or that he was sending the boys to that group to train them to be suicide bombers.

"You think Axelrod set fire to The Gateway House?" John asked.

The couple shifted, nervous again. Mrs. Ellington cleared her throat. "He called saying he had placements for the brothers staying with us now. I told him I wanted to know details about the adopting parents. But he went ballistic. Said he was doing these kids a favor, saving them."

"Saving them?" John asked.

"That's what he said. He was put on earth to save kids because no one saved him."

"Do you have a way to contact him?"

Mr. Ellington went to the camper, returned a minute later, and handed John a business card.

The card indicated Axelrod was a social worker with a group named Safe Haven. It was also the same number on the card for Sonny Jones. At least one of the names was phony.

When he punched the number into his phone, a message said the number was out of service.

John called the forensics lab and asked the tech team to trace the number.

Maybe they could narrow down a location where he might have been calling from.

———————— , ————————

Amelia entwined her fingers to keep from fidgeting. "Tell us more about the baby the Baylers adopted. How did he come to you?"

Mrs. Ellington picked at her fingernails. "Like I said, a woman left a note with the infant."

"How do you know it was a female?" John asked.

"The handwriting and . . . the things she said. She sounded upset, scared."

"What exactly did she say?" Amelia asked.

"That she had to leave the baby with us to keep him safe. She swaddled him in a baby blanket and left a rosary with him, and asked us to find him a good loving home."

"A rosary?" Amelia asked.

Mrs. Ellington nodded. "I figured she was a religious person."

Amelia's pulse jumped. The rosary Papaw had left led them to Sister Grace. Was this the same baby? Frustration mushroomed inside her. Sister Grace had disappeared so they couldn't ask her.

"Did Axelrod place the little boy with the Baylers?" John asked.

Mrs. Ellington fidgeted with her hair. "Yes. I thought it was a little odd since he normally placed older children, but he said he was doing a favor for a friend who couldn't take care of his baby."

Amelia's dream flashed in her mind. What if Mark was her baby? Had the Commander arranged for them to take Mark until he could come for him?

She gestured toward the camper where the two little boys had ducked inside.

"Who are the kids?" Amelia asked.

"They're brothers. Their parents were killed a couple of months ago in a car accident. Unfortunately they didn't have any family. And they don't want to be separated."

Amelia tugged at her scarf. "Do you have a family who wants to adopt them?"

"Not yet. It's more difficult to place older children, especially two from the same family."

Mr. Ellington folded his arms. "We decided to keep them and raise them as our own."

Amelia pictured them traveling from town to town, always looking over their shoulders, hiding out. "You can't raise them on the run."

Tears filled Mrs. Ellington's eyes. "I know, but after the fire, we're afraid to back to Slaughter Creek."

"Do you think Axelrod might contact you about them again?" John asked.

"I don't know, but he was upset when we said we planned to keep the boys," Mr. Ellington said. "We think he set fire to The Gateway House to get them. But we managed to escape before he could take them."

"Can you give a description to a police artist?" John asked. The couple nodded.

"Good, I'll set it up." John paused. "What kind of car was he driving?"

Mr. Ellington pulled his coat up over his ears. "A black sedan once. Another time I believe he was driving a white van."

Amelia's heart hammered, as John reached inside his pocket for his phone. "Help us, and we'll provide protection for you."

"What about Timmy and Clayton?" Mr. Ellington asked.

John narrowed his eyes. "First, if your story about the boys checks out, we'll help you get custody and start a new life with them somewhere else."

Mrs. Ellington clutched her husband's arm. "What do we need to do?"

"We need to monitor your phone. If Axelrod calls, we can trace his location."

Mr. Ellington put his arm around his wife. "Is that it?"

"Once we make an arrest, you'll need to agree to testify against him," John finished.

Mrs. Ellington looked at her husband, and he gave a small nod.

John agreed. But Amelia was more concerned about finding the Baylers.

Mark just might be her son.

———————— , ————————

John phoned his chief and made arrangements to put the Ellingtons into protective custody, then collected DNA samples from the boys to verify the couple's story. He'd learned long ago not to trust anyone.

Coulter met them at the TBI office, where they gave a description to the police artist. He sent it to Brenda Banks as well as national databases for law enforcement authorities, airports, train stations, bus stations, and port authorities.

Coulter escorted the couple to a safe house. Arianna phoned that she'd heard chatter on the social media sites linked to SFTF, suggesting a possible location for the other militia group.

"I'll drop you off, then go," he told Amelia.

"That's ridiculous," Amelia said. "It would be way out of your way. Besides, I'm not crazy about going home alone, not after what I found at my house the other night."

She was right. Worse, the attack at the Baylers and the fire at The Gateway House proved that whoever they were dealing with was dangerous.

His stomach tightened. He wasn't crazy about leaving her alone either. But confronting this group could be dangerous.

"You can ride with me, but you have to stay in the car," John said.

Amelia agreed, and he drove deeper into the mountains toward the coordinates Arianna had sent him.

Tall pines and oaks surrounded them. The road was deserted, the night sounds echoing in the air, adding to the eerie feeling that they were heading into trouble.

He turned onto a narrow dirt road that literally cut through the forest, the trees obliterating any remaining daylight.

Questions ticked through his mind—had the Ellingtons told the truth? Or had they sold the children to Axelrod for a profit?

And if they had, did they know where the man was hiding? Had they known he was grooming boys to be suicide bombers?

If so, they had to pay for their crimes.

"Look, I see a light down there," Amelia said as he maneuvered through the dense woods.

He spotted it, too. A run-down shack, a couple of outbuildings, another shack out back.

Desolate, surrounded by the mountains. Dark. Off the grid.

He slowed, searching for vehicles, but he didn't see any. The place looked deserted.

Dammit, had someone warned the group that the police were looking for them?

"They're gone," he said as he shifted into park.

"You think they knew we were coming?"

"Either someone warned them, or they picked up enough on the Internet chatter to know we were closing in on them. Stay here. I'm going to look around."

"I can help," Amelia said.

"I said to stay here," John said. "They may have left someone behind to ambush us."

Fear flicked in Amelia's eyes. "Be careful, John."

He gave a clipped nod, then pulled himself from the SUV. Dirt and leaves crunched beneath his boots as he walked toward the building. Instincts on alert, he removed his gun from his holster and clutched it at the ready.

He scanned left and right, searching the darkness, half expecting an army to be hiding at the edge of the woods. But nothing moved. Not even the air.

In fact, it seemed strangely silent. His senses kicked in.

The quiet before the storm.

Shoulders tense, he slowly approached the front door, then decided to look inside the window instead. He pulled his flashlight from his pocket and shined it into the dust-coated window.

Bare minimum furniture. Except . . . there were chains dangling from chairs. Chains connected to several twin-size metal beds lined in a row like a barracks—or a prison. A rancid odor seeped through a broken windowpane. Raccoons skittered across the floor.

Fury railed inside him, and he walked back to the door and turned the knob. A click sounded, and he realized too late that the door was wired.

He turned to run just as a bomb exploded.

The boat rocked Zack back and forth, back and forth, the wind beating at the sides. His head felt funny and his stomach hurt. The air smelled yucky, too. He wished the rocking would stop . . .

He crawled through the darkness and pulled himself up to look out the tiny window. But all he could see was water. Icy gray waves that chopped up and down.

The voice in his head started again. He'd heard it before.

A boy's voice. It sounded like it was coming from him.

What was wrong with him? Sometimes it was the banshees. Sometimes the other boy.

No, it was *him*.

The boy who came to him in his dreams. The one with the mommy and daddy. The one who lived in the house with a swing set out back. And he had baseball bats and a soccer goal and normal stuff . . .

Not like the place where he and the other boys lived.

But this time the boy was crying. Great big wails that sounded like he was dying.

Where was he?

He closed his eyes trying to see. The mountains. Somewhere. Trees and weeds rushed past.

He wasn't with his mommy and daddy anymore.

This time he was in a bad place, too. A place that was just as dark as the place where Zack stayed most of the time.

He wanted to go back and help the boy.

But the boat was taking him farther and farther away. He could swim a little but not enough to make it across the ocean. Besides, if he jumped in, the sharks would eat him.

He thought about yelling for help, but no one would hear him.

No one ever heard him.

Chapter Twenty-Five

———————— o ————————

Amelia watched in horror as the building exploded. Wood splintered and popped, pieces flying, flames bursting from the structure shooting against the gray sky like orange spikes. Fire crackled and shot upward, thick smoke clouding the air.

Where was John?

She jumped from the SUV and screamed his name, searching the flames and rubble as she ran toward it. Her boots dug through the snowy ice, but heat seared her as she neared the outer edges of the blaze, smoke clogging her lungs.

Seconds later, she spotted John lying on the ground, face down. Wood from the building lay in fiery patches around him.

He wasn't moving.

Dear God, he couldn't be dead.

She wove to the right to avoid a burning patch of debris and knelt beside him. "John?" She gently turned him over to see if he was breathing. Relief filled her when she felt his chest rise and fall.

He had a couple of cuts on his face from the wood and glass, and a nasty-looking bruise on his cheek.

But he was still the most handsome man she'd ever known.

"John?" A wave of intense heat scorched her side from the flames, but she ignored it and stroked his cheek. "John, please talk to me."

He moaned, then slowly opened his eyes, disoriented.

"I'm calling an ambulance." She scanned the burning debris, wondering what had caused the explosion.

"No, I'm fine. It just knocked the wind out of me."

She touched his forehead. "You're bleeding."

"It's nothing." He pushed her hand away from his forehead and tried to get up but swayed. "What happened?"

Amelia caught him. "You went up to the door and the whole place exploded."

"Hell. A bomb." John gripped her hand and allowed her to help him up, although his eyes still seemed blurry. He looked around at the patches of flames and debris surrounding them. "Come on, let's get away from the heat."

He leaned on her as they hurried away from the fire. When they reached the SUV, she helped him into the driver's seat.

She ran around to the passenger side to retrieve her phone, but John was already calling a crime team by the time she got in.

When he hung up, he called his partner. "That group was gone, Coulter. They must have known we were coming."

Amelia hugged her arms around her middle as the roof of the building collapsed with a roar. God help them. Was her little boy living with this group?

———————— , ————————

John's head throbbed, but he was too angry to give in to a migraine. He had to catch the son of a bitch who planted that bomb. If Amelia had followed him up to the house, she could have been hurt.

Lieutenant Maddison met him at the edge of the blaze. "Did you see anyone when you arrived?"

"No, no one. They must have gotten word that we were coming."

"How?"

"I don't know," John said. "But see if you can find anything in that mess that will help us figure out where they'd go next."

"Another remote location," Lieutenant Maddison said.

"I'll call Arianna and ask her to check the Internet chatter."

He left Amelia at the SUV and followed Maddison over to the rubble. The flames were starting to die down, wood still crackling as the embers continued to burn.

Maddison stooped down to examine something, then looked up at John. "Looks like a homemade bomb. See this pipe? He probably filled it with gunpowder."

John turned and scanned the forests and ridges, wondering if the bomber had been watching. Was the explosion meant to kill him, or to hide evidence of the group?

————————— , —————————

Amelia watched John, Lieutenant Maddison, and the other CSIs comb the area, collecting evidence. In spite of the fact that John had been knocked unconscious and still looked pale, he refused to allow her to call the medics for him.

Lieutenant Maddison stepped aside to answer a phone call, then walked back to John and gestured toward her. Amelia tensed. Judging from the expression on his face, he had bad news.

She steeled herself as they approached. "Ms. Nettleton," Lieutenant Maddison said. "I got the DNA back from Davie Miller and Eddie Sweeny."

"And?"

"Neither one of them matches your DNA."

Amelia exhaled, and John stroked her arm. "I'm sorry, Amelia."

"What about the Bayler boy?"

"We don't have those results yet."

John's eyes darkened. "Sheriff Blackwood just called. Two bodies were found on Rocky Ridge."

Fear seized Amelia. "Children?"

John shook his head. "No, a woman and man. I'm going there now."

Amelia nodded, then addressed Lieutenant Maddison. "Let me know as soon as you get those results."

Amelia followed John to the car, desperately trying to hold on to hope, but at every corner they were hitting a dead end.

John veered onto another road that took them out of the isolated area where the camp had been. Then he wound down the mountain, tires grinding against the sand and icy pavement, slowing as they passed over the bridge and crossed Slaughter Creek.

Amelia spotted Jake's police car on the embankment as they approached the accident. John parked behind him, and they met Jake at the edge of the ridge. A team was already there, working to lift the couple from the ledge below while an ambulance waited to transport the bodies.

She wrapped her scarf around her head to keep the wind from freezing her ears as she watched them work. The drop-off to the ridge was steep, the guardrail intact.

Meaning they hadn't gone over in their car. They could have jumped, but had probably been pushed.

The rescue team laid the bodies on stretchers, and Jake leaned over the man's corpse. Both bodies were stiff with rigor, although the frigid temperature had slowed decomposition

"Gunshot wound to the back of the head," Jake said after examining the man.

John checked the woman, noting bruises on her wrists and arms. He angled her head sideways and pushed her hair back, gritting his teeth at the sight of the bullet hole in the center of the back of her head. "Same with the woman."

Jake dug in the man's pocket, removed a wallet, and flipped it open. He muttered a curse as he read the man's ID.

"Eugene Bayler," Jake said.

The woman had no ID on her, but Jake found a photograph of the couple in the man's wallet. Another picture showed the couple with the little boy they had adopted. Mark Bayler.

Amelia's heart sank. The Baylers were dead. Where was Mark?

———————— . ————————

John moved aside to allow the medical examiner to examine the bodies. Dammit, this had to stop.

The body count was rising. And he still hadn't connected all the dots.

Amelia looked shell shocked as she huddled in her coat, but she didn't retreat to the car, as if she refused to run.

"Both of the vics bled out due to the gunshot wounds," the ME said. "Shot at close range. Died instantly."

"It sounds like a professional hit," John said.

Jake's brow rose. "Or someone with military training."

The ME turned the woman's hands over and indicated her jagged nails. "It looks like she fought, and fought hard. I might get some DNA from beneath her fingernails."

John gestured toward the man's knuckles. "Looks like he fought as well." He looked down at the steep drop-off. "No car up here or down there. The shooter shot them and dumped them over the ridge hoping no one would find them."

Jake pointed to skid marks on the side of the road leading to the overhang. "Looks like he was in a hurry."

"Who discovered the bodies?" John asked.

"A trucker called it in. She pulled over at the overhang for a smoke. Dropped her cell phone and bent to pick it up. That's when she looked over the ridge, saw the couple, and phoned it in."

"A female driver?" John asked.

Jake nodded. "I questioned her and took down her contact information. She was pretty shook up. Said it was the first dead body she'd ever seen."

Lucky her.

Jake stooped to examine the road. Tire tracks marked the sludge and led to the shoulder near the ridge. Only one set, meaning somehow the killer had been in the same car as the couple. He tried to piece together a possible scenario.

A car hijacking? The unsub had surprised the couple at a gas station or motel, then forced them to drive out there, where he shot them and dumped their bodies, thinking no one would find them.

Or he'd ambushed them at their home and forced them to go with him at gunpoint?

What about their little boy? So far the serial kidnapper had only snatched children at opportune moments. No murder involved.

This was different.

Because the Baylers had run? Because they knew the kidnapper and could identify him? Because Mr. Bayler had handled the adoptions and the kidnapper was afraid he'd talk?

"I assume you're looking for the Baylers' car," John said.

"An APB's been issued, and there's an Amber Alert for Mark Bayler," Jake said.

John turned to one of the CSIs. "Take a plaster cast of that tire print to narrow down what kind of car the unsub is driving."

The CSI went to the crime van to retrieve supplies, while the medics loaded the bodies in the van to transport to the morgue.

"I'll search for next of kin," Jake said.

Amelia walked away, the worry in her body palpable as she tapped her fingers up and down her arm. Her nerves looked frayed now, making him want to comfort her.

Unfortunately he knew what she was thinking. A cold-blooded killer had taken Mark Bayler.

The little boy she thought might be her son.

Exhaustion tugged at Amelia as John drove her back to her studio. His buddy had done a rush job to install the security system, and he showed her how to set it.

Her ears were still ringing from the explosion, and she couldn't erase the image of the Baylers' dead bodies from her mind.

Whoever had shot them was a cold-blooded murderer.

She shook off her jacket as they entered, the painting of Sadie and Ben drawing her gaze.

Was she crazy to think she might have that someday? To want love for herself? To want the little boy she'd given birth to?

She looked up at John, and her heart melted with longing and need. The dream she'd had of him teased her, and her body warmed.

But the thought of the Baylers' little boy in the hands of the ruthless person who'd killed the couple made her tremble.

If Mark was her son, and the Commander hadn't taken him all those years ago, Mark's birth father might have returned for him.

"Amelia, are you all right?"

Dried blood darkened his forehead and the bruise on his cheek looked stark. "I should ask you that. Come on."

She took his hand and led him to the bathroom, then gestured toward the toilet. "Sit."

"What?"

"I'm going to clean your wounds," she said. "You really should have gone to the hospital."

"I'm fine."

She gently shoved him onto the seat. "I said sit. I want to take care of you."

His dark gaze met hers. "I should be saying that."

"You have taken care of me," Amelia said.

She wet a cloth and wiped at the blood on his forehead. His skin felt hot to the touch, his breathing growing heavier as she tended his wound.

She raked his hair back from his forehead to apply antibiotic ointment and a butterfly bandage, and he gripped her hips with his hands. "You're driving me crazy."

Another smile tugged at her mouth. So he *wasn't* immune. He felt the heat between them, too.

Instead of pulling her to him though, he stood and clutched her hands in his. "Enough."

"Why?" Amelia asked, an angry note to her voice.

His gaze latched with hers, a flicker of regret there. "You're too good for me. You're strong, resilient, beautiful."

Amelia's pulse clamored. No one had ever said that to her. "So are you, John. You almost got blown up today, and I was attacked. For all we know, we might die tomorrow, so why not comfort each other tonight?"

Emotions glittered in his eyes as if he wanted to walk away, but in the heat of the moment, her argument made sense.

She lifted her hand and squeezed his arm. "I don't know how you do what you do, John. It takes a special man to risk his life to save strangers."

"They're children," John said gruffly. "Innocent kids." He cradled her hand between his. "Just like you were."

The cries and screams of the CHIMES echoed in Amelia's head. "I'm trying to forget that time."

"Forgetting isn't all it's cracked up to be," John said.

She swallowed at the anguish in his voice. "You sound like you know that firsthand."

He sighed wearily. "I do. A few years ago, I had an accident and lost years of my life." He dropped his head forward with a pained sound. "I don't even know what my real name is."

She'd forgotten days and nights, but John had lost years where he had no knowledge of where he'd been or what he'd done? Or if he even had a family?

At least she'd had Papaw and Sadie, and they had loved her unconditionally.

Touched by the anguish in his eyes, she cupped his face between her hands, stood on tiptoe, and pressed her lips to his.

One touch of his mouth to hers set her body on fire with need and hunger.

He moaned low in his throat, a sound so raw that it sent a thousand erotic sensations cascading over her body.

But he started to pull away again.

"Why are you always shutting down?" she whispered.

"I don't know how to do this," he said gruffly. "How to be what you need. What you want." He dropped his head forward. "What you deserve."

"You are exactly what I need right now." Amelia looped her arms around his neck and brushed her lips across his heated skin. "I need your hands, your mouth, your lips . . . "

His breath brushed her cheek as he trailed his hands down her hips and coaxed her toward the bedroom.

Raw passion and hunger drove John to succumb to his need for Amelia.

The moment he'd seen her, he'd wanted her.

He'd been lying to himself when he said he wouldn't take advantage of her. He'd seen snippets of himself as a killer. But he wasn't that man anymore . . .

He would do anything to keep her safe.

She kissed his neck, and his skin burned with an ache that only she could assuage. He eased her back on the bed, passion exploding between them in a rush of pleasure and moans as they tore at each other's clothes.

Her satiny skin glided against his as he rose above her. This time she whispered his name in a guttural groan, and he trailed his fingers over her breasts, teasing her nipples to hard buds that he drew into his mouth.

She raked her fingers across his back, urging him closer, and he suckled her until she lifted her hips in silent invitation. Stoked by the way she rubbed her foot up his calf, he kneed her legs apart, his thick cock pulsing between her legs.

"I want you, John," Amelia whispered against his neck.

God help him, her feminine scent was intoxicating.

Dammit, he wanted her, too. Wrong or right, it didn't matter. He had to have her. Be inside her. Feel her body joining with his.

At the last minute, common sense kicked in, and he dug a condom from the pocket of his jeans, rolled it on, and thrust inside her. Amelia cried out his name as he filled her to the core.

She wrapped her legs around him, and he lifted her hips, pulling in and out, teasing her clit with his cock, then filling her again and again. Together they built a frantic rhythm, naked bodies sliding against one another as the tension built.

Her body quivered, and she trailed her fingers down his back as the first shudders of her orgasm gripped her. John ran his hands over her breasts, toying with her nipples as she met him thrust for thrust. Finally he gripped her hips and plunged harder, deeper, the heat waves building inside him, emotions teetering on the surface as his release claimed him and he poured himself inside her.

———————— , ————————

Shudders tore through Amelia as her orgasm gripped her, but images of John and her together hit her as the waves receded.

John holding a gun on her. John ordering her to obey. To be quiet.

Locking her in that room.

John saluting the Commander and keeping her hostage. John aiming a gun at her and ordering her back inside the hospital room.

Tears flooded her eyes, fear and horror clutching her.

Amelia rose from the bed, her body shaking. Dear God, John hadn't been her lover. Not even her friend.

He had worked with the Commander. Had held her prisoner.

And now what was he doing? Had he lied to her? Was he playing some kind of sick game by insisting he had amnesia?

Bile rose to her throat, and she raced to the bathroom, slammed the door, and fell to her knees in front of the toilet.

Thoughts tumbled through her brain . . . if he worked for the Commander, had he gotten close to her to keep an eye on her?

Maybe he even planned to get rid of her as the Commander would have done . . .

———————— , ————————

Fuck. He stared at the sketch the newscaster flashed on the television screen, his blood boiling.

That picture was him.

Goddamn son of a bitch. He threw a beer bottle at the screen and watched the bottle shatter.

Agitated, he stood and paced to the window and looked out. He was safe for now.

But he'd need to change his appearance soon.

Become someone else so those asinine cops couldn't catch him.

Or stop him from finishing what he'd started.

Laughter gurgled in his throat. He was going to make the world a better place.

And if it didn't work, at least everyone would know his name when he was gone.

Chapter Twenty-Six

———— o ————

John's heart pounded. What the hell had just happened?

One minute he and Amelia had been entwined in each other's arms in the throes of passion, and the next she'd run from the bed as if she was terrified of him.

He scrubbed his hands over his hair and felt the Band-Aid Amelia had applied with tenderness.

Emotions tightened his chest. God, he wanted her again.

But something was wrong.

He tugged on his jeans and walked over to the bathroom door, then paused to listen. It sounded as if Amelia was retching.

Sweat broke out on his brow, dread clenching his gut. He had a bad feeling, but he forced himself to knock anyway.

"Amelia," he said in a low voice. "Are you okay?"

Silence.

"Please open the door."

"Go away," she said in a shaky voice.

"No, tell me what's wrong."

She suddenly swung the door open, her eyes red-rimmed and swollen. She looked pale and angry and scared.

"I remembered something."

She'd dragged on a robe that she wrapped tighter around her as if the thought of the two of them naked turned her stomach.

"You . . . you worked for the Commander. All this time I thought my dreams about you meant . . . " Her voice trailed off.

Shock bolted through John. "You dreamed about me?"

"Yes." Her mouth twisted into a grimace as she released a bitter laugh. "But now I see you were there to help him. To keep me prisoner."

John felt as if he'd been kicked in the gut. He'd had snippets of memories, but not that he'd held her captive.

Had he worked for Arthur Blackwood?

"I'm sorry, Amelia, I had a head injury—"

"Did you help him steal my baby?" Tears tumbled down her cheeks. "What did you do with him, John? Is that the reason you agreed to work with me, to keep me from finding out the truth?"

"No." He shook his head in denial, but how could he be certain of anything when the past was a void? When some of his memories didn't make sense?

"That's it, that's the reason you came to Slaughter Creek, to watch me, to make sure I didn't find my baby."

He reached for her. He had to comfort her, reassure her she was wrong. But she shoved him away, betrayal hardening her eyes.

"That's not true, Amelia. Think about it." He forced a calm to his voice, desperate to convince her, to convince himself. "You came to me, remember? You asked for my help."

She paced across the room, tapping that same rhythm on her arm as she gained momentum. "Because I thought you were one of the good guys. But hell, that was probably some show, a setup." Her voice stung him. "You helped the Commander torture us, didn't you?"

"No. I . . . I don't remember everything from my past. I had an accident six years ago and have amnesia."

"How convenient," Amelia said.

Jesus, he should have told her sooner. "It's true. I work for the TBI. I'm investigating the kidnapping case."

More than anything, he wanted to defend himself. Assure her he wasn't the monster she believed him to be.

She backed away, her eyes wild with panic.

"But you were there, you held a gun to my face and locked me in that hospital room. I saw you with the Commander."

How could he deny it when he'd wondered if he'd done something bad in his previous life?

"I'm not that person anymore," he said, his voice hoarse. "When I woke with amnesia, maybe I joined the TBI to atone for what I'd done."

Amelia pointed to the door. "Get out. Or does that not fit with your plans? Did you come here to get rid of me once and for all?"

"Of course not," John said. "I care about you, Amelia." More than he should.

"Care about me?" Her voice bordered on hysteria. "For all I know, you got me in bed so you could kill me in my sleep."

"Amelia, no—"

She threw up a hand to stop him from speaking, then wiped at the tears streaming down her cheeks. "Please leave."

He reached for her again. He wanted to hold her so badly he ached. "I told you I'm sorry. I may have been that person before—"

"You *are* that person." Anger sharpened her voice. "And I was a fool to fall in bed with you. But I won't fall for your tricks or lies again."

She pointed toward the door, and he decided he should leave. She needed time. Hell, they both did.

He grabbed his shirt, holster, and gun and strode from the bedroom, self-recriminations beating him up as he left.

———————— , ————————

Amelia paced the studio, so overcome she could barely breathe.

John had lied to her. Betrayed her.

While all this time, she'd been falling in love with him.

What was she going to do now?

Was he trying to find her son or trying to keep her from discovering the truth?

For all she knew, he could have warned the Baylers to leave . . .

A hollow emptiness opened up inside her. What a fool she'd been. All her life people had used her. Now, just when she thought she was strong and independent, she'd let John slip under her defenses. She'd thought he even cared, that they might have something special between them.

She would never trust another man in her life.

Blinking back tears, she removed the paintings of John from the closet, grabbed a knife, and slashed the drawings she'd done of him. They were filled with emotions, her memory that the two of them had not only been lovers, but that they'd been in love.

That he was her savior.

What a lie.

She had to find her baby herself. But how?

Brenda. Brenda had befriended her when she'd written those profiles on the CHIMES subjects. She'd been a straight shooter. She wanted the story, but she also respected the subjects and had been sympathetic to their suffering.

Swiping away her tears, she retrieved her cell phone and pressed Brenda's number.

———————— , ————————

John didn't want to leave Amelia, especially knowing she hated him. But how could he blame her?

His phone buzzed. Arianna. He snatched it up. "Yeah?"

"Agent Strong, the tech team has just picked up something from the buzz on the Internet."

"What?"

"Another bombing is planned. Tonight."

John went cold inside. "Where?"

"UT Knoxville. Apparently there's a protest rally there this evening."

"What kind of protest?"

"Something about overturning the government, restructuring the social-welfare system."

John mentally thumbed through the other target sites. A women's clinic. A DFACS office.

"It's not SFTF," she said. "Roper was right. They advocate defending the country but are not terrorist oriented. This other group is the opposite. They think making a bold public statement is the only way to be heard and to make changes."

"Call ahead and alert the local authorities that Coulter and I are on our way. They need to beef up security for the event."

"Done."

She hung up, and he phoned Coulter and explained the situation. Coulter agreed to meet him at the TBI headquarters.

John flipped on his siren and raced through traffic. Coulter was waiting for him outside, and they rushed toward Knoxville. John flew around cars on the interstate while Coulter phoned ahead to the local law enforcement agencies and explained their suspicions. Nick Blackwood was going to meet them there, too.

"We need plainclothes security teams interspersed through the crowd. Also alert campus security at UT," Coulter said to the chief of police. "We believe the attack will occur tonight at the protest rally. We also believe the bomber will be an adolescent or teenage boy who's been brainwashed into believing he's on a mission for his people. In the last situation, the killer strapped dynamite to his body. In the first instance, he put a pipe bomb in a backpack and set it down. But the bomb exploded before he got too far away, and he died in the explosion."

Anxiety knotted John's shoulders as he drove, but finally they arrived in Knoxville. They went straight to the UT campus and parked near the protest rally. Already hundreds of students had gathered, carrying signs advocating government changes, some shouting that the breakdown of society and the family was the government's fault.

A podium was set up for speakers to take turns, and the press roamed the crowd, taking photographs and interviewing individuals. The rally seemed peaceful at the moment, but a group of nonsupporters had gathered at one end and were shouting at the others to go home.

The peaceful protests could erupt into violence at any second.

———————— , ————————

John would be furious when he found out what she was doing.

But Amelia no longer cared what he thought. Or what anyone else thought, for that matter.

She'd been a puppet on a string when Arthur Blackwood had experimented on her, and she'd kept her silence afterward because of her therapy, and out of respect for Sadie.

But her son's life might depend on her finding him.

After all, the Commander could have used him as he had her and the others. God knew he'd abused his two sons, Jake and Nick. Sadie had confided in her that he'd subjected them to extreme physical tests of survival as well as mental tests to turn them into soldiers and the kind of men he deemed soldier worthy.

Ignoring the warning that another hailstorm was imminent, she met Brenda at the local TV station, and they chatted for a moment, then Brenda directed her cameraman to set up for the interview.

"Are you sure you're up to this?" Brenda asked. "The last few months must have been difficult for you."

"They have been, yet I feel like I've gotten my life back, Brenda. At least my sanity, so if you're worried I'm going to fall apart on you, don't. I'm stronger than I've ever been."

"I never doubted that," Brenda said with a squeeze to her hand. "And I'll do whatever I can to help you."

"Thank you. You've been a good friend." She hadn't trusted Brenda to begin with, but Brenda had definitely been loyal and treated her with kindness. Brenda had also respected her privacy, and the profile she'd written had painted her in a positive light.

"Then let's do this," Brenda said. "I'll start with a brief introduction, then prompt you with questions. Also, the station set up a tip line connected to the police department. We'll give out that number at the end."

"Did Jake agree to this?" Amelia asked.

"Yes. It took some doing, but Sadie convinced him."

Of course. Jake would do anything for Sadie.

She'd started to fantasize that she and John might have that kind of love. Stupid on her part. Six might have been mentally ill, but at least in his own way, he really did love her.

Before her interview, Brenda gave a recap about the Bayler couple being found dead.

Then she escorted Amelia to two chairs set up in front of the camera, and they both took seats.

"We've been following the story about the investigation into the Slaughter Creek experiments and the crimes that resulted from them," Brenda said after introducing herself. "Today, we have one of those subjects with us." Brenda angled herself toward Amelia. "This is Amelia Nettleton. She suffered at the hands of Commander Blackwood, but Miss Nettleton has undergone therapy and made great strides in recovering from the drug therapy and abuse she endured. That said, there is a new development to the story." She hesitated. "I'm going to let her tell you why she felt the need to speak up today."

Nerves fluttered in Amelia's stomach, but she'd come too far to back down. There had to be someone in Slaughter Creek who knew something about her baby. Someone who wouldn't be afraid to come forward now that the Commander was dead.

"Hi," Amelia said, forcing a smile at the camera. "Miss Banks is right, I have worked hard in my recovery. The process has also triggered memories that I'd lost years ago."

She barely resisted tapping a rhythm on her leg. "In fact, I recently learned that while I was locked in the hospital, I gave birth to a son. It seems impossible, but I have proof that it's true." Sorrow and fear clogged her throat, but she swallowed them back. "Commander Arthur Blackwood took my baby away from me at birth. My son would be six years old now.

"I've traced his disappearance to a local church and The Gateway House, but haven't determined where he is at this moment."

"Do you think Arthur Blackwood used him in another project?" Brenda asked.

"That's a possibility," Amelia said, shivering at the horrid thought of her baby being subjected to the same kind of abuse she'd suffered.

But she latched onto another possibility. "It's also possible that a couple may have adopted him. That couple, the Baylers, were found dead. But their adopted child was not with them and is missing." Amelia swallowed hard. "If you have any information about this child, please contact the police. Mark's life may be in danger."

***

Mark Bayler rocked himself back and forth against the wall of the room where the bad man had locked him.

Red flashed in front of his eyes. So much red.

Blood. His mommy's and daddy's. A scream sounded in his head. His mama's. His own . . .

The bad man had shot them in the back of the head. Killed them for no reason.

Then tossed them over the mountain like rag dolls.

Now they were gone forever.

Mark stared down at his ragged nails. He'd tried to scratch the bad man and make him stop. But it hadn't done any good.

The man slapped him so hard he'd flung him across the floor.

Tears leaked from his eyes and ran down his chin. Snot bubbled in his nose. His throat hurt from screaming for help.

But no one had heard him.

He wanted to go home. Wanted his parents back. Wanted to make the bad man go away forever.

The door screeched open. A scraping noise sounded. The man walking.

He was half dragging his leg like something was wrong with it.

Mark looked at the gun. It was shiny and big. That gun had killed his parents.

If he could grab it, he'd make the bad man die, too.

The man knelt in front of him and held up the gun. "You want to shoot me like I shot your mother and father, don't you?"

Even his voice sounded mean. And his smile was evil like the monsters he'd seen on TV.

The man pressed the gun to Mark's temple. Mark tried to be still, but his legs were jumpy.

"You do, don't you?" That nasty smile again. "You want to blow my brains out."

Mark hated him so much that he nodded.

"Good," the man said with a laugh. "You're going to be perfect."

Chapter Twenty-Seven

---◦---

John and Coulter slipped through the crowd, studying the faces in search of a potential bomber. Nick had gone to the roof of a nearby building to get a better view.

A gloomy gray settled over the area, shadows plaguing the sidewalks and streets from the storm clouds while the wind roared around them.

Unfortunately the rally was composed mostly of young people, hundreds of college students, which made picking out a teenage boy even more difficult. John recognized campus security and the numerous local police, but there were supposed to be dozens of undercover cops and security teams working the scene as well.

Groups of protestors shouted that the government needed to be changed, that new leaders needed to be put in place.

An argument erupted somewhere in the crowd, and John saw Coulter move closer to check it out. One of the local police noted an abandoned backpack, and John's breath hitched as he watched the officer kneel and slowly unzip the bag.

Seconds later, the officer gestured that the bag was clear.

A young man with shaggy brown hair wearing a denim jacket walked up to the podium. Perspiration beaded on his fore-head, and his hand trembled as he reached for the microphone.

John inched forward in the crowd, eyes glued to the podium.

To the left, a popping sound erupted. John spotted a scruffy young guy in a denim jacket aiming a gun into the crowd.

Coulter jumped the guy from behind. They dropped to the ground in a fight, and several cops rushed to surround them.

John jerked his gaze back to the podium, his pulse stuttering when he saw the young man on stage lift his hand and push his coat to the side. A maniacal smile curved his mouth.

Dynamite was strapped to his chest.

Damn. The boy was going to blow himself up onstage. Judging the distance between him and the crowd, he'd take several lives with him.

John spoke low into his mic, his voice crackling in the wind. "Suspect on stage has a bomb. Clear the area immediately."

The boy's eyes suddenly latched onto John.

A black emptiness hollowed out the boy's face, yet his gaze didn't waver as he slid his hand toward the inside of his jacket.

"Don't," John mouthed.

"Bomb!" someone shouted.

Panic ensued, and students began running in all directions, screaming and pushing and shoving in their haste to escape.

The last thing John wanted was to kill this kid. He'd probably been brainwashed for years.

But he couldn't let him take out the crowd.

He aimed the gun at the boy's head. "I said don't do it."

For a brief second conflicting emotions flashed on the young man's face, but another heartbeat and his fingers touched something that looked like the trigger.

John had no choice. He gripped his gun and fired.

Everything was unraveling. All the lies and secrets . . .

Except John still hadn't figured it out.

Helen Gray sat outside Amelia Nettleton's house, her heart in her throat. The storm outside raged violently just as the one inside her took root and built in intensity. All those years ago, she'd done what she had to do.

More than anything she'd wanted to fight Arthur Blackwood. But that had been impossible. He had been too strong, had too much authority.

He was ruthless.

He was dead though, and it was time for her to tell the truth. To come out of hiding.

Sister Grace had contacted her, frightened, saying Amelia was asking questions. Then she herself had run out of fear.

Amelia's heartfelt plea on the news had torn Helen up inside. The poor girl had suffered unbearable torture at the hands of the Commander, yet she'd survived.

And she was still suffering.

Helen was a mother herself. She knew exactly how it felt to lose a child. To have the baby ripped from her arms, because Arthur Blackwood had done the same thing to her. He'd taken her son from her and destroyed her life.

Amelia was begging for help, and she had to step up, even if it got her killed.

———————— . ————————

Mass pandemonium reigned as the crowd raced for cover, and campus security and local police worked to clear the area.

John ran up to the podium and caught the young man before he collapsed onto the floor of the stage. He'd shot the kid in the shoulder, just enough to take him down. Quickly he secured and handcuffed him before the teen could trigger the explosive.

The bomb squad raced over to dismantle the homemade device.

John stood by while the team worked, and within minutes, they'd removed the dynamite from the boy.

John zeroed in on the tattoo on the boy's wrist—a string of *B*'s. What did it mean?

Nick joined them, his expression full of rage.

The kid looked up at them, dazed and confused, blood seeping from his shoulder. "You aren't going to kill anyone today," John said.

"There are others to carry on the mission."

John dug his hands into the boy's arm. "What mission?"

"I am a loyal soldier," the boy said, a deadness to his eyes.

"You're not a soldier," Nick said. "And the people here are not terrorists."

"Everyone needs to take notice. We are important. Changes have to be made."

John shook the young guy. "Killing innocent people is not the way to make change."

"But we have to make people wake up, make them see the breakdown of the family. Teenagers having babies, hookers getting pregnant, families throwing their kids out on the street."

John growled in disgust. "You may think you're delivering a message, but you aren't saving families. You're murdering kids and innocents."

"We had to get attention. No one cares about family anymore. The whole government needs to be burned down."

It was useless to argue with him.

Nick gripped him by the collar. "Who sent you?"

"Our father. He saved us and now we will save others." Then the boy clamped his mouth together as if he'd said all he was going to say.

John cursed again. When he looked up, he saw Coulter approaching, shoving the other young man toward them. He was handcuffed and secure, his eyes flaring with the same kind of dead look the other boy had.

"He was a diversion," Coulter said in disgust.

Dammit. How many more were there?

Nick shook the kid again. "Where are the others? Where's your leader?"

The boy jerked his head up, eyes spitting rage. "We will never betray him."

John and Coulter pushed the boys toward the police van. Except for a few curious stragglers, the area had cleared. "I'll take him in and interrogate him," Nick said. "He'll break."

But John spotted an older man in the group, watching, his face grim, his features hidden by a hat. Something about the man struck John as familiar.

Maybe his military stance.

"Put them in separate cars," John told one of the officers. "And separate them when we get to the station."

The officer nodded, and John released the kid to him, then sprinted toward the man in the crowd.

Their gazes met, and a sinister smile creased the man's face as if he were sending a message that he'd enjoyed the mass chaos. The suspect broke into a run, but his limp slowed him down.

John picked up his pace, but the suspect darted around a building. Adrenaline surged through John, and he elbowed his way through the onlookers in pursuit.

John spoke into his mic, alerting security and locals that he was chasing another suspect. "I think I may be onto the leader. White male, forties, dark-gray trench coat, a limp."

John lost sight of him, and climbed the steps to one of the campus buildings for a better look. He scanned the area, and spotted the suspect duck into the dining hall. The man's limp grew more pronounced as he picked up his pace.

John took a shortcut through a walkway to a clearing, then entered the building. He rushed through a maze of hallways, then to the central cafeteria. Anger slammed into him when he saw the man in a low conversation with another teenage boy. The kid looked nervous and was fiddling with his fleece jacket as if he might also be wired. A tattoo encircled his wrist, a row of several B's connected together. The other teen had had one, too.

John gripped his gun at the ready as he approached from behind.

"Watts and Samuels failed," the man said to the kid. "It's your turn to step up, Bluster."

"Yes, Father," the boy said.

John spoke into his mic again. "Request backup in the dining hall asap. We have another bomber. Repeat: We have another bomber."

He inched up behind the older man and shoved his Sig Sauer into his back. "It's over. Tell the kid to call it off."

A sinister laugh rumbled from the man's chest. "It will never be over."

The kid tensed, eyes wide with fear as he realized they'd been caught.

"Yes, it will," John snarled. "You're going to stop it now."

He dug the barrel of his weapon deeper into the man's back. Instead of complying, the man motioned for the boy to trip the bomb. The teenager slid one hand inside his jacket, and John spotted the dynamite strapped around him.

Coulter and one of the bomb experts approached slowly from behind.

"Do it," the man ordered.

Coulter attacked the kid from behind, sliding his arm around the boy's throat in a choke, immobilizing him. Seconds later, Coulter yanked the teen's arms behind him and snapped handcuffs around his wrists.

John searched the dining hall for an accomplice, but the room was empty.

The bomb expert hurried to dismantle the bomb while John handcuffed the man with the limp and dragged him outside to another police car.

At the station, he would get some answers. Between this bastard and the three teens, one of them had to talk.

———————— , ————————

Amelia found another disturbing canvas when she entered the guesthouse. Anger suffused her. She hadn't even been gone long this time.

And that security system was supposed to be foolproof. But obviously it had failed.

This painting depicted a small grave with a teddy bear in it.

More vile words had been written on the wall in red paint. *Whore. Tramp. Lunatic.*

She grabbed a knife from the counter and ripped the canvas into pieces. Shaking with rage, she took the strongest cleaner she could find and began to scrub the walls. The red paint faded and spread like blood.

Someone wanted her to think she was going crazy, but she wasn't. She remembered the truth now—she had delivered a child and John had been there, but not to calm her and love her as her partner. He might have even taken her child and given him to someone else.

Because she knew for sure that he'd held her hostage for Arthur Blackwood.

Pain shot through her. How could she have let down her guard and trusted him? How could she have taken him to bed?

A knock sounded, and she wiped her hands on her smock, then tossed the cleaning rag into the sink and hurried to answer it.

Hoping it was Sadie with little Ben and Ayla, she swung open the door. But Helen Gray stood on the other side, her features strained as she shivered in the wind.

"Helen, come in out of the cold."

The wind swept the woman's hair around her face, and she brushed it back. "Thank you, we need to talk."

Amelia's heart picked up a beat. "Of course. Do you have more news for me?" She waved her in and offered her tea. Helen accepted, her gaze sweeping the studio and lingering on the painting of Sadie and Ben.

A frown marred her face when she noticed the smeared red paint on the wall.

"What happened?"

Amelia ushered her toward the kitchen, away from the mess. "Someone broke into my house and left a crude message on the wall."

Helen's face paled. "Has it happened before?"

Amelia nodded. "Ever since I started looking for my baby, I've had break-ins and threats."

"I'm so sorry," Helen said, sympathy in her eyes.

Amelia put the teakettle on, then turned to her while the water heated. "But no one is going to deter me."

Helen claimed a seat and folded her hands on the table. "That's the reason I'm here."

Amelia studied her for a moment, wondering what she meant. She gathered tea cups, sugar, and milk and set them on the table.

The woman looked nervous. Did she have bad news for her?

The teakettle whistled, and Amelia grabbed it and poured them both tea. Her heart hammered as she joined her guest.

"What is it, Helen? You have news?"

"Not exactly. I saw you on the news pleading for the little Bayler boy." She traced a finger along the edge of her cup while she blew on the hot tea. "I should have spoken up sooner, but I wasn't sure about him and I was afraid."

Amelia sipped her tea. "I don't understand."

"You're going to hate me when I tell you who I am, and what I've done, but it's time." She fiddled with the sugar packet, then ripped it open and dumped it in her cup.

"Please, just tell me, Helen. Do you know where Mark is?"

Helen shook her head, a sadness flickering in her eyes. "No, but I am afraid for him."

Amelia folded a napkin on the table. "Go on."

Helen inhaled a shaky breath. "I . . . was at the hospital when you gave birth."

Amelia gasped. "Why were you there?"

She hesitated. "Because I knew Arthur Blackwood. I'd become suspicious about what was happening at the hospital. Little things just didn't add up.

"One day I was snooping around Arthur's office and found a file. It was about the CHIMES project." Her voice cracked. "I was so shocked, I wanted to tell someone. But he found me with the file. I told him I was going to go to the police. But he threatened me and my son."

Amelia frowned, trying to follow her. "So you stayed quiet."

"Yes. You have to understand. I didn't care if he killed me, but I didn't want my child to suffer."

"You said you were there when I gave birth?

She nodded. "Arthur wanted to put your baby in an experiment, but I took him from one of the nurses and ran."

Shock squeezed the air from Amelia's lungs. "You took my baby? Who did you give him to? Where is he?"

"I don't know where he is," Helen said. "That's the reason I joined the social services agency. I've been looking for him myself."

―――――――― , ――――――――

The boat rocked and swayed, making Zack so dizzy he could barely see. Zack heard the other boy's voice in his head again. He was scared.

"It's time you think about whether you want to live or die."

"I don't want to die," the boy cried.

Who was the boy talking to him? And where was he?

Was he on the boat, too?

Zack dragged himself up. He gripped the windowsill and stood on tiptoe to see out the tiny window. Surely the boat would stop soon. They had to get to wherever they were going.

But all he could see was water. Miles and miles of ocean. Waves crashing. Sleet slashing down from the sky.

He'd heard one of the guards say they were going to an island. One nobody knew about.

A place where no one would ever find him.

Chapter Twenty-Eight

———— o ————

John spread the photos of the missing children across the table in the interrogation room, watching Axelrod's face for a reaction. Axelrod and Sonny James were one and the same. The man who'd worked with the Ellingtons, the one who'd called the school and dental office with phony information so he could snag Danny Kritz.

Axelrod had the audacity to smile. "They were lost, but I saved them."

"Is that what you really think?" John asked, struggling not to slam his fist into the man's head and beat him senseless.

Axelrod lifted his head, the scar above his right eye distorted with his grin. "Yes. Those kids were stuck in homes where they were neglected. Tossed around like sacks of garbage. No one loved them or really cared about them." He rubbed his bad leg and gestured toward it. "I know. I've been there."

"So you took it on yourself to rescue them?"

"That's right. I turned them into men, into people who'd make a difference. Now their names will be remembered."

"But innocent people died in those bombings."

"No one is innocent, not if they stand by and just let it happen. If they don't do something to make the system work better. To stop teenage girls and hookers from having unwanted kids and stop the system from putting them in terrible homes where they starve and get beat."

John's head reeled. This guy was so warped that he really believed he was saving these kids and that he'd bring attention to his cause by using them as suicide bombers.

"There are right and wrong ways to go about making changes," John said bluntly. "Using kids as killers sure as hell is not one of the right ways." He gestured toward the string of B's tattooed around the man's wrist. "What does that stand for?"

"The Brotherhood," Axelrod said. "We've bonded and created our own family."

"Who are you working for?" John asked.

The man's beady eyes flashed with an evil warning. "I'm not working for anyone. I'm the leader."

"But you had help in the abductions?"

"I hired that buffoon Billingsly, but he was a moron. So I figured I'd best be on my own."

John tapped the pictures one by one. "Where are the other boys?"

"That I will never tell you."

"Then you have someone else working for you?"

Another sly grin slanted the man's mouth, but he refused to speak.

John gripped the bastard by his shirt, choking him. "Tell me where the kids are. Where are you holding them?"

"They're somewhere safe," he growled. "Just waiting to take their turn for the cause. And when we finish and burn everything down, we'll take over as leaders and everything will be different."

This man needed psychiatric care. He was totally demented. "So you think beating boys into doing what you want is better than foster care?"

"I taught them to be strong, to be men, just as my mother taught me."

John knew that abuse victims often became abusers. The cycle continued.

But this man was a killer, too. He shook him hard. "Do you have a little boy who belonged to Amelia Nettleton?"

"That crazy bitch from the sanitarium?"

John's protective instincts roared to life. "She's not crazy. Arthur Blackwood abducted her son. Do you have him?"

"I don't know what you're talking about." Axelrod massaged his leg, leaning back in the chair with another chilling smile.

The bastard still thought he was winning. Playing a game and teaching the world a lesson.

John stood and exited the room before he shoved the barrel of his gun into the man's mouth and made him eat it.

———————— , ————————

Ten minutes later, John texted photos of each of the perpetrators in the UT bombings to Arianna. Thanks to facial recognition software using age progression, she sent back their names and details about their abductions within half an hour.

The three they had in custody were—

Leonard Watts, the boy John had shot.

Jim Bluster, the teen with the bomb in the dining hall.

And Bailey Samuels, the boy Coulter had subdued.

"Find their families if they have any," John said. Although judging from the victimology he didn't expect much. "The young men have been brainwashed to obey orders and protect the group's secrecy. Maybe someone from their past can reach them and convince them to talk."

"I'm on it," Arianna said.

Watts was in surgery to remove the bullet John had put in his shoulder. Coulter was interrogating Samuels, and Bluster was in a holding cell.

John studied the information on the last boy, hoping time in a cell would pressure him to talk, although the kid had probably endured worse.

A memory struck him, and he saw himself in the military, marching, saluting his Commander, raising his weapon to fire.

Holding someone in a cell.

Amelia.

God . . . was she right?

He saw the Commander's face as if it were yesterday. *"Do as I say, son,"* Blackwood said. *"Do not disobey me or you'll regret it."*

His pulse spiked. Could it be true?

No wonder he'd blocked out his past. No wonder he'd felt uncomfortable in church, as if he needed to pay penance. The Commander had been a monster, and so had he.

Nausea rolled through him.

Somehow he had to make things right for Amelia.

Finding out where the boys were being held might lead him to Amelia's son.

She might hate him now, but if he found her little boy, at least she could have the family she wanted. The one she deserved.

He studied the file. Jim Bluster was seventeen now, but he'd been seven when he was kidnapped. Ten years he'd been missing, at the mercy of a madman. Ten years that madman had had to warp his mind.

No telling what he'd told the boy. Or what he'd done to him. Physical and psychological abuse. Possibly drug therapy or torture.

He read further. Jim used to like baseball. He'd played on a little-league team, and had been a leader. He hated spelling and English, but he'd liked math.

Of course that was in first grade. Probably wouldn't help much now.

His phone buzzed. Arianna. "Yeah?"

"Mrs. Bluster is on her way. She's ecstatic that we found her son. Oh, and I told her to bring some family photographs, I thought you might want them to jog his memory."

"That's great, Arianna. Thanks. Did you tell her where we found him?"

"No, I thought I'd let you handle that."

"How about the others?"

"The kid you shot, Leonard Watts, is an orphan. His parents were killed before he was abducted. He went through that home for kids, The Gateway House."

Where Axelrod took him from the Ellingtons under the guise of placing him in a loving home. "And the third?"

"Bailey Samuels was in foster care because his mother was a drug addict. She overdosed three years ago."

"What about his father?"

"Not in the picture. I found a grandmother. She's on her way."

He thanked her and disconnected. Another agent knocked on the office door, then poked his head in. "Mrs. Bluster is here to see you."

John stood. "Show her in."

The agent disappeared down the hall. Seconds later, John heard crying, and frowned as the woman rushed in.

"Agent Strong, I got a call. You found my son . . . "

John nodded and coaxed her to sit down. "Yes, ma'am, we believe so."

"Where is he? I need to see him." She brushed away tears with a tissue, a hysterical sob escaping her. "It's been so long . . . My god, I thought he was dead . . . I'd given up . . . "

John squeezed her hand. "Mrs. Bluster, I know this is a shock, but we really need to talk."

"What's wrong?" She sniffled, worrying the zipper of her jacket with her fingers. "Is he all right? Where has he been all this time?"

"We're still trying to determine that," John said. "Now, I need you to stay calm."

"Oh God, he's hurt, isn't he?" She lurched up from the chair. "Take me to him."

"I can't, not yet." John urged her to sit back down and began to explain.

Her reaction was just as he expected. Shock mingled with anger and grief.

"You say he was going to set off a bomb?"

"Yes. We believe a group has kidnapped boys for years. They're training the victims to become suicide bombers to make a statement about the sad state of families these days," John said. "We caught three of them, your son included, at a protest rally, where they were wired with explosives."

She dropped her head into her hands on a sob. "Oh Lord . . . no."

"I'm sorry." John's heart ached for the woman. "Your son is here, but he won't talk to the police. Unfortunately, there are more kids missing who we haven't located yet." John hesitated, letting his words sink in. "We will get your son therapy, Mrs. Bluster, but we also need to find this group's base camp. Other lives depend on it."

Turmoil strained her features as she lifted her head, and she ripped at the tissue in her hands. "And you want my help to find them?"

"Yes. But I have to warn you—your son has been brainwashed and may not remember you at this point. But I need you to try to talk to him anyway."

"You're going to put him in jail after all he's suffered?" she cried.

John adopted a neutral expression. He needed her cooperation, even if he had to lie to get it. "He will be evaluated by a therapist and most likely be held in a facility where he can receive psychological treatment to help him reorient to society and to life in general. It may take some time to undo the damage done to him."

Sorrow wrenched the woman's face, making John hurt for her. She'd obviously suffered all these years her son had been missing.

"I'm so sorry, but it's important we convince him to talk. The sooner we track down where he was kept, and the people who held him, the sooner he can start healing and we can reunite the others with their families."

She nodded miserably.

"We have to work fast," John said. "This group may be planning another attack any minute."

"John tried to save you and the baby."

Shock rolled through Amelia. "What? But he helped guard me."

"At first, yes, but when he realized what was going on, he tried to save you and get you out of the hospital. Arthur fought with him. He had him subdued and threatened to kill him if either of us went to the police."

"John tried to save me?"

"Yes. He told me to take the baby. He was adamant I get him away from Arthur. So I took the baby to a church and dropped him off. I thought they'd find him a good home. I knew they worked with The Gateway House. That's the reason I was looking into them when I started at the agency."

"You left the rosary beads?" Amelia asked.

Helen nodded. "It was the saddest day of my life, but I thought I was doing the right thing."

Confusion clouded Amelia's head as she tried to comprehend the string of events Helen was describing. "Did Commander Blackwood find him?"

"I . . . don't know. All these years, I'd hoped he was adopted. But Arthur had far-reaching contacts and was ruthless. I wanted to follow up and find where the baby was placed, but he was watching me, and I didn't want to lead him to your son." She rubbed her hands together. "When the story broke about the project, I thought it was time to come out of hiding."

A knock sounded at the door, and Helen paused. Amelia pushed her teacup away, and stood, half expecting John to be on the other side. But when she opened the door, shock immobilized her.

A man stood on the other side with a gun in his hand. Dear God . . . it wasn't possible . . .

Helen rushed up behind her, and he fired the gun. Amelia gasped as Helen collapsed, blood gushing from her chest.

Amelia turned to run for her papaw's shotgun, but suddenly the butt of the gun slammed against her head and she collapsed, the world fading.

Helen's cries echoed in her ears as she lost consciousness.

———————— , ————————

John studied the teen's face for a reaction as his mother entered the room. His sandy brown hair was cropped short, the tattoo of the string of connected *B*'s marring his wrist stark beneath the fluorescent light.

But it was the dead, flat look in his eyes that was haunting.

"Jim, it's me, your mother," Mrs. Bluster said as she slid into the chair across the table from the boy. She reached out to touch his hands, which were handcuffed to the table, but he jerked back, the handcuffs rattling.

Mrs. Bluster startled, hurt, but she recovered quickly. "I know you've been gone a long time, Jim, but I never gave up looking for you. I called the police every week to see if they had any leads."

He adopted a sullen look, anger radiating from him.

"They told me you might not remember me. That you've had a rough time." Her voice faltered. "But I don't care what you've done or where you've been, you're my son and I love you. I always will."

The boy's eyes twitched as he stared at the woman. But he showed no other reaction.

She dragged out a photo album and turned it so he could see. "I thought you might like to see some pictures of when you were little, when you lived with me and your father, before he died."

The boy glanced at the book, then crossed his arms. "You've got the wrong guy, lady. My parents didn't love me. They didn't want me."

"That's not true," she said softly. "You have your father's eyes, Jim. And that mole on your neck. It was there when you were born." She flipped several pages of the album, describing the story behind each photograph. The first time his father had taken him fishing at age five at a stocked pond.

A camping trip they'd taken where the tent had washed away. One Christmas when they'd gone skiing, the birthdays they'd celebrated.

The last of which the father was missing from.

"We lost your father that summer," she said, grief making her voice quiver. "He died of a heart attack. It was sudden and the doctors said he didn't suffer, but you and I did. I didn't handle it very well, and you cried every night."

The pictures stopped after that birthday party.

"I let you down back then," Mrs. Bluster said. "I was lost in my grief, and started drinking too much. That's when social services intervened. The day you disappeared I was devastated." She wiped at more tears. "The police searched everywhere, and they put out an Amber Alert, and . . . and I straightened up then. I joined AA and started looking for you myself . . . looking for you was all that kept me going. All these years . . . "

Jim swallowed hard as he studied the pictures, his face stricken with grief and confusion and the realization that he'd been lied to by his abductor. Somehow her love had gotten through to him.

"Honey, I know you've suffered, and you have a right to blame me." She pushed her hair from her eyes. "But you're here now, and I want to help you. I want you to come home."

He folded his hands into fists, obviously still torn, troubled.

"I understand you're loyal to the people where you've been, but your father would want you to talk to the police. He didn't believe in violence, honey, he'd want you to stop anyone else from getting hurt."

A single tear rolled down his cheek, then he gave a quiet nod.

John cleared his throat. "There are other boys who've been brought into the group, boys stolen from their homes." John paused to let that register. "You can save these kids from suffering like you did."

Mrs. Bluster laid her hand over Jim's, and he started to pull away, but she stroked his hand with her fingers, and this time he squeezed hers in return.

"Please, Jim, tell them where to find them."

The boy gulped, then reached for the pad and pen John had laid on the table.

John, Coulter, and Nick Blackwood led the attack team to the location Jim Bluster had given them. He'd drawn a detailed map of the site of the group's new compound. Apparently the group had caught wind of John's investigation from the Internet and moved earlier, but hopefully this time John's team would surprise them.

Jim said the place was primitive, but they'd been trained as soldiers, ready to die for the Brotherhood, and the accommodations didn't matter.

John and Coulter called on all their resources. Helicopters flew in, dropping a tactical team along with SWAT, and John and Coulter geared up and hiked in on foot.

At first glance, there was no sign of the boys. Dammit, had someone heard about the arrests and moved them again?

But as they approached the main building, he heard noise.

They swarmed the camp, police charging in, catching the group off guard. According to Jim Bluster, the group held a nightly meeting. John and the team strategically timed their attack, so most of the group would be contained in one area.

Protective gear saved the front team as they shot three grown men dressed in camouflage guarding the compound while the meeting took place. Others charged through the door and windows, taking the group by surprise.

The team moved quickly and efficiently, storming the main camp.

Rayner, the man left in charge and Axelrod's second-in-command, was tall and imposing, the look of a psychopath in his eyes.

John jammed his gun in the man's face. "You son of a bitch."

"You may have me," Rayner said in a stone-cold voice. "But there are others who will take my place. Others who follow the Commander and Axelrod. Others who believe in what we're doing."

"You're nothing but a coward," John said between clenched teeth. "Killing innocents for no reason. Forcing children to do your dirty work so you can make a name for yourself."

"I'll be famous just like Commander Blackwood and Axelrod," Rayner said.

John wanted to pull the trigger bad. "Not if I have anything to do with it."

The man spit at him. "Go to hell."

"That's where you're going." He raked the barrel of the gun across the man's forehead.

"Go ahead. Shoot. I'm not afraid to die."

John hissed. "That would be too easy for you. You're going to suffer in prison for the rest of your sorry life."

He whipped the man around and handcuffed him. "Where are the boys?"

Instead of answering, the man simply laughed, a sinister sound that made John's skin crawl.

Nick strode toward him, his jaw set in rage. "I'll take him. Go look for the boys."

John was glad to leave him with Blackwood. Blackwood had his own brand of justice. Maybe he'd beat the truth out of the bastard.

Wind and the cold bit at him as he and Coulter split up to search the compound.

John shined his flashlight across the property, finally spotting a pile of brush. Too neatly stacked for it to have been from the storm.

Someone had put it there. To hide an opening?

He yanked away the brush, twigs and limbs scraping his hands. When he lifted the last piece, he spotted a wooden lid. He pried it open and shined his light down into the hall.

"Coulter, over here!"

His partner ran over, and John led the way down the steps, shining his flashlight to illuminate the darkness. The sound of banging and cries for help echoed from below, and he took off running through the tunnel.

Several hundred feet in, he and Coulter found an underground cell.

Chaos erupted, the boys shouting all at once.

"Help!"

"Get us out of here!"

"Where is he?"

John shined his flashlight inside the cell. He recognized little

Mark Bayler and Danny Kritz from the pictures he'd seen. The others were probably on the missing children list. Maybe nine kids altogether, ranging in age from six to thirteen.

Most of the kids were dirty and scared, and some looked malnourished. His flashlight shined just enough to reveal bruises and scars. Three were chained to a pipe at the back. Probably the ones who'd fought back.

"Hang on, guys," John said. "We'll get you out of here."

He waited with them while Coulter ran back through the tunnel for tools and backup. Two officers returned with them, one carrying an ax to break the lock on the cell.

Over the next few hours, John and Coulter oversaw moving the kids to a secure facility, where they were evaluated by doctors for physical and psychological trauma.

Some were treated for burns and other minor injuries, but thankfully there was no evidence of sexual abuse.

Rayner was locked up as well, although he wasn't talking. But the younger kids who hadn't been brainwashed yet revealed everything.

Apparently Rayner worked for Axelrod. He'd beaten them into submission because he'd been beaten himself. Beating was the only thing that made him strong, Rayner had told them.

He had maps drawn up of future areas to target, and had already picked his next heroes, suicide bombers, for the mission.

Each boy had his own horror story of how he was abducted, where he was kept, and the mind games Rayner had played with him.

"I want DNA samples taken from each of the victims," John said. Maybe one of them was Amelia's son. And he needed to learn the identity of the others to reunite them with family.

John's phone buzzed as he was about to sit in on the interview with Mark Bayler. It was Amelia's number. "Amelia . . . "

"Help . . . " a woman cried. "He has Amelia."

John's blood ran cold. "Who is this?"

"Helen Gray. Hurry. I've been shot."

Chapter Twenty-Nine

John clenched the phone. Helen Gray had been shot? Amelia was missing . . .

"I'll be right there." John disconnected, told Coulter where he was going, and called an ambulance to meet him at Amelia's as he raced outside to his SUV.

The sleet had stopped, but the wind beat at the trees as if a tornado might be coming. A car turned in front of him, and he slammed the brakes and hit his horn as he swerved to avoid it. He righted his SUV and raced on, his heart hammering.

Who had taken Amelia?

He had just arrested the leader of the Brotherhood and his second-in-command.

Of course, her missing son might have nothing to do with this Brotherhood group . . .

Ominous clouds rumbled above, icy patches slowing him down, but he drove as fast as he could up the mountain. Fear gnawed at him as he swung onto the road leading to Amelia's. He spotted a black sedan in her drive and Amelia's Mini Cooper.

The ambulance hadn't arrived yet.

He threw the SUV into park, pulled out his Sig, and scanned the area in case he was walking into a trap. Nothing evident, but he remained on guard as he approached the front door. When he checked the door, it screeched open.

Instincts on alert, he inched inside, then spotted Helen lying on the floor. Blood soaked her abdomen and shirt, seeping around her.

She was unconscious.

He ran to the kitchen and grabbed some towels, knelt beside her, and pressed the towels to her wound with one hand to stem the blood flow.

The wind chimes clanged in the background. Cold air swept through the house from the front door. He took her hand in his free one. Her fingers felt icy and frail, but she slowly opened her eyes. "Helen?"

A weak nod. "John, he has Amelia. You have to save her."

"Who has her?" John asked.

"He . . . he must have followed me here," she cried. "I saw her on the news, pleading for information about her son. And I had to come."

Sweat beaded on John's forehead. "You know where her son is?"

"No . . . "

She was fading again, and he gently shook her. "Helen, where is she?"

"I don't know," Helen murmured. "But you need to know the truth. The accident you had, your amnesia."

John's heart thundered. How would Helen know about that? "What about it?"

"You challenged him and tried to save Amelia, and he couldn't have that. I heard him give orders to subdue you, to make it look like you had an accident, to brainwash you so you wouldn't remember Amelia."

Confusion swirled in John's head as he tried to remember the events she described. "I tried to save her?"

"The night she delivered," Helen said. "But he caught you and took you away. Then he erased your memory."

A coldness swallowed John as a memory surfaced. He was with Amelia, she was crying, screaming, in labor . . .

Then . . . everything went blank.

"Did I work for Arthur Blackwood?"

Her breathing grew erratic. "You helped him because that's all you ever knew, but then you fell in love with Amelia and wanted to get her away from him."

So he had guarded her. Damn, no wonder she hated him now.

"I begged him to let you go," Helen said. "But he said he'd kill you if I interfered."

Her eyes fluttered, her voice growing weaker. He was losing her. Where was that damned ambulance?

"How do you know all this? Did you work for Blackwood, too?"

She shook her head, her eyes suddenly desolate, as if she thought she was going to die. "No." Tears rolled down her face. "I didn't know what he was doing," she whispered. "I didn't. I swear. But now he's back. He was supposed to be dead . . . "

John went stone cold still. Supposed to be dead? "Helen, God, what are you saying? Blackwood is alive? He has Amelia?"

She nodded, gasping for a breath.

A siren wailed. The ambulance was finally coming. The color had faded from Helen's face, and her eyelids looked heavy. She needed help, surgery, fast or she wasn't going to make it.

"Was I one of Blackwood's subjects?" John asked.

A sob escaped the woman. "No, John. You're his son."

———————— , ————————

Amelia stirred from unconsciousness. Fear hammered at her as she realized she was strapped to a chair.

Her head swam from whatever drug he'd injected her with. She blinked to focus and glanced around the dark basement, shivering from cold and fear.

He walked toward her, a leer on his face. "Hello, Amelia."

Her mouth was so dry she felt as if it had cotton in it. "You bastard. You're supposed to be dead." She gulped back tears. "How did you survive?"

His laughter echoed in the dark. Then he held his hand up in front of her, fingers splayed. His thumb was missing. "I was a soldier. I cut off my thumb and left it in that chopper. I knew those fools would find my DNA and assume all of me had blown up in the explosion."

Amelia shivered. "But Nick and Jake saw you get in the helicopter."

"I have followers," he said in a voice filled with self-love. "They will do anything for me."

"One of them posed as you to throw off the police?"

"Yes. He was honored to be a decoy."

"How could anyone follow you?" Amelia said in disgust. "You're a monster."

"And you're a sick, mentally ill girl," the Commander said. "You always will be."

"No, I'm strong now," Amelia said. "Your experiment failed."

His footstep clicked as he came closer. "I never fail."

Fear choked her. She wanted answers. "What did you do with my baby?"

A wry chuckle rumbled from the bastard. "You weren't fit to be a mother."

"Because you drugged me." She struggled against the bindings. "Where's my son?"

He gave her an odd look as if he wanted to say something, then a sinister leer appeared on his face. "You said I failed, but I didn't. You don't remember everything."

"I remember giving birth."

"To one son." He circled her, eyes boring into her. "Not two. You had two boys, Amelia. Twins."

His words roared in Amelia's ears, sending her into shock. Twins? Just like her and Sadie . . .

She wanted to scream in frustration. "What did you do with them?"

"Don't worry. My grandsons are safe."

Her stomach clenched. "What do you mean, *your* grandsons?"

Another laugh. "You haven't figured it out yet? I thought that was the reason you and John Strong were working together. That's the reason you went and saw Sister Grace and got that Jayne woman to help you."

"You killed them, too," Amelia gasped.

"Just the Jayne woman. The nun . . . I let her go. But I don't think she'll be back."

Amelia's mind spun as everything sank in. What did he mean? Then the truth dawned on her. John had been working with the Commander. She'd thought they had been in love.

And they had had sex.

John was the father of her babies.

And he was the Commander's son.

Tears blurred her eyes.

Her babies were related to Arthur Blackwood, the man she hated most in the world.

"You called me, didn't you? You tried to make me think I was losing my mind by talking about Viola?" Her head swirled as she pieced together the facts. "You put that bear in my house. You tore up my journals."

Blackwood laughed. "You're such an easy one to manipulate, Amelia. Such a malleable mind."

"Why do you keep tormenting me?" Amelia cried. "Why can't you just give me my children? Then die?"

"Because I'm invincible," he said with an eerie laugh. "And your children are Blackwoods. They need to be made into men."

Amelia steeled herself. "You may think you're God, but you're not. And one day someone will take you down." She hoped when they did, he'd suffer, too.

He untied her right hand and shoved a pen between her fingers, then laid a notepad in front of her.

"Now write a good-bye note to John."

"Why? So you can kill me and make it look like a suicide?"

"Of course. No one will be surprised. Poor Amelia, she suffered from delusions. Dissociative Identity Disorder. Depression because she was delusional. Even your shrink will testify you were unstable. That you came to her claiming you had a baby who I took away."

How did he know her doctor would testify?

The truth hit her like a fist to her chest. "My doctor—Dr. Clover works for you?"

Another evil grin. "Of course. You didn't think I'd forget to watch you, did you?"

Nausea climbed Amelia's throat. She had trusted Dr. Clover. Confided her secrets to the woman. Respected her opinion.

Had poured out her heart about Bessie's bear and the journals . . .

And Dr. Clover had used them against her.

Just like she'd trusted John.

But he was Arthur Blackwood's son.

Helen said he'd tried to save her though. That he'd loved her. That the Commander had destroyed his memory.

Where was John now?

"Write," the Commander ordered.

———————— · ————————

The paramedics rushed in and began working on Helen, taking her vitals, applying blood stoppers, and easing her onto the stretcher.

John squeezed her hand. "Helen, can I call someone? Do you have family?"

She had lost consciousness though and didn't respond.

He jogged beside them as they loaded her into the ambulance. She stirred and reached for his hand.

"John, save Amelia."

"How? Where is she?"

"I don't know," she said in a broken voice.

"Do you have any idea where Blackwood would take her?"

She tried to speak, but her voice came out a guttural sound, then she passed out again.

"Get her to the hospital," John told the medic. "I'll check in later."

John climbed in his SUV, then punched Sheriff Blackwood's number as he squealed from the parking lot. "Jake, this is Agent Strong. You aren't going to believe this, but your father is alive."

Moments passed as Jake absorbed the news. "What? That's not possible."

"But it is," John said, hating it as much as Jake did. "And the bastard has Amelia. I need your help."

"Christ . . . How the hell did he survive?"

"I don't know, but he must have faked his death. We have to find Amelia before he kills her."

Another tense heartbeat passed.

"Listen, Jake, I know this is a lot to take in. But we have to hurry."

Jake cleared his throat. "Right. I'll call Nick and alert all the authorities to be on the lookout for him," Jake said. "We'll look into that website for the Commander's followers. Maybe one of them knows where he'd go."

"Thanks. I'm going to question Axelrod."

Fear seized John, nearly immobilizing him. Arthur Blackwood was a monster, a man who'd nearly destroyed Amelia.

What was he going to do to her now?

John faced Axelrod in the interrogation room, rage eating at him, at the evil oozing from the man's pores.

"Have you been in contact with Commander Blackwood?" John asked.

Axelrod's bushy eyebrows rose. "You've seen him? He's alive?"

"You didn't know?"

Axelrod shook his head, then leaned back in the chair, looking oddly satisfied. "No, but I'm not surprised, I suppose."

"He kidnapped a friend of mine." *The woman I'm in love with.* "You worked with him?"

"I protected him before CHIMES. And as I saw what he did, I decided to form my own group of followers. I'm going to be as famous as he was when the reporters start covering my story."

Sick, twisted fuck.

John leaned forward, hands on the table. "You want the reporter who covered the CHIMES project to write about you?"

Axelrod's eyes lit up with excitement. "Yes, Brenda Banks. She'll make me famous."

"I can arrange for her to talk to you," John said. "That is, if you tell me where Blackwood took my friend."

Axelrod's expression taunted him. "Where do you think he would take her?"

"I never said my friend was a woman."

Axelrod laughed, a throaty chuckle that grated on John's last nerve.

"We both know you're working with Amelia Nettleton, looking for her baby. And she was the Commander's pet project."

Hatred surged through John. "Do you know where she is?"

Fear flashed in the man's eyes for the first time since he'd been arrested. "No. But I did hear he had a special child some of his followers were watching. That he didn't want anyone to get the kid."

"Where did he hide him?"

"They moved him to my compound for a while." Axelrod rubbed at his leg. "But the Commander had someone take him to a safe place."

"Where?"

"I don't know the location."

John wanted to choke the man. "Where would he take Amelia?"

"Use your head," Axelrod said. "Where was the one place he inflicted the most damage on Amelia?"

John's heart hammered as it hit him. The sanitarium.

Body pulsing with frustration and fear, he turned and strode toward the door.

"You're going to send Brenda to see me, aren't you?" Axelrod asked.

John shot him the same kind of evil look Axelrod had sent him. Their gazes locked, filled with animosity.

He walked out the door, leaving the bastard stewing over whether John would keep his word.

To hell with the man. He refused to do anything to glorify a killer.

Ice crunched beneath this boots as he climbed in his car. He pressed the accelerator and sped down the drive, tires screeching on the slick asphalt as he turned onto the road leading into the mountain.

A bleakness fell over him. What if he didn't find Amelia in time? What if the Commander had Amelia's son and he never found them?

Then the child might end up tortured and abused like his subjects . . .

And Amelia . . . how could he go on if he let her die?

No, he couldn't lose her.

She was the only thing that mattered in the world to him. The one person who made him want to be a better man.

He maneuvered the winding road, climbing higher into the

mountains. The sanitarium looked like an ancient haunted castle set on the hill in the midst of the sharp ridges and thick trees. They should have shut down the place after the experiment was revealed, but they'd tried to clean house, reorganize, make it a viable psychiatric hospital again.

A sarcastic laugh bellowed from him. There were patients being treated there now.

But the basement where the Commander had conducted his experiments had been locked and closed off.

John met security and got a passkey to get through secure areas, then instructed the team to comb the building.

An eerie silence mingled with the echoes of terrorized patients' cries in the halls.

And triggered a litany of flashes behind John's eyes. Memories of being there. Watching the Commander issue orders.

He headed to the basement where the Commander had performed his experiments. And where he had almost killed Sadie.

He eased open the door, his pulse jumping. Was Blackwood holding Amelia there in the dark?

Slowly he crept down the steps, his gun drawn.

But the sound of a gun clicking made him freeze.

Dim light from a bulb far across the basement room offered just enough light for him to see a shadow.

"I've been expecting you, son."

John's lungs tightened. Of course Blackwood was waiting. It was too easy, a setup.

And he'd taken the bait.

Blackwood had lured him there so he could kill him and Amelia together.

Chapter Thirty

———— o ————

J ohn stared into Commander Blackwood's steely, hard eyes.
Suddenly memories assaulted him. Six years ago, he'd confronted Blackwood just like this.

To save Amelia and the baby.

Per his father's orders, he'd helped guard Amelia for months.
But during that time, he'd fallen madly in love with her.

And he'd realized that his father was a sick monster.

The day she'd gone into labor, he'd rushed to her room.
"Come on, Amelia, I'm taking you someplace safe."

*She rubbed her belly, but gave him a beautiful smile. Minus
the narcotics they'd pumped into her for years, her eyes were clear,
her face full of color and life.*

*He took her hand and helped her step from the room where
they'd been keeping her. At the door, he motioned for her to wait,
and he peered into the hallway.*

*She suddenly clutched her abdomen, and heaved a deep
breath. "John . . . I think the baby's coming."*

*Dammit, she wasn't due for two more weeks. He should have
broken her out sooner. If she delivered there, his father would take
the child.*

His baby.

He had to save the baby and Amelia.

He took her hand and coaxed her down the hall, his gun at the ready. If they could make it to the end, he could help her into a wheelchair. Then he could roll her out of there.

But just as they neared the corner of the corridor, his father stepped from the shadows, his gun drawn.

"You're not taking her anywhere, John."

"Let her go, Commander," John said through gritted teeth. "She deserves to be free now."

Footsteps pounded. More of the Commander's minions.

Amelia screamed and doubled over, breathing through a contraction.

"Get her to the delivery room," the Commander ordered.

The guards surrounded them with guns, and they rushed Amelia onto a bed and wheeled her to the delivery room. John latched onto her hand.

"It'll be all right, Amelia. I promise."

By the time they got in the sterile room she screamed again. "The baby's coming!"

The guards grabbed his arms to hold him back from being with her. He heard Amelia in agony, pushing. A baby's cry rent the air.

His baby . . . A boy . . .

John had to save him from his father.

He tried to reach him, but the guards jerked him back. Then the Commander took the baby. Amelia was crying, screaming, begging to hold her son.

"Let me have him," John snapped.

But something hit him hard in the back of the head, then a needle jabbed his arm.

The memory faded, the dank basement echoing with another scream.

Amelia's.

Amelia's scream brought him from his memory to the present. And then he knew that Amelia's son . . . was his son.

For a moment he couldn't move. Couldn't breathe. The room swirled out of control.

Slowly Amelia's cry broke through the haze clouding his mind.

Dammit, he had to stop the madness.

"Let her go, Father," John said between clenched teeth. "It's over."

The Commander's bitter laugh filled the room. "I see you're still thinking with the wrong side of your brain."

"No, with my heart," John hissed. "But you wouldn't understand since you don't have one."

"Emotions make a man weak."

"No, they make a man human."

Another bitter laugh, then the Commander laid a hand on Amelia's shoulder. John's gut clenched at the sight of her tied to that chair.

"No one will be surprised to find that Amelia killed herself. Not with her history."

His father wrapped his arm around Amelia's throat, the gun pressed to her temple. Her panicked look wrenched him from the inside out.

Once she'd looked at him with love and trust. Yet, somehow in spite of everything his father had done to tear them apart, they'd found each other again.

This time he wouldn't let her down.

"Release her," John said, a warning to his tone.

"You can still come and work with me, John. You made a good soldier once."

"I said, let her go."

"She ruined everything," the Commander said. "Now it's finally going to end."

He cocked the gun at her temple, and John jumped him, tearing him away from Amelia. The gun went off, fired into the air, pinging off the ceiling. It was so damn dark John couldn't see if she'd been hit.

Then he felt blood seeping down his arm. He'd been shot.

The Commander slammed the butt of his gun against the side of John's face, but John fought back. He lost his Sig in the tumble, and heard it slide across the concrete.

A sob tore from Amelia's throat. "John!"

John cursed himself. He'd been trained well as a sniper. He should have fired a bullet into his father's head.

The Commander jerked him by the neck and slammed his gun against his face again. John tasted blood, pain shooting through his eye and temple.

He shoved his fist into his father's stomach, causing him to cough, then tried to shove him off of him. But his father fought back, and they rolled on the floor, trading punches.

John managed to jab a hard knock to his father's throat, causing him to fall backward. He pounced then, and clawed for his gun. But the Commander kicked him in the gut and John doubled over.

The Commander lurched to his feet, swinging the gun at John, then ran toward Amelia. He untied her feet, keeping the gun trained on John, then took Amelia's arm and dragged her from the chair.

She cried out, and John rolled toward his gun. His fingers connected just as the Commander fired again. John rolled sideways to dodge the bullet, snagged his gun, and let off a round.

Bullets pinged off the floor and walls as the Commander ran for the steps. He was pushing Amelia up the stairs when John tackled them. He knocked the Commander off balance, away from Amelia. She fell down the steps, and he rushed to see if she was okay.

In that split second, the Commander disappeared through a back door that John hadn't even known existed.

"Amelia." John knelt to see if she was okay. He could hear her breathing. "Are you all right?"

"Yes," she cried. "Go after him, John. Don't let him escape."

John helped her sit up, then jogged toward the corner where the Commander had disappeared.

But just as he stepped outside into the frigid air, the sound of a helicopter roared in the night. He looked up and saw its lights flashing as it soared above the treetops and whirled away.

———————— , ————————

Amelia doubled over to catch her breath and crawled to the steps to wait on John. He had to catch the Commander. Make him tell them where her sons were.

But seconds later, John ran back into the basement. "Amelia?"

"I'm here. On the steps."

His footsteps clattered on the concrete as he strode toward her. She reached for him in the dark, and he slid his arms around her.

"Dammit, he got away," John said in a gruff voice.

Amelia collapsed into tears against him. If he was gone, they might never find her little boys.

Her heart squeezed. *Their* little boys.

John stroked her back, rubbing her hair, soothing her. "It's okay. I'll find the bastard and kill him."

"John, he said there were twins. I had two baby boys, not just one."

John's pulse jumped. "Twins? Dear God . . . "

Tears blurred her eyes. "I remember more now, John. Everything." Amelia cupped his face between her hands. "The twins are yours. You're the father of my babies."

Even in the dark, she saw a tear roll down his cheek.

"You were right," he said gruffly. "I wasn't just working for him. I remembered that day, you going into labor. I tried to get you away, but he attacked me."

"I know."

John's voice choked. "I . . . I'm his son, Amelia. I'm the bastard's son."

Despair threatened to overpower her. The details were blurry, but he had held a gun on her once.

He'd also tried to help her escape. "He caused your memory loss," she whispered. "He wanted you to forget me."

"And I did for a while. I forgot everything." His voice rattled with self-recriminations. "I should have tried harder to remember."

"It wasn't your fault, John." Through the haze of her fear, she felt something damp against her. John's shirt. Blood.

"You've been shot." Sticky blood oozed from his arm. "We have to get you to a doctor."

"I'm fine, it's just a flesh wound." He searched her face. "You're sure you're all right?"

She nodded again, her heart in her throat. John had tried to save her and the babies years ago. And he'd saved her that night.

But now the Commander was on the run, and he might do something drastic to her little boys.

"I need to call Jake and Nick," John said. "Tell them what happened."

She clutched his arms as he helped her to stand, and they climbed the steps to the first floor together. Amelia waved a nurse over to bandage John's arm, and he relented, but urged the nurse to hurry.

"We need to talk to Helen," Amelia said as the nurse finished taking care of John's wound. "John, she might know where the Commander is going."

———————— , ————————

John phoned Nick and Jake on the way to the hospital to see Helen.

"The Commander got away," John said. "Left the sanitarium in a chopper."

"We've got all the authorities looking for him," Nick said.

"Any idea where he was going?" Jake asked.

"No, I'm hoping Helen Gray might know."

"Who is Helen Gray?" Nick asked.

"A social worker," John explained. "She was at the hospital back when Amelia gave birth. Just let me know if Blackwood is spotted anywhere."

He ended the call, debating whether or not he should have told them they were related.

But he was still trying to get used to that realization himself.

When they arrived, he checked in with the nurse's desk. "We need to see Helen Gray. She was brought in for surgery earlier. How is she?"

"Let me get her doctor." She punched a button and paged the doctor, who appeared five minutes later. He introduced himself and shook John's hand.

"We just moved her to a room from recovery. She's going to be all right, but she'll be weak and sore for a while."

"Can we see her?" Amelia asked.

"Just for a few minutes," the doctor said. "Try not to upset her. The gunshot wound and stress of surgery took its toll."

John paused to study the woman's face as they entered her room. He'd been talking with her about the case for days now, but hadn't remembered knowing her years ago. Although if she was at the mental hospital, he must have known her.

He walked over to her bed, and Amelia followed him. The beep of the machines hooked to Helen sounded in the quiet.

Amelia squeezed his hand, and he swallowed hard. After all Amelia had been through, she seemed worried about him. She was amazing. No wonder he'd fallen in love with her years before.

And again these last few weeks.

"Helen," he said in a low voice. "It's John."

She breathed deeply as if still in the throes of the anesthesia, so he claimed one of the chairs beside the bed, sat down, and took her hand in his. Amelia settled beside him, silent, watchful, tense.

An hour bled into two as they waited, and neither spoke, both lost in fear and desperation. The Commander had their little boys. No telling what he'd done to them.

Finally Helen opened her eyes. She blinked several times, trying to focus, her breathing slightly labored. "John?"

"Yes," he said gruffly.

She squinted, then smiled when she saw Amelia beside him.

"You saved her," she murmured. "Thank God."

"Yes, but the Commander got away. And we still don't know where he took the boys."

Regret, grief . . . guilt clouded her face. Then a flicker of surprise. "Boys?"

"There were twins," he said gruffly. "You didn't know?"

She shook her head, her voice strangled. "I ran out after the first baby was born. Arthur threatened me, and I knew I had to leave town, to get away from him."

"Do you have any idea what he'd do with them?"

The color faded from her cheeks. "No . . . I . . . don't know."

"You were working with him back then, weren't you?" he said harshly. "You must know something more."

Helen opened her eyes, a deep sadness permeating the depths. "I wasn't working with him, John."

"But you were there when he took the babies."

"Yes," she said. "I was there because of you."

John's heart thundered. "I don't understand."

She squeezed his hand, her voice a raspy whisper. "I was married to him, John. Before I knew what was he was doing. What he was." Her breath stalled. "I'm your mother."

———— · ————

Amelia saw the shock on John's face at Helen's statement.

"You're my mother?" John said in a pained voice.

She nodded. "After you tried to help Amelia escape, Arthur took you away. He faked that car accident and brainwashed you so you wouldn't remember anything. Including me."

"You came to Slaughter Creek to look for our baby, didn't you, Helen?" Amelia asked.

"Yes, I knew Arthur sent him somewhere, but I didn't know where. Just that your son was my grandbaby and I loved him." Helen's lip quivered, and Amelia took her hand in hers. Then Helen looked at John. "I also wanted to see you, John. I hoped that once we met and you talked to me, it might trigger your memories."

John stood, obviously confused by the revelations. "I need some air." He looked back at Helen from the doorway. "Call me if you think of someplace he might have taken the boys."

Amelia squeezed Helen's hand. "Give him time."

"I don't blame him if he hates me. I should have gotten him away from Arthur years ago."

"We'll be back," Amelia said, then ran from the room to find John.

He was standing by the elevator, his body rigid, his mouth a straight line. Emotions warred in his eyes.

She reached up to comfort him, but he squared his shoulders and pulled away. "I'll drive you home now."

She decided to give him some time to process all he'd learned, and followed him to his SUV. They drove back to her studio house in complete silence, the sound of the wind and more sleet battering the road and vehicle.

When they entered her house, she froze at the sight of the blood on the floor from Helen's gunshot wound.

"John, Blackwood said my therapist Dr. Clover was working with him. Either she or the Commander put that bear in my house and tore up my journals and wrote on my mirror. They were trying to drive me crazy."

"Son of a bitch." He pulled his phone from his pocket. "I'll have her arrested and charged. Maybe she knows where the Commander is."

Amelia walked toward the sink. She had to clean up the blood.

But John caught her hand. "I'll clean up. Go ahead to bed, Amelia."

She started to argue, but the sight of the blood resurrected memories of being held by Arthur again, and she started shaking, so she ducked into the bathroom to wash the stench of his hands off of her.

By the time she emerged, John's expression looked even bleaker. "He must have warned Dr. Clover. Jake said she cleaned out her office and house and she's gone."

Disappointment and fatigue weighed on Amelia. She wanted John to wrap his arms around her, and for the two of them to make love again.

But so much had happened between them . . .

He looked even more distant than when they'd first met. So she retreated to her room to give him some time to come to terms with the truth about who he was.

An hour later she lay in bed staring at the ceiling, wondering what would happen, if they'd ever find the twins. She'd accused John of helping his father and obviously he had at some point.

But he'd lost his memory because he'd tried to save her.

Still, Arthur Blackwood's blood flowed through his veins.

But he loved you and risked his life to save you and his sons.

And she had loved him.

She knew it in her heart.

Chapter Thirty-One

———— o ————

John sipped coffee while he stared at the woods behind Amelia's as morning light broke through the dark clouds. The forests looked ominous, the trees dripping with ice. When he was a kid, he thought monsters lived in the trees.

But the real monster had lived with him. His father.

And now he'd escaped.

Again.

He had to find him. The bastard might come back to hurt Amelia if he didn't.

Damn. He'd wanted to join Amelia in bed when they'd gotten back that night, to hold her and love her all night, to assure her he'd bring their sons back to her.

It was difficult to fathom. The entire time he'd been helping her, they'd been looking for *their* sons.

But he'd failed them all.

He poured himself some more coffee, then stood outside and watched the morning come to life. Deer scurried about. Squirrels foraged for food. The wind shook sleet from the tree limbs, scattering twigs across the white ground. Icicles broke off, cracking and shattering like glass.

Helen was his mother. She should have told him sooner.

Then again, she'd probably been terrified of his father. With good reason, too. Still, she'd risked her life to help him and Amelia find their children.

Could Amelia ever forgive him for what his father had done to her? For his part in keeping her a prisoner?

His phone buzzed. Coulter. "Yeah?"

"John, Lieutenant Maddison wants us to meet him. He has news about the case."

"I'll be right there." He took his coffee mug inside, rinsed it, and put it in the dishwasher, then glanced at Amelia's bedroom door.

More than anything he wanted to tell her he loved her. That in spite of his amnesia, they'd found their way back to each other.

But how could Amelia love him when the Commander's bad blood pumped inside him?

He yanked on his coat, grabbed his keys, and headed outside. He wouldn't stop looking for the twins. If he found them, maybe he could beg her forgiveness.

———————————————

John was gone.

He hadn't even said good-bye.

Amelia sipped her coffee, then made a decision.

She was going to talk to a therapist about the RMT. She'd put it off, too terrified to revisit that time in her past or subject herself to drug therapy, but if it meant possibly finding the twins, she'd do it.

Dr. Clover's face teased her. The idea that she'd trusted the therapist who'd worked for Arthur Blackwood was more than she could bear.

She called Sadie and told her everything. The two of them cried together.

"We won't give up until we find your little boys," Sadie assured her.

"I want to try RMT," Amelia said. "Can you refer me to a therapist?"

"Sure. There's a woman I worked with in California who recently moved here. Let me make a call."

Amelia ended the call and paced the studio, the portrait of Sadie and Ben haunting her. What did her boys look like? Did they have John's dark hair and eyes? Were they identical like her and Sadie?

A few minutes later, Sadie texted her the new therapist's number. Sadie had set an appointment up for her.

Amelia dressed in warm clothes, then drove to the therapist's office. Dr. Marley was a young woman in her early thirties with a tender smile. And she'd agreed to do the treatment in her office, not the sanitarium.

"Sadie filled me in on your history, Amelia. Are you sure you're up to this?" Dr. Marley asked.

Amelia took a deep breath. "Yes." Nerves made her voice quiver. "You're going to put me in a hypnotic trance?"

"Something like that, yes," Dr. Marley said.

"But you will bring me out of it?"

The doctor rubbed Amelia's arms. "Yes. You do trust me, don't you?"

Amelia debated on an answer. Trust was difficult for her. But finding her children meant everything.

So she nodded and sank onto the couch. The doctor prepared a hypodermic needle, and Amelia prayed she would get answers.

"What's this about?" John asked Lieutenant Maddison as he met the man at the facility where they were holding the boys who'd been found at the compound.

The ones with family had been reunited with them, although ongoing therapy and in-house treatment was mandatory.

It was too early to tell if the effects of the brainwashing could be reversed or if one of them might try to carry through with a bombing.

"We have DNA results back," Maddison said. "Considering the circumstances, I called in some favors and put a rush job on the tests."

John narrowed his eyes. "And?"

"The Bayler boy shares the same DNA as Amelia Nettleton."

John's heart jumped. If Mark Bayler was Amelia's son, that meant the little boy was *his*.

God . . . Emotions he thought he'd never feel surfaced, throwing him off balance.

"Did you hear me?" Maddison asked.

He nodded slowly, adrenaline making him feel antsy. "Can I see him?"

"Of course," Maddison said. "But he's confused, John. Upset. His parents are dead."

Except they weren't. At least not his birth parents. They were very much alive.

Only how could he explain that to Mark?

His hands were sweating as he followed Maddison to the playroom, where several of the boys had gathered. One look across the room, and the gravity of the situation hit him.

All these kids had been traumatized. Reuniting with their families and helping them become emotionally stable would take time.

Gaining their trust would be complicated.

He spotted Mark Bayler in the corner at a table where he was drawing. He looked solemn, sad, haunted. How could he not be? He'd witnessed his parents' murder.

Except this little boy wasn't alone anymore. He was *his*.

He studied his facial features, and realized he should have seen it sooner. Mark had his dark hair, his wide cheekbones, and square jaw. And his eyes were just as dark as John's.

Damn his father. He had betrayed him by robbing him of his own child. Of the twins. By depriving him of a life with Amelia.

Tamping down his anger, he slowly approached the boy. "Mark?"

Mark looked up at him with big brown eyes that mirrored his own. Sad eyes, confused and scared.

"Hi," he said in a low voice. "Mind if I sit down? I have a story to tell you."

The boy shrugged, but stopped his drawing. John glanced at it, troubled by the images.

Mark had drawn a picture of the ocean with an island in the middle, the waves choppy, the sky bleak. In the middle of the island, he'd drawn a castle that looked dark and haunted.

"Who are you?" Mark asked.

"Mark, did your parents tell you that you're adopted?"

Mark nodded. "Do you know where my other parents are?"

John smiled at the kid and began to tell him.

Amelia came to, slightly dizzy and disoriented.

Immediately she knew that the therapy had worked, because she remembered everything. Dr. Marley handed her a tissue, and she wiped at her eyes, aware she'd been crying at times, begging for help at others.

"Are you all right?" Dr. Marley asked gently.

"I will be," Amelia said. "But I have to call John."

"Who is John?"

"The agent I've been working with to locate my son. I mean, our sons. John is the boys' father."

She thanked the doctor, then retrieved her phone from her purse and rushed out the door. She pressed John's number, anxious to talk to him.

"Amelia?"

"I think I know where the Commander took the boys."

"Where?"

"The same place he took the CHIMES when we were little. An island off the coast of Georgia."

John made a low sound in his throat. "I'm going to text you an address. Meet me there."

He didn't wait for a response. He hung up, leaving her wondering.

Wasting no time, she rushed to her car and fought the storm as she drove to the facility. John met her outside and escorted her into the building and through security.

"What's going on?" Amelia asked.

"There's someone here you need to meet."

Her heart stuttered as he led her into a small playroom, then over to a little dark-haired boy sitting at a table. The moment he looked up at her, tears burned her eyes.

It was her son.

He looked just like a miniature version of John. Same dark hair. Same dark eyes. Same sharp cheekbones and chin.

She sank onto the small chair beside him, aching to pull him into her arms.

"This is Mark," John said with a lopsided grin. "Mark, this is your mother."

———— · ————

John barely managed to maintain his calm as he watched Amelia reunite with their child.

"You gave me away?" Mark asked in a low voice.

Amelia shook her head. "No, sweetie. It's a long story, but someone took you from me. I've been looking for you though because I love you and want to be with you."

He studied her for a long moment with a childlike innocence, yet a world-weariness also lingered on his face. No telling what kind of life he'd led.

Although at least he'd been with the Baylers, not with the Commander.

Mark's twin might not have been so lucky.

"I know this is a lot to understand," Amelia told Mark. "And we can take it as slow as you want, Mark. But I want us to be together as a family."

Mark looked around the room. "Then I won't have to stay here forever?"

"No, oh, no," Amelia said softly. "You'll have a real home again."

The boy looked back and forth between John and her, then down at the picture he'd drawn. "What about him?"

"Who?" Amelia asked.

He pointed to the window in the dark castle on his drawing. "The little boy who talks to me in my head."

John zeroed in on the child in the window. He hadn't noticed him before. But he looked like Mark.

"Is that you?" John asked.

Mark shook his head. "No, his name is Zack."

Amelia gasped softly, and traded a confused look with John. But the truth slowly dawned on her. Zack had to be Mark's twin brother. "How long have you known Zack?"

"Ever since I can remember." Mark shrugged. "He talks to me all the time."

Amelia tapped the sketch. "That place, the island. Have you been there, Mark?"

He shook his head. "No, but Zack is there. He doesn't like it. He asked me to get help."

Amelia looked up at John. "That's the place I told you about, the island where he took the CHIMES when we were smaller."

John angled himself toward Mark. "Listen, Mark, I'll go check out that place, and then come back. Okay?" He had to. If the Commander was there, it might be his chance to catch him. To stop him.

To kill him once and for all.

Until he was dead, Amelia would never be safe.

And if his other son was there, he had to rescue him before the Commander moved him someplace where they'd never find him.

Mark pasted on a brave face, reminding him of Amelia, and John's throat clogged.

"You need to hurry. He's scared."

Amelia planted a kiss on his forehead. "Sweetheart, I have to go with John and show him where that island is." She looked up at the counselor sitting in the corner. "Will you be okay here until we get back?"

Mark nodded. "Save him. He's never had a mommy and daddy."

John looked at Amelia and saw the anguish in her eyes. They had to hurry.

Amelia's heart swelled with love as she hugged her son, and they left the room. She couldn't believe he was alive and that they'd finally found him.

And that he had a twin brother.

"I don't understand how Mark knew about Zack," John said. "Do you think they met at some point?"

Amelia hesitated. "Maybe he has a connection with his twin like Sadie and I do," Amelia admitted. "We don't always know each other's thoughts, but sometimes we sense when the other is in trouble."

John seemed to stew over what she said as they got in his SUV.

"I hate to leave him alone," Amelia said. "Especially when we just found him."

"I know," John said. "But he's safe, and if he's right about the Commander having his brother, we need to find them."

"I think I can lead us to that island," Amelia said.

"Good." John squeezed her shoulder. "I'm going to line up a chopper and team for backup. We'll get him out if we have to storm the place."

———————— , ————————

Zack stared out the window at the endless sea of water. Chop, chop, chop, the waves crashed back and forth.

Outside his room in the hall, it was quiet.

An eerie quiet as if he were alone in the castle.

Then loud footsteps. Voices. Men hurrying. Something was wrong.

He jammed his notepad beneath the mattress of the cot in case they came in. He'd been drawing, trying to show his friend where he was.

That kid is just in your head.

No . . . he was real, wasn't he?

Or was he crazy like the Commander said?

Chapter Thirty-Two

———— o ————

John and Amelia flew to Savannah, then took a chopper with Nick and Jake riding along for backup. The Blackwood brothers had been shocked to learn John was their half brother. At least as shocked as one could be when the Commander kept surprising them. But both had admitted they'd suspected the Commander had had another family during the years he was presumed dead.

And they wanted their father gone for good as badly as John did.

Amelia showed them where the island was on the map, then called Sadie to tell her about finding Mark. He had no idea what Sadie had said to her, but Amelia seemed pleased when she'd hung up.

Now worry pulled at her face again. John understood her concerns.

The closer he got to the coast, the more familiar the area seemed.

He had been to this island before, too.

Probably when he was guarding Amelia.

That thought soured his stomach, but he inhaled deeply to calm himself. He had to finish this for Amelia and for his sons.

He studied the map spread across his lap, the details of his visit blurry, but he easily guided the pilot toward the remote island.

Amelia sat with her hands clenched in a death grip, staring out the window, scanning below just as he was. Every minute counted.

The top of a building caught his eye through the fog, and he remembered Mark's drawing. Although this place looked nothing like a castle, it was the only building on the island, and he vaguely remembered it from years before.

"There," he said, pointing out the building to the pilot.

The pilot gestured toward a clearing about a quarter of a mile away. "I'll try to land over there." But the wind was so strong, the chopper rocked sideways. The side brushed the tops of some trees, sending it spinning.

The pilot tried to correct it, bobbing up and down in the turbulence.

Finally he brought the bird down, the engine sputtering. Reservations nagged at him for bringing Amelia. Finding Zack could be dangerous.

But if he was traumatized, Amelia might be able to help.

"Stay here with the pilot," he told her. Gordon was former military and trained with a weapon.

John secured his Sig Sauer, adding a knife to an ankle strap under his pants leg. Jake and Nick were checking their weapons as well. But suddenly the sound of guns cocking echoed nearby.

"Don't move, you're surrounded."

John froze as men dressed in camouflage stepped from the shadows of the trees, automatic rifles aimed at him, Amelia, Nick, Jake, and the pilot.

"You're holding a child here?" John asked.

A laugh rumbled from one of their captors. He was big, rough-looking with a tattoo of an eagle on his lower arm. "We'll take you to him."

The hair on the back of John's neck prickled. That was too easy. There was no way these men would turn over the child without a fight.

The man with the tattoo gave John a warning look. "Give up the weapons."

John, Nick, and Jake exchanged looks, then handed over their guns. The pilot tried to reach his, but one of the men shot him, and he fell to the ground, the bullet piercing him right between the eyes.

Amelia gasped, and John cursed.

"Anyone else want to be a hero?" the shooter growled.

John shook his head, and Jake and Nick played it cool.

The leader gestured toward a path. "That way."

Another man aimed a gun at Amelia's back. "Go, lady."

John cursed himself for bringing her along. If they both got killed, little Mark would be left completely alone in the world.

———————— , ————————

Amelia followed close behind John, with Nick and Jake behind her. The poor pilot . . . he was dead because he'd tried to help them.

There were at least eight men with guns, which meant they were outnumbered. And now John and the Blackwood brothers were unarmed. If anything happened to John, she'd never forgive herself.

A chilly breeze ruffled the trees, and waves crashed at the shore as they followed a path up to the building.

One of the men opened a heavy wooden door, and the troops ushered her and the others inside. The entryway was dark, cold, as if the place had been deserted for some time. Cracks in the walls and poor lighting added to the eerie feel.

They followed the men up a staircase, then through a set of double doors and down a corridor.

They came to a door, which one of the men unlocked.

Her pulse thumped when he opened it and ordered her to go in. Amelia's heart squeezed at the sight of the little boy sitting by the window with a sketchpad in front of him.

Then he turned toward her, and her heart melted. He looked exactly like Mark.

They were identical.

She and Sadie had had a connection all their lives. Had sometimes drawn the same pictures.

Her sons also shared a similar kind of connection.

This little boy had been drawing the same picture Mark had drawn, a sketch of the building with him inside looking out the window for help.

John didn't like this setup at all.

The only reason they'd brought them this far was because they planned to kill them.

Dammit to hell.

The door slammed shut behind them, locking them in. John's heart hammered at the sight of the boy. He looked just like Mark.

"Damn my father for keeping them both from us," he muttered.

Nick strode across the room to check the window while Jake looked for a vent to escape through.

Amelia stooped down beside the child. "Hi, my name is Amelia. Are you Zack?"

The little boy jutted up his chin. "Yes, how did you know?"

John gently touched the boy's shoulder. "Mark sent us to get you."

A tiny smile pulled at Zack's mouth. "I knew he would help me."

Amelia squeezed his arm. "Zack, we're here to take you to a nice home. Would you like that?"

He looked wary but he nodded. "Can I meet the other boy? The one who lives in my head?"

John soaked in his son's face. But anger for all he and Amelia had missed consumed him.

"Yes," Amelia said. "And he's not just in your head. He's your brother, Mark."

Outside the room, footsteps pounded, then John heard shouts.

Nick cursed. "Damn, they're leaving."

Keys jangled outside the door, then it opened again, and the Commander appeared holding a semiautomatic, an evil leer splitting his face. "Hello, my sons. So nice to have you all here together."

"You son of a bitch," John growled. "Just let us take Zack and we won't even bother looking for you."

Blackwood's hearty laugh rumbled in the cavernous space. "We all know that's a lie. Besides, Zack is going with me."

He aimed the gun at Amelia, and John, Jake, and Nick went stone still. Then he crossed the room and jerked Zack up by the arm.

"Please don't take him," Amelia cried.

"Leave him," John said, his fists knotted.

But Blackwood dragged Zack toward the door. Zack yelled and kicked at him, but the Commander fired a shot into the air. Amelia screamed and Zack froze, then went limp and let Blackwood drag him from the room.

Amelia sobbed and ran to the door and started beating on it. John caught her and pulled her into his arms. "Shh, we'll get out and find him. I promise."

Nick rushed to the window. "They have a chopper. It looks as if they're escaping."

John's adrenaline surged. Damn bastard was going to get away again.

He released Amelia, removed the knife from his ankle, and used it to pick the lock. It took him several tries, but he managed to open the door.

He waved them to the door. "Come on."

But as soon as they made it into the hallway, a bomb exploded from below.

Amelia cried out. The walls shook. Smoke seeped upward. John forged ahead, knowing they had to hurry.

He led the way down the hall. They came to a halt at the double doors, which were locked. Nick slammed his body against the doors, and John joined him. Three tries later, the doors splintered, and they started through.

Smoke clogged the stairway and the hallway. Flames licked at the floor and doorways.

Jake removed his jacket and so did Nick, and they beat at the flames as he and Amelia raced through the fiery patches and hurried to the bottom floor. Fire shot up across the front entryway, and John pointed left.

Amelia coughed as smoke clogged her lungs. He jerked a handkerchief from his pocket. "Here, cover your face."

She took it and did so, while Nick plowed ahead, beating at the flames licking the walls to make a path. Jake took up the rear.

Part of the roof crashed in with a thunderous roar, and burning pieces rained down. One caught Jake. Nick ran back to help him.

"Go on. Get Amelia out of here!" Nick shouted.

"Go after the Commander!" Jake yelled

John didn't want to leave his half brothers, but he had to save Amelia and his son.

Another explosion blasted, rocking the walls and shaking the foundation, and the building began to crumble down around them. Amelia screamed as burning rubble pummeled them. He dragged her behind him, keeping her close until they made it to the outside.

They were both coughing, but he eased Amelia to the ground a few feet away. He spotted the Commander climbing into the helicopter, pushing Zack in front of him.

"Go get him, John!" Amelia shouted.

He ran toward them and caught Blackwood by the leg. "You're not going anywhere!"

The Commander slammed his gun back, hitting John in the face. He grunted, but rage fueled him, and he punched his father in the lower back, catching him in the kidneys.

The Commander dropped down in pain. The chopper was just about to lift off. Zack clung to the edge, looking terrified. "Jump, Zack!"

Zack shook his head, fear paralyzing him.

John held out his arms. "Come on, son. I'll catch you, I promise."

The boy was shaking, but he lunged into John's arms. John caught him, hugging him hard. Zack's little body shook against his, then John grunted again as Blackwood kicked him in the knees.

His legs gave way as his knees buckled, and he went down, Zack still clinging to him.

"Run, Zack!" John released his son and pointed toward Amelia. She was running toward them, screaming his name.

Smoke and flames hurled upward, filling the sky, creating a hazy fog behind her.

John rolled over and saw the Commander trying to make it to the chopper again. But he lunged up, caught him around the knees and dragged him to the ground. "You son of a bitch, did you give Zack to Axelrod to turn into a suicide bomber?"

The Commander snarled in his face. "Hell, no. I had his men take him someplace safe until I could get him."

"How did you find Mark? Were the Baylers in on your scheme?"

"Axelrod was prepared to search every shelter in the state, but lo and behold, a baby boy showed up in Slaughter Creek's very own Gateway House right away. Your mother was never very bright, and she was certainly no criminal mastermind."

John's nostrils flared.

"DNA proved the match, and the Baylers were only to be involved for several days. But I kept having to deal with . . . distractions . . . and by the time I came for Mark, the Baylers were attached, continually subverting me and ignoring my demands. So they had to die. Fools." A ruthless smile curved his mouth. "I always planned to reunite Mark with Zack and raise them myself." His father hissed. "Somebody had to teach them to be men."

John hated him for everything he'd done, for what he'd put him through, for the way he'd hurt Amelia and their boys. "You're never going to get them."

He slammed his fist into his father's face. But the Commander aimed the gun at him, ready to pull the trigger.

Rage hit him, and John snatched it and slung it over the cliff. Below the ocean crashed and roared.

He and the Commander traded blows, rolling near the edge. Blood spurted from his father's nose and mouth.

"You can't kill me," Blackwood growled.

John grinned this time. All the fury eating at him collided, fortifying his strength.

"Watch me." He kicked Blackwood in the gut, causing him to cough blood, then grabbed him and slung him over the edge of the cliff.

Blackwood bellowed his name. "You have to save me. I'm your father."

John stood on wobbly legs, staggered to the edge, and looked down where Blackwood was clutching the sharp, rocky cliff. His body dangled over the edge, the raging water beckoning below, waves crashing in a thunderous roar.

"Good bye, Commander." Hatred for his father burned through him, and he stomped on his father's fingers, bones cracking. The Commander struggled to hang on, but John stomped them again, bones and cartilage shattering, then he kicked the

Commander in the face with his boot so hard the man let go and plunged to the water below.

John stood, staring down into the sea, searching for him to emerge, to somehow surface on the shore.

But a sliver of moonlight illuminated the ocean, and he spotted a wave catching his body and tossing it out to sea.

"John!"

He spun around and saw Amelia hugging Zack, the two of them trembling and hurrying toward him.

He ran toward them, then pulled them into his arms. They hugged each other, Amelia and Zack crying against him.

But the fire thundered behind them, orange flames lighting the sky.

He leaned over and gave her a quick kiss, then kissed the top of Zack's head. "I have to find Nick and Jake." They were his brothers.

Amelia nodded, and he raced back toward the blaze.

Amelia hugged Zack to her, grateful to have found her sons. The poor little guys had been through so much. She just prayed they could all be together and be a family.

She wanted John to be part of that family, too.

Fear seized her as he ran into the building. Fire and smoke consumed the structure, and it was crumbling down. The roof collapsed with a big boom, the walls cracking and splintering, erupting into a big ball of flames.

"Is he coming back?" Zack said, his nails digging into Amelia's arm.

"Yes," Amelia said. They'd been through too much to lose each other now that they'd finally found the twins.

But as seconds turned to minutes, her hopes evaporated. What if John didn't survive?

What if she'd lost him for good?

—————— . ——————

John found Nick trying to drag a flaming board off Jake. The ceiling and walls were collapsing around them, the smoke so thick he could barely breathe.

He jerked off his jacket, wrapped it around his hands, and pulled at the plank. Together he and Nick finally lifted it, then slapped at the flames on his sleeve.

"Let's get out of here!" John shouted.

He and Nick helped Jake up, and they ran through the fire, dodging more debris and jumping over patches of embers as they escaped.

When they made it outside, they were all heaving for fresh air. John searched through the smoke and saw Amelia and Zack waiting by the water.

"Did you get him?" Nick asked, his voice hoarse from the smoke.

"He went over the cliff," John said. "The waves caught him and carried him out to sea."

Amelia called his name again, and he ran toward her, wiping soot from his sweaty forehead as he approached. She was holding Zack, the two of them clinging to one another.

It was the most beautiful sight he'd ever seen.

"John . . . I was so afraid I'd lost you." She choked on tears, and threw herself at him again.

He hugged her and Zack to him, and buried his face into her hair. "No, Amelia, I'm right here." He would never let her go again.

—————— . ——————

Amelia thought they'd never get back to Slaughter Creek. Zack had been a trooper and seemed relieved to be away from the island. He'd already relayed some details about what had happened to him, how the Commander had tried to break him and turn him into a soldier, but he had escaped inside his head into a fantasy world of banshees and monsters and made the man think he was crazy so he'd leave him alone.

He was a smart little boy. But his way of coping reminded her of herself.

She'd gently explained that she and John were his parents.

"I have a mommy and a daddy," he said, his eyes big with wonder.

Amelia stroked his hair. "Yes, Zack. And you have a brother."

"Mark, the boy who talks to me?"

"Yes." Amelia squeezed his hand. "I've been looking for you for a while now. We're going to take you to see your brother, and we'll go home."

Tears blurred her eyes as he curled up against her. "I'm finally getting a real home. And Mark and I can play together."

"Yes, sweetie, you're going to have a real home." And so would she.

Amelia swallowed her tears as he closed his eyes, curled against her, and fell asleep.

John glanced at him with an odd expression, emotions riddling his face. Sighing, he put his arm around her and pulled her and Zack up against him. She laid her hand on his chest and closed her eyes, comforted by the beating of his heart and grateful to finally have found all her boys.

When they landed, John carried Zack to his SUV. It was late, but she and John agreed that they had to reunite the twins that night.

"Mark helped show us where you were."

"He's my brother?" Zack asked again, as if he still couldn't believe what they'd told him.

"Yes, you're twins just like me and my sister, your aunt Sadie. When we were little, we shared a connection. I think you and Mark do, too."

John smiled at her, and the three of them walked inside hand in hand. He spoke with the guard, then the psychologist in charge, then they walked to Mark's room.

Amelia knocked softly, then pushed the door open. Mark was in bed, but he had a smile on his face. "I knew you were coming."

Tears filled her eyes. She knew how empty and lost she'd felt without Sadie all those years. Her sons must have felt the same way.

"I tried to talk to you," Zack said. "I saw the pictures you drew, too."

"The banshees are scary," Mark said.

Zack crawled onto the bed beside his brother. "I know. But I think our daddy killed the monsters."

Amelia's heart gave a pang. Yes, John, the boys' father, had killed the biggest monster of all, his own father.

And he'd done it to save her and their sons.

John rubbed her shoulder. "Do you think they're going to be okay?"

A sense of peace enveloped Amelia. "Now that they've found each other, they will." She touched his cheek. "And now that they have a real father."

His eyes darkened, flaring with a wariness that tore at her heart. But there was need there, too. Need and hunger and the raw desire she'd felt between them years ago.

And again these past few days.

"How about us?" he murmured against her ear. "Will we be okay?"

She looped her arms around his neck. "What do you think?"

"Can you forgive me for what I did years ago? I . . . am the Commander's son."

"He was a sperm donor, nothing more. You are your own man." She traced a finger along his jaw. "You're brave and honorable. You tried to save me and the twins years ago. And now you've brought us back together again."

John's throat ached. "I love you, Amelia," he whispered. "I always have. I just forgot it for a while."

A slow smile curved her mouth. "It's all right, I forgot who I was, too." She cradled his face with her hands. "But none of that matters. We have a family together. Two little boys who need us. We've already missed so much."

John's dark gaze met hers. "I don't want to miss another second. I want us to be together."

"I want that, too."

The boys looked up at them, identical faces, the connection between them as strong as if they'd never been separated at all.

Amelia felt that way with John. All her life she'd been looking for love, family, a home. Only she'd thought she didn't deserve it.

But she had actually found it a long time ago when she was still in that sanitarium. And now she'd found that same love again.

She fused her mouth with John's, savoring his kiss because it felt like she was finally coming home.

And she was. She was finally going to have that family with John and their sons.

Maybe one day she'd even get to put that wedding ring quilt on her bed for her and John to sleep under.

Acknowledgments

———— o ————

I want to thank Lindsay Guzzardo for her editorial insight and suggestions—she made this book so much better! And to Maria Gomez, my fabulous editor, who lets me write dark.

Also thanks to Reba Bales, my sister, who answered questions regarding the prison system and mental illness.

And as always, thanks to my critique partner, Stephanie Bond, and fellow writer Jennifer St. Giles for their brainstorming ideas and willingness to read any version.

Last but not least, thanks to the fans of the Slaughter Creek series who asked for Amelia's story!

About the Author

—————— ○ ——————

Best-selling author Rita Herron has written more than sixty romance novels and loves penning dark, romantic suspense tales, especially those set in small Southern towns. She earned an *RT Book Reviews* Career Achievement Award for her work in Series Romantic Suspense, and has received rave reviews for the Slaughter Creek novels *Dying to Tell* and *Her Dying Breath*. She is a native of Milledgeville, Georgia, and a proud mother and grandmother.

23406296R00198